Christmas at the Little Cornish Bakery

Jennifer Bibby is an author of warm and heartfelt community romances. Her debut novel was a contender for the 2022 RNA Joan Hessayon Award. A lifelong lover of stories, she enjoys exploring the everyday lives of modern women through literature. Jennifer is happiest by the sea and loves dinosaurs, travel, classy cocktails and medieval history.

Christmas at the Little Cornish Bakery

Jennifer Bibby

ZAFFRE

First published in the UK in 2025 by
ZAFFRE
An imprint of Bonnier Books UK
5th Floor, HYLO, 105 Bunhill Row,
London, EC1Y 8LZ

A CIP catalogue record for this book is
available from the British Library.

Paperback ISBN: 978-1-78512-664-2

Also available as an ebook and an audiobook

1 3 5 7 9 10 8 6 4 2

Typeset by IDSUK (Data Connection) Ltd
Printed and bound in Great Britain by Clays Ltd, Elcograf S.p.A.

FSC
www.fsc.org

MIX
Paper | Supporting
responsible forestry
FSC® C018072

The authorised representative in the EEA is
Bonnier Books UK (Ireland) Limited.
Registered office address: Floor 3, Block 3, Miesian Plaza,
Dublin 2, D02 Y754, Ireland
compliance@bonnierbooks.ie
www.bonnierbooks.co.uk

To my own grandmothers, Nanna Rowley and Nanna Bibby, with love xxx

Prologue

Outside it was trying to snow. Flakes drifted against the windowpane before disintegrating, the weather depressingly symbolic of the situation Lola found herself in on Christmas Eve. Not just Christmas Eve, but her birthday, and the last one of her thirties at that. Topping up her glass of Baileys, although the temptation to just guzzle it out of the bottle was strong, Lola settled back on the sagging rust-coloured sofa and tried to smile through the pain. It could be worse, she reminded herself, she could still be with Jared. Shuddering at the thought of his betrayal she ignored the notion that being with him would at least mean she wasn't alone.

Lola whispered to herself, 'Inner happiness is much more important than company. Happiness and contentment.' She repeated it like a mantra, hoping if she said it enough, she'd believe it. 'Cheers! Happy birthday to me!' She swigged her drink.

Putting down her glass, Lola reached for her phone, opened her messaging app and scrolled through all the unopened texts from him. She wavered slightly, memories of the good times they had assailing her, before

1

highlighting his number and blocking it. The satisfaction was instant.

Lola glanced around the poky studio flat that was positioned slightly wonkily above the Oxfordshire bakery she'd waltzed into four weeks ago – right when they were in the middle of a complete flap due to their baker having broken their arm at an ice rink. Spying the urgent advert in the window, Lola had stepped inside. Armed with a little bit of her natural charm, her always up-to-date food hygiene certificate and a CV as long as her arm, Lola had managed to convince the harried owners that she was just the woman to step into their breach. A light as air Victoria sponge and a round of fruit scones had quickly sealed the deal. The bakery wouldn't have to cancel orders in the run-up to Christmas and Lola would be able to pause and take stock.

Pulling the patchwork quilt snuggly around her knees, Lola counted her blessings. She'd had the good fortune to be in the right place at the right time, she had a roof over her head that did not leak (many years of travelling around the country, of camping and cramming herself into dreadful flats had taught her a watertight roof was a luxury) and although she had chosen to spend Christmas alone, she had been invited to join various people the following day. The kindness was overwhelming, but Lola felt very much that this Christmas needed to be done solo. Her heart and mind were all muddled up and she knew come the middle of January she would have to move on, but where to?

She loved the tight-knit community she had found, the way the locals hurried in each morning to buy their bread, the way they'd filled their baskets with mince pies, gossip and good cheer. All the compliments about her cakes and bakes filtered through into her borrowed kitchen and it didn't take much for Lola to reconnect with her childhood dream of having her own little bakery, full of cheery locals, piles of fat scones and the rumblings of local news. If circumstances had been different, she would have stayed on in Oxfordshire, tucked away in the biscuit-coloured villages with their sloping roofs and undulating hills, the smell of wood fires on the chill night air. It was an uncomplicated life; the locals were content and they loved Lola's cakes. Although thrilled with her success, Lola hoped the original baker didn't get wind of how well she was doing. She never, ever wanted to step on anyone's toes.

The fire flickered in the grate and Lola shuddered. It was the call of the wind, the echo of change. There was a week left of this old year, a week left to find her next adventure. The year had had a mighty good go at knocking Lola off her feet. If the pain of discovering her long-term partner, Jared, had been cheating on her, hadn't been enough she was then felled by the sudden passing of her beloved Nannie Ruby. Her grandmother may have lived to the grand old age of ninety-three and would have been much annoyed to find Lola grieving – after all, she'd had very good innings, as she liked to say – but that didn't make her passing any less painful. The grief still sliced through Lola's heart, causing her to catch her breath and stem her tears as best she could.

Lola felt utterly lost without her grandmother to call up for guidance. Ruby had always been on the end of the phone, lapping up her granddaughter's adventures, dishing out advice and comfort when needed. Ruby had taught Lola everything she knew. Their bond had been so tight – like two peas in a pod – that her mum, Bridget, had confessed to feeling squeezed out.

Determined not to cry at the memory of Ruby, Lola reached onto the bookshelf, pulling down an old wooden box, the surface worn smooth through years of handling it. Lola sniffed back tears; Ruby would not be impressed with her if she started to cry. Certainly not on her birthday. Birthdays had always been marked with towering home-made cakes and glasses of fizz.

Lifting the lid, Lola peered at the contents; they always made her feel close to Ruby when the pain threatened to engulf her. A box of tarot cards, the gilding worn off the edges, a blue sprigged teacup. Lola held the teacup up, checking for cracks or chips, but it was perfect in its delicate beauty. The saucer was similarly undamaged. White with pale blue flowers painted around the rim, it was the cup Ruby had used to read people's tea leaves. A skill Lola had never quite mastered, although it fascinated her and she had, on occasion, given it a go.

Cradling the cup in her hands, Lola closed her eyes, allowed the memories of sitting in Ruby's dining room on dreary Saturday afternoons, listening as her grandmother

4

peered at the formations of leaves left at the bottom of the cup before imparting her wisdom. Lola had once asked Ruby how she knew the future, only to be met with a half-shrug and the cryptic response that people always wanted reassurance. Lola placed the teacup on the table and lifted the next package out of the box. Ruby's tarot cards.

The box was scuffed and slightly damaged through use. Lola held it briefly to her lips before tipping out the cards, worn smooth and still smelling faintly of Ruby's perfume. Ruby had carried them everywhere, offering divine guidance on the bus or in the local library. She'd been a bit of celebrity in their home-town for her predictions and sage advice, which Lola's mother had found frankly embarrassing as she didn't believe in all that hokum. Lola knew her mother would have loved to have curtailed Ruby's influence over her, but her mother also enjoyed spending long hours at the hair salon or shopping and Ruby had been a conveni-ent babysitter.

Lola lifted out the contents and shuffled the cards, their weight comforting as she dealt a hand for herself, as she had done many times in her life for others looking for guidance. Turning the cards over, Lola was not sur-prised to see the same combination she had been getting for the past ten days, ever since she'd started to think about moving on. Strong indications of new beginnings, of happiness, of love even, although Lola was not ready or looking for a new relationship. The thought of ever giving her heart away again terrified her. However, the message from the cards comforted her, made her feel closer to her grandmother. Gave her hope.

With a smile Lola reached into the bottom of the box and pulled out a brown leather-covered notebook. The well-thumbed and slightly greasy pages contained all of Ruby's recipes and had been a constant companion to them both throughout Lola's childhood. Ruby had called it her spell book because she knew true alchemy was in baking a perfect sponge cake, not turning dross into gold. Cake, Ruby had always reminded Lola, was happiness made real. Lola closed her eyes and thought of this, of how she could spread love and happiness through her baking. She indulged in the fantasy of having her own little café, with an awning and bunting and children coming in to choose gingerbread men. It was a dream she'd harboured since she was a child, one Jared had scorned and made her suppress. Well, as she now knew, following him had been a bad decision, and anyway, he was gone, her future was whatever she wanted it to be, cake-scented and sugar-dusted. But where?

Lola flicked through the notebook, past recipes for rock cakes and lemon drizzle sponge, mince pies and apple strudels, her mouth watering until something fell out. She picked it up, an old-fashioned postcard of a tiny beach with fishing boats washed up on it. Lola turned it over, her excitement fading as she realized there was no message on the back, just a description and a date: *Fishing Boats at Polcarrow Bay, Cornwall, 1950.*

Why on earth had her grandmother kept a postcard with just a date on it? Ruby had been an unsentimental woman, not prone to keeping souvenirs or writing gushy messages in birthday cards, but she had always had a fondness for Cornwall. There had been a few allusions to a summer spent by the sea there, all recalled with a wistful smile, before the subject was quickly changed.

Peering closer at the faded colours, Lola felt a nip of cold air at the nape of her neck and her tiny apartment was filled with the scent of the sea. 'Polcarrow, Cornwall,' the name triggering a memory. 'Polcarrow,' she repeated. She'd seen it before somewhere. She tapped her fingers on the postcard, running the name through her brain until it clicked into place.

Lola frantically flicked through the pages of the notebook until she came to the scone recipe. The paper was smudged and soft from use, the ink mired by sticky fingers from baking, but there it was, next to the word 'Scones', written in tiny curling letters in faded pencil: *Polcarrow*. A memory assailed Lola, sunlight filtering through yellow kitchen curtains, flour-strewn countertops, the scent of something baking in the oven. Lola recalled tracing her fingers over the unusual word, forming the letters with her mouth before asking her grandmother what a Polcarrow was.

Lola still remembered the way Ruby had frozen before quickly pulling herself together, tugging the book from Lola's hands and cramming it back on the shelf. 'A place,' she'd said, 'somewhere I went a long time ago. Now, what colour shall we ice the cakes? Blue or pink?'

Polcarrow had been tucked away in Lola's mind after that, pretty much how the postcard had been hidden in the book. Her younger self had thought nothing of the way Ruby had changed the subject, but now Lola's intrigue got the better of her. She picked up her phone, typed the name of the village into the search engine and watched as the screen filled with photos of a tiny fishing village tucked into the ragged edge of Cornwall's coast. Blue skies and sunshine shone down on the harbour, bouncing off a row of adorable ice-cream-coloured cottages. The photos reminded Lola of childhood holidays, sticky ice creams on the beach, sand between her toes, endless, perfect days.

Lola's sixth sense twitched. Deep down she sensed Polcarrow must have been somewhere special to Ruby. Why else would the card have appeared when Lola was searching for guidance? Was it mad though – to drive all the way to Cornwall on a whim? Hadn't she done madder things? Packed up and gone travelling around Portugal at a moment's notice, set up a mobile cocktail bar to tour the summer festivals?

Propping the postcard up against the TV, Lola decided she'd leave it there, see if she was still called to travel to Cornwall in the morning. They'd been when she was a child, but she couldn't remember the name of the town they'd stayed in. Only the seagulls threatening to steal her pasty and the luminous turquoise sea.

8

Maybe Cornwall was worth a chance, if nothing else? Change of scene.

Three days later, Lola was trundling down a steep, cobbled road in her pink Mini. There'd been no rooms in the pub in Polcarrow so she'd found a cheap holiday apartment in a nearby town, arriving late the previous night to black skies and sea, like a shroud across the world. Turning off the radio, Lola allowed the squawk of the gulls to lure her towards the sea. She made her way past picture-perfect whitewashed cottages, their doors painted in jolly, primary colours and wound her way down past the church towards the seafront. After pulling up along the harbour, Lola got out of her car and glanced around. So this was Polcarrow.

With the sky and sea merging into a grumpy grey, it was hardly the beautiful village of her internet searches. Lola's heart sank as her eyes ran along the slightly dilapidated seafront. The whole village had an air of being slightly uncared for, as if forgotten about. However, as she took in the pastel cottages, the pub sign swinging in the sea air, the sun briefly broke through the clouds and something lifted in Lola's heart. On a summer's day she imagined there would be nowhere quite like this quaint little village with the sun sparkling on the sea.

Her eyes skimmed the seafront before falling on the café across the road. It was tired, old and had a 'To Let' sign above its burgundy awning and a hopeful possibility bloomed in her heart. Studying it, she repainted the dark, flaking windows a pale grey, imagined chairs with parasols outside, the door open, sunshine streaming in and people buying cream teas to eat on the beach. She was so engrossed in mentally redecorating the café that she didn't hear someone draw up beside her until they spoke.

'Be a shame to lose that—' the old man indicated to the café '—Scruff and I always get a tea and a bite to eat after our morning walk, don't we, boy, although, between you and me, the scones are usually a bit stale. Think she buys them in.' The old man gave her a long, considered look. 'You interested?'

Lola turned to him. 'Well my scones would always be home-made and never stale,' she promised.

'Well, if you're serious about that place, I'll hold you to it. Come on, boy.' He whistled, and the fluffy sheepdog followed him.

Lola watched them amble down the harbour front and head towards the pale-yellow cottage. A smile spread across her face. Polcarrow, it seemed, was a village in need of a baker.

Chapter One

Now

'We are gathered here today to remember the young lives lost when *The Maid of the Seas* perished during a storm on 17th November, 1950,' Tristan, Polcarrow's vicar, intoned in his gentle, guiding voice.

The wind ruffled Lola's hair and glancing out to sea, where the waves were crashing furiously against the harbour wall, she shuddered at the thought of being out in a fishing boat in this sort of weather. Tristan's voice washed over her as he uttered a short prayer, her mind anticipating the storm that was predicted to hit over the next few days. The village had already begun to batten down the hatches in preparation. Lola glanced at Alf. The elderly fisherman had his head bent in prayer and remembrance.

'Such a waste of life.' Alf's voice was choked with sadness. 'Thomas Penwith, we always said he had nine lives, never thought he'd come a cropper at sea. He was a fool though to go out in weather like this. They all were, but we can't change that now.' He reached forward and ran his fingers over the third name on the memorial – Charles Tremaine. 'It wasn't like Charles at all. My brother was the sensible sort. Love drove him to it. Love and greed, nothing good comes of either.' Alf sighed. 'Well, maybe love if it's done right.'

Alf laid a few flowers at the foot of the small memorial and bowed his head in his own prayer. Lola caught Tristan's eye, a look passing between them, a mutual understanding that always existed whenever they were close. Tristan gave a nod and Lola stepped forward, placing a comforting arm on Alf's shoulder.

'Shall we go somewhere warmer?' she suggested gently.

Alf nodded and raised a hankie to his eye. 'I'll be with you in a minute.'

'I'll go and put the kettle on.' Lola gave his arm a gentle squeeze before escaping the bitter November wind that was whipping over the sea and howling around the churchyard. Lola hurried ahead along Polcarrow harbour front to her café.

She unlocked the door, sighing with relief to be out of the cold as she stepped into the warmth. No one else knew but as well as the memorial to the lost fishermen, it was also the one-year anniversary of Nannie Ruby's passing. Wiping away the tears from her eyes, she turned the lock on the door and headed into the kitchen in search of a few moments of reflection before everyone else arrived. She'd light her own candles for her grandmother later. Hanging up her coat in the kitchen, she wiped the rain away from her face, grateful that the inclement weather had been able to hide her own tears.

Taking a few breaths to steady herself, Lola pressed her palms together in prayer, directing her gratitude towards her grandmother. It was down to Ruby that Lola had inherited enough money to make her dream of owning a café come true. The secret that Lola kept tucked tight up against her heart was her reason for coming to Polcarrow. She had told no one that she'd arrived on a whim after discovering the postcard matched the place name alongside Ruby's scone recipe. That she had packed up her car and headed off in search of a new adventure. That this search for something unknown would bring her a whole life – a café, friends and a community that she adored. Ruby had led her to the only place Lola had ever felt was home.

Tying the apron behind her back, Lola used the mirror hanging on the back of the door to check the victory rolls in her bright red hair were still in place. Miraculously, they'd been unruffled by the wind. After reapplying her signature red lipstick, Lola stepped out of the kitchen, her eyes brimming with happiness rather than sadness as she took in the cosy, vintage-style café she had created. Lola wished Ruby could see what she'd achieved. The café was decorated in soothing shades of pale grey and yellow, the counter had a view of the sea and was covered in glass domes full of tasty baked treats ranging from a classic Victoria sponge to bars of chocolate tiffin and, of course, no Cornish café would be complete without a generous offering of scones. She'd kept her promise to Alf that her scones would never be stale.

A knock on the café door brought Lola back to the present. Wiping away her tears, she hurried to unlock it, happiness spreading across her face as her eyes met those of Tristan. The sight of him always lifted Lola's heart and right now, seeing him was like the sun coming out after a storm.

Burnt out from working in a tough inner-city parish, Tristan had been sent to Polcarrow as the new vicar, arriving mere weeks before Lola had rocked up with her pockets overflowing with recipes and tarot cards. Both new to a village that was wary of incomers, but chronically nosey about their business, Lola and Tristan had quickly become friends. Together they'd weathered the curious looks and questions of the locals, and had won them over far more quickly than they'd expected.

Every morning since Lola had opened the café, Tristan joined Alf and Scruff for tea and toast. Lola knew from the way he always lingered that it wasn't just the particular blend of Earl Grey she stocked that kept him coming back for more. Tristan was kinder and sweeter than any of the men Lola had ever met before and his admiration that simmered with the desire for more than just friendship delighted and terrified Lola in equal measure. It was a barrier she'd once have leaped over, but the fact that her heart was still bruised from Jared and that her friendship with Tristan was invaluable, made her pause. She was wary of giving her heart away again.

'Lola, are you OK?' Tristan stepped through the door into the café, worry flashing across his face as she wiped away her tears.

'Yes, I'm fine, it's just . . .' She trailed off. 'Been a bit emotional.' It was on the tip of her tongue to tell him about Ruby but she realised this was Alf's day for mourning so tucked her own memories away.

Tristan unzipped his coat but the concern in his eyes didn't dissipate. He hesitated before laying a comforting hand on Lola's arm. As she leaned into the touch, heat bloomed through her and she wished he'd just pull her into his arms and give her a big hug. The desire to be held by him was strong, but she froze rather than making the move and instead gave his hand a grateful squeeze. Glancing up at him, her heart skipped the same beat it had been skipping since the first time he'd popped in to check she was OK and welcome her to the village just after she took ownership of the café. From the very first moment she had met him, Lola had instinctively known she could trust Tristan.

'Where's everyone else?' she asked, feeling untethered as their brief contact ended. She touched her arm where his hand had been, as if to preserve his gentle reassurance.

'They're coming with Alf,' he said as he followed Lola to the counter, pushing his damp blond hair off his forehead – an action Lola's hands craved to do. 'I warned them that if they took too long I'd nab the biggest scone.'

'Oi, I make all my scones the exact same size,' Lola scolded him, 'there is no biggest scone. But I do have extra-special scones for you all to try.'

Tristan raised an eyebrow, which caused Lola's insides to somersault as if they were on a trapeze. In her opinion, a vicar had no business being as handsome as Tristan was, but she never felt she could complain about that fact for long, not when they had become such firm friends. Lola swore she was done with love after her last relationship had crashed and burned in spectacular, heart-breaking fashion. Although, as she shared smiles with Tristan this notion was becoming increasingly difficult to uphold.

'Sometimes I can't believe I've already been here nearly a year,' he said. 'It feels both much shorter and as if I've never been anywhere else.'

'Maybe it's because you don't want to be anywhere else?'

'Maybe. Even on days like this—' he gestured towards the sea through the window '—it's sort of thrilling, isn't it?'

'From the safety of dry land. I can't imagine what those young lads were doing going out in weather like this. Or what it must've been like to suddenly realise you were in big trouble out at sea. It doesn't bear thinking about.' Lola shuddered and shook her head sadly.

They both took a moment to reflect on the ferocity of the weather swirling outside the window before Tristan turned back to Lola.

'I still remember the first morning I came to investigate what was going on and found you in the middle of the floor, sanding down the chairs. You were so flustered and . . .' He trailed off, his own face flushing as he grappled for the right word.

Lola hung on to the possibility of whatever he was going to say. 'And?' she asked, leaning towards him.

'Determined,' he settled on, 'determined to get it right.'

Lola nodded, her heart sinking, wishing he'd picked something a little bit more flattering. 'Yes, I really was. I hope I have.'

'You have, Lola,' Tristan said, leaning over the counter and giving her a long, ponderous look. 'I always wonder what drew you here, of all places.'

All Lola had ever told anyone was that she had been travelling around when she'd stopped in Polcarrow, seen the café and risen to Alf's challenge to keep him supplied with fresh scones. That had been the moment she knew deep in her soul that she had to come and live here. Lola hadn't told anyone anything about Ruby, about the connection she was sure her grandmother had with Polcarrow. Somehow it felt fanciful. Why else would she have kept a postcard hidden? Lola had expected to find something of Ruby in the small fishing village, but there had been nothing. Then again there was no reason for there to be. However, there was a sense of home, something that Lola had been searching for for a long time, and that, she had decided, was enough.

Lola flashed a smile at Tristan and repeated the same response she'd uttered on numerous occasions, 'I was called here, on the wind, you know. My sixth sense heard there was a village in need of tea and cake and I answered the call.'

Tristan laughed. It was the answer she'd always given when travelling, had loved the way it kept her shrouded in mystery. No one she'd met on her travels had really revealed their true self to anyone and it had become habit. However, now, seeing Tristan turn her response over in his head, the urge to tell him everything was growing stronger. How wonderful it would be to confide in someone, to reveal her true self.

'One day I'll find out the truth.' He flashed a heart-melting smile at her and Lola wondered how he hadn't been snapped up by anyone yet. Generous of nature and six foot tall with broad shoulders, his sea blue eyes and blond hair were a winning combination. Lola had always thought she preferred dark-haired men, but Tristan had completely overruled this preference.

Lola wished she could find the words to unravel her whole life to him, the way he was currently unwinding his damp winter layers. She watched him hang his coat up, drank in his strong, tall frame, the whole unexpect-edness of how much she liked him. The urge to cross the friendship barrier tingled in her fingertips. There was a pause as they took each other in, sneaking that extra look they so often found themselves doing, before the moment was broken by Scruff's barking as Alf, Freya and Angelo came through the door.

'Ugh, Scruff, no, not in here!' Alf groaned as the dog gave himself a shake, sending water droplets all over the floor and anyone unfortunate enough to be close to him.

Freya made a face. 'Yuck, I'll go and get the mop.'

Was that disappointment in Tristan's eyes, Lola wondered as he went to help Alf out of his coat. At almost ninety, retired fisherman Alf was considered the unofficial head of the village. He didn't go any-where without his dog, Scruff, who in turn liked to go anywhere he might be slipped a treat. Alf and Scruff had adopted Lola's café as their second home and Lola would not have had it any other way.

Coats all hung up to dry, everyone settled themselves at the table. Freya mopped the floor and Lola pulled out her pad. 'What is everyone having?'

'Earl Grey, please,' said Tristan.

Alf pulled a face before turning to Lola. 'I'll have a mug of strong fisherman's tea, a proper brew, that is. Not that muck you drink, Vicar.'

'It's what I like!' Tristan protested, glancing at Lola for support.

'There's nothing wrong with the comfort of familiar-ity,' Lola said diplomatically, even though she sometimes wanted to ruffle Tristan's habits, see what was under-neath that neat, held-together exterior. 'What's everyone else having?'

Taking down Freya and Angelo's orders, Lola retreated behind the counter to get started on the drinks, only to be followed by Freya.

'I'll do Angelo's coffee and my hot chocolate; I want lots of marshmallows. You make the teas,' she said as she began the process of steaming the milk. Lola was grateful for all of Freya's help, employing her had been her best decision since opening. Freya ran the front of house leaving Lola free to bake and provide tarot card readings from the kitchen door.

Lola had invited Freya to stay with her over the summer after her life in London had imploded. They had been friends for years, bonding over a summer working in a terribly run cheap cocktail bar. Freya's skills with the coffee machine, coupled with the rugged Cornish seaside that inspired her paintings, had helped her decide to settle permanently in Polcarrow. Freya was currently renting the spare bedroom in Lola's quaint cottage, but Lola knew it was only a matter of time before Freya moved in with Angelo up at Bayview House. Angelo, a sculptor currently on sabbatical, had been another summer waif and stray Lola had taken under her wing, and she prided herself on matchmaking the artistic couple.

Lola placed the teapots and cups onto a tray, including Alf's trusty blue and white Cornishware mug, and carried the drinks over to the table, setting them down in front of Alf and Tristan.

'What was your brother like?' Tristan asked as he poured out his tea.

Alf shook his head disapprovingly at the pale colour, stirred his own tea, poured it and showed the dark brew to Tristan. 'That's what you need, Vicar. Charlie? Well, it's strange because in a way he'll be forever twenty-two and I'm nearly ninety. He's more of a memory now than a person. Seventy five years is a long time.' He took a satisfied slurp of his tea. 'My ma was heartbroken, inconsolable, carried his photo everywhere in a locket. Broke the family up. My sister moved away, couldn't face it here anymore. He wouldn't have been on that boat if it wasn't for the woman he was planning on running away with.' Alf shook his head bitterly. 'We never mentioned her again. Nor him really, too painful. I had to get on with it, running the business, fishing, stepping up. I know he had dreams but maybe I did too, and they got put aside. I had responsibilities I never expected. No time for sentiment. I missed him, God, did I miss him. His guiding ways, his good nature. It's been so long sometimes it feels like he was never here.'

Lola reached out and squeezed Alf's hand. Her own loss was rawer. Not that she'd told many people about Ruby, part of her wanted to keep the memories to herself.

'Enough of all this sadness, what's been has been, it doesn't do to dwell on it. I don't understand people's desire to keep dredging up the past,' Alf said after a few moments of silent reflection. 'Come on, Lola, it's halfway through November, what are your plans for Christmas?'

Lola clapped her hands together in delight. 'I'm so glad you asked! Before meeting you earlier I whipped up some special scones I'm hoping to trial. Hang on, let me get them.' Darting into the kitchen, Lola emerged moments later with a plate piled high with golden scones. 'Cranberry and orange,' she explained, placing them onto the table, 'with brandy infused cream.'

Passing around plates, napkins and knives, everyone tucked into the scones, which received thumbs up and sighs of delight. Lola chewed thoughtfully and made a mental note to add a pinch more cinnamon.

'Lola, that scone was smashing, I hope they stay on the menu.' Alf patted his middle. 'Your scones remind me of the ones my mother used to make. Or at least they're the closest imitation I've ever found.'

Lola froze. Should she tell him the recipe came from Polcarrow? Could it have been Alf's mum who'd shown Ruby how to make the scones? Even the thought was ridiculous, so she decided not to say anything. She didn't even have any proper concrete proof Ruby had spent much time in the village. 'They're one of the first things my grandmother taught me to make after fairy cakes. She used to make scones every Sunday for tea.'

'These are divine, Lola,' Tristan said almost in awe.

Giggling, Lola replied, 'I'll take that as God's approval then. Alf?'

Alf crumbled up a bit of scone and let Scruff lick his fingers. The dog barked his approval and Lola gave him a quick scratch behind the ears. Scruff loved everything she baked, even if he wasn't meant to get his paws on it.

Lola let out a sigh of relief. 'Glad they pass the test. Angelo? Freya?'

'I like them,' Freya said as she helped herself to the half Angelo hadn't eaten. He wasn't one for indulging in too many sweet treats. 'What else are you making?'

Warming to the theme, Lola rattled off a list of all the things she was planning on serving in the café. 'Chocolate logs, themed cupcakes and mince pies of course.'

'I bet your pies are better than any supermarket,' Alf said, 'they're my favourite after scones. I can't wait to try them.'

'Alf, I'll make as many mince pies as you can possibly eat,' Lola promised.

'That sounds like a challenge, Lola, one that I am happy to accept.' Alf's eyes twinkled.

'I'm also going to make Christmas cakes and I'll decorate them however you want. Freya, could you possibly make me a poster to put in the window please? What do you think? I don't know how many people make their own anymore. I was helping in a bakery last Christmas and they did a roaring trade in them. Do you think anyone will want one?'

'I think that sounds marvellous,' Tristan reassured her. 'I'm sure people would much rather buy a locally baked cake than something off the supermarket shelf. We used to get inundated with them at my old parish – so much so that last year we did a taste test. Poor Mrs Mulligan prided herself on her fruitcake only to be pipped to the post by a supermarket one. We didn't have the heart to tell her. Put me down as your first order.'

'And me, but don't skimp on the brandy,' Alf warned her.

Lola reached into her apron pocket and pulled out her notebook. 'Excellent, my first customers, how would you like them decorated?'

'Not much surprises me at my age so I'll leave it up to you.' Alf winked.

Lola cast a glance at Tristan, pen poised.

'Ooh, I'll have a surprise decoration too.'

Lola glanced at Freya and Angelo, who shook their heads. 'I'll make a poster though,' Freya promised.

'Excellent, thanks.' Lola slipped the notebook back into her pocket. 'I love Christmas. What was it like here in the old days, Alf?' she asked. 'I'd love to know all about a traditional Polcarrow Christmas and maybe try and honour that somehow.'

'Old days, hey, you make me sound ancient! We didn't have all this fancy stuff to be sure. Midnight mass, Christmas Day drink in the pub, carol singers.' Alf sat back and thoughtfully regarded Lola and Tristan. 'I know its a cliché to say it, but it was a much simpler time. People just want rubbish now, stuff for stuff's sake. We didn't have much but my ma always used to make a Christmas cake, silver sixpence and everything in it, or was that the pudding, I forget now. She made sure whatever happened we enjoyed ourselves. That was until, well, you know . . .' A shadow passed over Alf's face as he silently recalled his memories. 'But there's no point dwelling on the past, is there? We've done enough of that for one day. I'm more interested in seeing what a modern, Lola Christmas looks like.'

Alf held up his mug and Tristan chinked his cup against it. 'I second that.'

Chapter Two

Lola didn't have to wait long to find out what a modern day Christmas in Polcarrow would look like. On Wednesday morning, Sue Chapman, leader of the village committee, bustled into the café, half the contents of her overlarge handbag threatening to spill out as she pulled out a bunch of flyers and handed them to Lola.

'Festive festival?' Lola questioned.

'You know how successful reviving the Fisherman's Fair was in the summer?'

Lola nodded. It had been wonderful to see the village full of people taking part in the sandcastle competition, admiring the fishing boats and eating cream teas. The whole fair had created a bit of local buzz and after appearing in *Cornish Life* magazine, Alf had become a local celebrity.

'Well, we had the most wonderful idea to put together all the various festive events.' Sue pulled her multicoloured reading glasses from her head and put them on. Taking the top flyer, she explained to Lola, 'Last year we just sort of had a church bazaar but this year Tristan wants to hold a Christmas tree festival and I thought, what if we had a light switch on as well?' Sue passed the flyer to Lola before reaching into her pocket for her phone. Lola waited as she swiped through various screens before turning it to Lola. 'What do you think of that?'

Taking the phone from Sue, Lola studied the photo, which appeared to be of a stack of lobster pots fashioned to look like a Christmas tree. 'Oh, Sue, that is absolutely gorgeous! I love it. How are you going to make it though?'

'I thought I'd ask for volunteers to help,' she confessed. 'My husband thinks it's a bit bonkers and wonders what on earth is wrong with a real tree. But I love this—' she smiled fondly at the photo on her phone '—and if we can pull it off, I mean, how difficult can it possibly be to stack together some lobster pots and drape lights over them? I think it could be something really special.' Sue slipped her phone back into her pocket. 'So can I leave some leaflets with you?'

'Of course you can! I'll even stick one in the window.'

'Perfect! Now, while I'm here it'd be a bit rude not to have a gingerbread latte, wouldn't it? Even though it is still November.'

'It's never too early for a gingerbread latte, Sue,' Lola told her. 'Takeaway or drink in?'

Sue glanced over her shoulder. 'In. The laundry can't find me here. Add in one of those brownies too, please.'

After the lunchtime rush Lola made a cup of tea and flicked through the pages of her Christmas cake order book and smiled with satisfaction. Freya had made a poster advertising them, which was stuck in the window of the café. Tristan had also taken a copy to put on the church noticeboard. There'd been a flurry of interest which had been matched by orders. With every Christmas cake order she placed in her book, Lola realised she was doing much more than just baking cakes. Every villager grew misty eyed as they reminisced about Christmases past; from beloved childhood presents to comical arguments over cracker toys, to the bittersweet family memories the season conjured up. Lola realised that her job was more than just cake baker, but to provide a trip down memory lane.

The villagers spoke about the cakes they'd loved, ones bursting with brandy, or decorated with ornate piping and little silver stars. Some asked for space to be left to sit a family heirloom decoration on the top. Lola smiled at this. With her penchant for the styles of the 1940s and 50s, she loved delivering life with a huge heap of nostalgia on the side. The project excited her and filled her with warmth as she thought of the extra magic she would help bring to everyone's Christmas.

Just as Lola was figuring out when to start the baking and what quantity of ingredients to order to fulfil the orders she had taken, the café door was pushed open, letting in a blast of chilly November air, and a uniformed courier driver entered, a wrapped-up package clutched in his hand.

'Lola Curran?' he asked, glancing at his notes and then at her.

'Yes, that's me.' She darted out from behind the counter, wondering what on earth he was delivering. She hadn't ordered anything.

The man dumped the package on one of the tables and passed his electronic device to Lola. 'Sign here,' he said as he gave the café a cursory glance.

Lola did as she was asked before passing the device back to him. 'Can I get you anything while you're here?'

'Yeah, a coffee would be great, two shots please. It's been a long day.' He rubbed his face and followed her over to the counter, peering at the treats stacked in their glass domes. 'Oh I shouldn't, but I'll take a couple of those brownies – for the wife, you know.'

'An excellent choice,' Lola said as she put two in a bag, passed him his coffee and waited for his payment to go through on the card machine. As soon as he'd left, Lola hurried over to the package, armed with some scissors to cut through the sticky tape holding it all together. By the looks of things the sender had used a whole roll. Whoever had sent it had not wanted anyone to get easy access. Lola wrestled with the tape, puffing as she pulled it off. The contents of the package were wrapped in bubble wrap and on the top sat a white envelope. Curious, Lola tore into it. Reading the note she gasped.

We found these hidden in the attic. After talking to the solicitor, who got hold of your mother, we were advised to send them on to you as they appear to have belonged to your grandmother and it didn't feel right keeping them. I hope they mean something and arrive safely.

The note was signed by the new owners of Ruby's house with contact details. Lola swallowed to think of someone else having turned the empty shell of Ruby's house into their home.

Putting the note aside, Lola tore through the layers, like some sort of pass the parcel that contained trips down memory lane, not sweets. Her stomach clenched. Things that had been hidden rarely contained good news. The box smelled of secrets, of parts of a life that had been hidden away, dispersed around a house, never meant to be looked at again. There was the faint aroma of her grandmother's perfume, a whiff of damp, all of it triggering fresh memories of Ruby's house. She had been tasked with helping her mother clear it out, which had been terse, done quickly and with little time for sentimentality.

Lola had taken whatever she could find that had meaning, thinking of the recipe book, the 'magic' spoon Ruby had used in all her baking, her tarot cards and teacup and a set of pearls she'd probably never wear but that she remembered Ruby wearing on special occasions.

Once empty, Bridget had locked the house up for one final time and paused on the doorstep, the 'For Sale' sign looming over the hedge. Lola realised nothing would ever be the same again. It was like she'd packed part of her away in the boxes. Turning, she'd caught her mum regarding her, as if she was debating whether or not to say something.

'What is it?'

Bridget was silent for a while before saying, 'You two were always thick as thieves.'

'What do you mean by that?' Lola asked, puzzled.

'It's silly but I was always a bit jealous of your bond with Ruby,' her mum admitted, with embarrassment. 'She was delighted that you inherited her psychic abilities. I never did, even though I tried. Mum prided herself that it'd come through the generations, but it seemed to skip me,' she said sadly. 'She was always disappointed by that.'

Lola digested this. 'Mum, I had no idea. Is that why—'

'Yes, why I didn't want you spending so much time with her. No one should say this about their child but I felt like you'd taken my place. I also didn't like how she'd wheel you out to read the cards for her friends. You were just a kid. The mystical stuff never felt right to me. At school I was teased for my mother being a witch. I just wanted a normal mum like everyone else had, not one who'd read palms on the bus into town.'

'I had no idea.'

'Of course you didn't, you weren't supposed to,' she sighed, reaching into her pocket, pulling out a packet of cigarettes. 'Now, come on, it's cold, let's go. I need to pack for my return flight.' Bridget had walked down the driveway, a box tucked under her arm, moving away from any questions Lola had. They had never spoken of it again. Bridget had flown back to Spain and remained there, soaking up the sun and loving the ex-pat life.

Now, Lola picked up one of the bundles, underneath the bubble wrap it was encased in brown paper. Tears sprang to Lola's eyes as she thought of whoever had put the box together, taking great care of the contents, knowing they would mean something to the recipient. Lola glanced around the café, at the evening drawing in early over the bay. It would soon be time for the post-school rush, not the ideal time to unwrap delicate mementoes. Lola gently replaced the bundle she'd extricated, refolded the bubble wrap and closed the lid. She'd take this home and go through it when she had the space and time to deal with whatever her sixth sense was telling her was lurking inside.

Chapter Three

As soon as the post-school rush ended, Lola quickly cleaned down the café, locked up and headed home, the package tucked safely under her arm. The storm that had been threatening the memorial service had blown through Polcarrow, bringing with it dark moody skies and sideways rain. Lola was looking forward to cold crisp days and would've been lying if she didn't admit she was crossing her fingers, hoping for snow. Who didn't love the romance of a white Christmas? Although with Cornwall's more temperate climate, snow was wishful thinking.

Sighing at the thought of snowball fights on the beach and warming up with luscious hot chocolates laden with cream and marshmallows, Lola reminded herself that a white Christmas in reality was usually a bit soggy. Romance would be nice though, she thought, having someone to curl up with in front of the fire, all safe and snuggled up warm. Her mind inserted Tristan into the image, the pair of them tucked up under blankets, throwing another log into the burner. Lola smiled at the thought and wondered how she could find the courage to turn the fantasy into a reality. Since March, when Lola opened the café, they had bonded over morning tea and toast. This had stretched well beyond the allotted breakfast time as parishioners realised they had more chance of catching their vicar in the café than the church.

Their friendship had grown from these morning chats, especially in the early days when they were both trying to figure out the motivations of various locals. They'd huddled together over the final slices of cake, swapping notes and exchanging past life stories. Lola had quickly found herself looking forward to the early starts because it gave her time with Tristan before anyone else got to him. Their bond had grown and she'd spent more time than she liked to admit wondering what it would be like to act on the impulses that sparked in her heart every time he stepped through the café door. They'd seen each other at pub quiz nights and other village events but their obvious attraction to each other hadn't made it out of these boundaries. *His friendship is much more valuable*, she repeated like a mantra, as she headed along the harbour front to her own little blue-painted fisherman's cottage.

Balancing the package on her hip, Lola fished the house keys out of her pocket. As she unlocked the front door the delicious aroma of something tomato-based slowly cooking greeted her. Lola paused. The smell of cooking and the lights on low meant that Freya must be in. The faint sound of voices from the living room confirmed this as Lola placed the box on the floor to remove her coat and rainbow-coloured scarf and hang them on the pegs by the door. After picking the box back up, she gave a gentle knock on the living room door before pushing it open. Freya and Angelo were sprawled on the sofa, halfway through a bottle of wine, a paint sample chart unfurled like a banner across their knees.

'Productive afternoon?' Lola asked, nodding towards the paperwork strewn across the coffee table. As part of his testament of love towards Freya, Angelo had purchased Bayview House, a very dilapidated old building situated right at the top of Polcarrow with views to die for across the bay. Lola adored the house with all its original 1930s features. The huge windows that flooded light into the rooms made it an ideal residence for two artists. It was such a shame the previous owners had left it to wrack and ruin.

'Ummhmm.' Freya shifted up on the sofa and signalled to the colours in the book. 'We're going to paint it white. Blank canvas, keep it bright and airy. I'm thinking of contrasting that with bright curtains and furniture. I mean, look at this sofa!' Freya leaned across Angelo to show Lola a photo of a stunning fuchsia sofa.

'That is gorgeous! You know I love anything with a bit of colour.' Lola glanced around her own living room, decorated in an eclectic style that combined the traditional cottage features with bright modern tones. Various trinkets she'd picked up on her travels were displayed, ranging from a shamanic drum to a sampler she'd found in a junk shop that had been completed by Edith in 1887.

'I guess that's two votes for the pink sofa now,' Freya said as she gave Angelo a kiss. 'You're out-voted, my love. You can't have everything in black.'

'I never said I wanted everything in black, I just don't . . .' Angelo trailed off and had another look at the photo Freya was brandishing. 'OK . . . you can be in charge of the soft furnishings. I'm not sure cushions are my forte and you do, erm, prefer a more varied colour palette than I do.'

Freya gave him another kiss and flashed Lola a triumphant thumbs up. Angelo was more of a sculptor than a painter, liking clean lines or working with metal and wood, elements he could get his hands on, manipulate. Freya much preferred opening her paints and creating bright seascapes and sunset scenes.

'What's in there?' Freya asked, nodding at the package.

'Oh this?' Lola glanced down at it, smoothing the rucks in the re-attached sticky tape. 'Just something I ordered,' she found herself saying, suddenly possessive of its secrets whilst she sorted out what it contained.

Freya nodded and asked no further questions. After all, it was the season of deliveries. 'Do you want some wine? Angelo's got an aubergine parmigiana baking in the oven. It should be done in about fifteen minutes.'

Lola shook her head at the bottle Freya was waving. 'Maybe with dinner, which smells divine!' She stood up. 'I'll just take this upstairs and change out of my dress.'

Freya nodded and turned her attention back to whatever Angelo was looking at on his tablet. Leaving them to their future building, Lola carried the box upstairs and plonked it on the middle of her bed, staring it out. Not quite ready to open it yet, she headed into the bathroom to remove her once expertly applied, but now rather smudged, makeup. She prided herself on always looking flawless and as a devotee of vintage styling she loved being dressed to the nines, even in the kitchen. Her bright red hair was curled into victory rolls which she knew would last another day if she slept with a hairnet on.

Smoothing in her night cream, Lola pushed away the thought that in a few weeks' time she'd be turning forty. It seemed such a huge milestone, as if life was about to flip over into a different era. She wondered where the last twenty years had gone. Had she spent them well? Made the right choices? Giving her cheeks one final satisfied pat, she decided there was no point dwelling on the 'what ifs'. She tried not to do regrets but as she got older, that was becoming harder to live by.

As she changed into some silky pyjamas, the package sat in the middle of the bed, almost demanding her attention. Lola opened it up and started to remove the inner packaging she'd stuffed back only to have her investigations stalled by Freya calling up that the food was ready.

Over dinner they discussed the storm that had thankfully left Polcarrow unscathed, Bayview House and Christmas.

'You OK?' Freya asked, tipping the last of the wine into her glass as Angelo cleared the table to wash up.

'Yes, why wouldn't I be?'

Freya shrugged. 'You seem a bit distracted.'

Lola opened her mouth and almost spilled out about the contents of the package but instead quickly changed track. 'Just busy thinking about all those Christmas cakes I'm going to be making, that's all, plus I need to find time to fit in knitting a Christmas jumper for Alf and a matching one for Scruff.'

'Oh my gosh, that's the cutest!' Freya gasped. 'I can't wait to see them. Hey, reckon we could get Angelo in a Christmas jumper?'

'That's a battle you can have. Maybe find one with a penguin on it, given the all-black thing he's got going on.'

'I could go even further and get him a penguin onesie.'

Lola laughed, picturing Angelo with his whole mad, bad and dangerous to know persona dressed as a six foot penguin. Freya was obviously having the same thoughts as she was, giggling into her wine.

'What's this?' Angelo asked as he came in. 'Did I hear "penguin onesie"?'

Freya composed herself. 'No, of course not, would I be so mean?' She reached out for him and quickly changed the subject. 'Are you staying tonight or going over to Bayview?'

Angelo looked at Lola and then back at Freya. 'Here would be nice if no one minds?' Freya and Angelo exchanged a heated look.

'Of course I don't mind,' Lola said and gave a pretend shiver. 'I've told Freya you're welcome to stay here as much as you like. I don't like thinking of you freezing up in that old, draughty house.'

'Don't worry, the first thing I did was have the boiler replaced. It's just everything else that's taking time or money.' He sighed and joined Freya on the sofa, where she began to reassuringly stroke his long hair. 'I need to raise a bit of extra funds.'

Silence settled over them. All three of them knew there was an easy way for Angelo to make some extra cash but he was still stubbornly refusing to resurrect his art career. Freya, on the other hand, had grasped the opportunities Cornwall had presented her with to develop her paintings and following a gallery night in the café back in the autumn, had started to finally make some money from her art. Lola was proud to see that Freya was determined not to let anything stop her.

Catching the looks Angelo and Freya were casting each other, eyes sparkling and edges blurred with desire, Lola made her excuses about needing to get her beauty sleep and having an early start and headed upstairs to bed.

Even though the night air was nippy, Lola pushed the bedroom window open to let some fresh air in. Her bedroom was at the front of the cottage and she loved nothing more than being lulled to sleep by the gentle whoosh of the waves. When it was stormy she loved knowing she was safe and warm while the elements battled it out.

She sat on her bed and regarded the package sitting in the middle of her favourite lilac-sprigged duvet cover.

Leaning forward, Lola lifted out the objects. Carefully, she unwrapped each one, taking her time to discover what was stowed away in the box. In the first was an ornate cross pendant Ruby had been given on her confirmation then never worn, a story Lola had heard when she'd found the beautiful cross as a child whilst searching through Ruby's jewellery box. Ruby had never gone to church either, much to her parents' dismay, citing that God could see you everywhere, that there was no point just being good on a Sunday morning. Tangled up with the cross was a tarnished ring set with a slightly dulled red stone. She lifted it to the light. A ruby? Lola slipped it onto her finger. She had never seen it before. Lola gave it a polish. Holding her hand out so it caught the lamplight, she wondered who had given it to her grandmother. Why had it been kept hidden? Ruby's engagement ring had sparkled with a trinity of diamonds but that had been passed to Lola's mother.

After pulling the ring off, she nestled it back against the black velvet and moved on to the next, bulkier package and found another set of tarot cards. These ones were smaller, fitting neatly in Lola's palm, the illustrations printed in primary colours, more basic looking than the deck Lola had inherited from Ruby.

Giving the cards a shuffle, Lola began to deal out a spread, amazed to see the same cards coming out in the same order from this deck as every other one she dealt from for herself. The priest, the priestess, the lovers, new beginnings. Lola considered them, her thoughts flitting briefly to Tristan. It seemed preposterous to think they had been led to this tiny village at the same time to . . . well, to what? Fall in love?

Face flushing, Lola tidied the cards away. It was too fanciful a thought. She was almost forty, not fourteen. Whatever she'd been led to Polcarrow for was surely something greater than her own love life. Love was a risk, one Lola wasn't sure she was willing to take again. Jared had gone from charming to toerag at record-breaking speed and had left deep scars. It still amazed Lola how long she'd stayed with him, how much she'd wanted to believe his empty promises. Especially as she would've advised anyone else in the same situation to dump him and move on.

She picked the cards up, restacked them and slipped them back into their case then set them aside. The next few bundles turned up a small box that contained theatre tickets, a pair of pearl earrings, and rather strangely, a single white satin glove. Why had Ruby kept one glove? Lola tried it on but Ruby had had slimmer fingers than her and a bit of a wrestle ensued to get it back off. Lola reached into the box but there were no bubble wrapped packages left. Instead, sitting at the bottom, nestled in brown paper, was a small stack of white envelopes tied together with a red ribbon.

Picking them up, Lola lifted them to her face and breathed in the scent of the past: old paper, slightly damp, love tied together and banished away. Holding them, Lola's heart rate picked up. Here was a secret, the writing on the front was not the neat slant of her grand-father, Ernest, it was looser, as if penned by a dreamer. Lola's fingers toyed with the bow before deciding to come back to the letters, for they weighed heavy in her hands with whatever secrets they would spill.

The final item left behind was a small cloth-bound notebook, red in colour. Lola picked it up and opened it. 'No way,' she exclaimed as she flicked through the pages. Written in neat, girlish writing on the front page was Ruby's name and address. Lola turned the first page and read:

1st January, 1950

It's a brand-new year and I have a lot of hope for the future. Things have to start getting better and I think they will. Out dancing with Ida and Joan last night, feet a bit sore today but it was fun. Think Ernest might be sweet on me, but I'm only eighteen, too young to get married. I want some adventures first. I have therefore decided that 1950 is going to be my year of adventure.

Lola gasped with delight. She had no idea Ruby had ever kept a diary. She certainly hadn't as an adult. Lola skipped through the first few entries, hungry for glimpses of a young Ruby. They were mostly complaining about the cold weather, her job as a typist, which was dull but gave her money for lipsticks and the dances she'd been to. There were notes about some of the tarot readings she had done as she set out on her life path of advice giving, although Lola wondered what advice an eighteen-year-old could truly impart, but Ruby had always had the air of someone who knew more than this life had shown her. As she flicked through descriptions of the spring, of galleries she'd been to, theatre shows she'd seen (and rated) a cream envelope fell out where it had been tucked in safely further along in the book.

It was unsealed. Untucking the flap, Lola pulled out an old black and white photo and studied it for a few moments as she tried to figure it out. It showed a group of young people sitting on a beach. Lola's eye honed in on Ruby, standing in the middle of the shot looking glamorous in a floral summer dress, her head thrown back laughing. She was flanked by two young men who were lifting her off the ground, whilst one of her friends looked on in amusement. Peering closely at the people, the hairs on the back of Lola's neck stood up and her mouth went dry. Did one of the men look familiar? No, it couldn't be, could it? Turning the photo over she gasped to see written in Ruby's neat handwriting: *Polcarrow, September 1950*. The same as next to the scone recipe.

'Yes!' Lola whooped to herself as she held proof in her hands that her hunch had been right. Ruby had been in Polcarrow. It had meant something!

Lola turned the photo back over. She never remembered seeing that sheer joy in any of the photos of Ruby and Ernest. Lola flicked through the book hoping for

42

more photographs, but there was nothing. Suddenly the paintings her grandmother had had hanging in the hallway of her house depicting cavernous coves and fishing boats took on a whole new meaning, as did the wistful look Ruby got every time she spoke of her youth, her love for Cornwall but her fear of going in the sea. Lola didn't need to tap into her sixth sense to know there was something more behind the laughter in that photo, behind the treasured postcard. Something carefree that spoke of summer abandonment and hopeful, young love.

Lifting up the letters, Lola squinted at the front of one of the envelopes. A Cornwall postmark was stamped in bold black. Lola glanced from the letters to the photo to the diary, as everything she had known about Ruby rearranged itself. Someone had written to Ruby, who had then tied the letters up with a red ribbon. Were they love letters? Lola wondered, but if they were, why had Ruby ended up back in London with sweet but slightly dull Ernest, with his smart suits and job in a bank and settled down far, far away from the sea?

Chapter Four

23rd August, 1950

Dear Diary,

I have the most wonderful news! Joan's uncle has invited us to spend a week in his house in Cornwall. Apparently the house is large, built in the art deco style (whatever that means) and overlooks a small bay. I have no idea what we'll do in some sleepy Cornish village but it's been so long since I saw the sea. Probably not since the war ended and that was only on a day trip to Southend and it rained. I've already bought some new fabric to make two new frocks, my ones are so tired. I wish rationing would end, it's very tiresome now. I've no idea what one needs to take with them to Cornwall. A bathing suit maybe, so it's a good thing I finally learned to swim even if I hate getting my hair wet! Mum made a face when I told her about the trip, as if she doesn't approve, but knows she can't stop me. Wild horses couldn't stop me. Or is it wild fire? Anyway, whatever the wild thing in the saying is, it won't and can't stop me. Apparently I can use the break to seriously consider Ernest. He's sweet on me, but it's only been a couple of dances and everyone is giving me the nudge, expecting us to walk down the aisle. There's nothing wrong with Ernest, I'm wise enough to know what sort of catch he is, but, I don't know, I want something more than just getting married, at least for now. Anyway, I'm sure my head is so full of the sea, of Cornwall and whatever goes on there to give Ernest much thought.

Give Ernest much thought? Lola repeated to herself the next morning, feeling perturbed on behalf of her gentle grandad, who'd adored his wife. She'd had an unsettled night and had woken early the next day to head to the café, where she was now dipping back into Ruby's diary. She turned over a few pages, the writing becoming increasingly erratic as Ruby scribbled about her holiday, but something niggled, telling Lola she needed to proceed with caution. This was her grandmother's life she was raking through. Judging by the photo, other people's pasts were tied up in it. Lola settled back against the kitchen counter reasoning another entry wouldn't hurt when the door being flung open made her jump so much that she almost dropped the book.

'Freya! You gave me a fright!' Lola exclaimed as she clutched the book to her chest.

'Are you OK?' Freya narrowed her eyes.

'Yes, of course, why?' Lola slid the book back into her pocket.

'You're being a bit weird, like jumpy weird,' Freya said. 'What's in that book?'

'Oh, nothing, just some notes I've been keeping about recipes,' Lola bluffed, not ready to broadcast to everyone the story of her grandmother's life in Polcarrow. Although, she had been hoping to catch Tristan that morning, show him the photo, see what he made of it all.

Freya gave Lola a long look before holding up two different types of bunting, having decided it was time to start getting the café looking festive. 'I was just wondering where you wanted these to go. And I might need help while it's quiet.'

'Definitely the gingerbread one around the counter,' Lola said, stepping forward. She picked up the second one, which had a robin motif. 'Maybe this around the window?'

The door chimed and Freya, trailing bunting, headed back into the café to help the customer. Lola took the opportunity to fire a quick text to Tristan:

Hiya, any chance you can pop over a bit later? I have something I'd like to chat about.

He responded immediately:

I can come now?

Lola almost swooned at his dependability and peering through the kitchen door window to where Freya was busy serving a young couple, texted back:

It's a bit of a private matter. Come at the end of the day, I'll save you some cake.

Slipping her phone back into her apron pocket, Lola joined Freya and whilst the customers concentrated on their coffees, she set about trying to work out the best place to put the Christmas tree so that it wouldn't be in anyone's way.

Lola let Freya go just after the post-school rush, which consisted of groups of teenage girls buying marshmallow-laden hot chocolates and occupying the sea view table pretending to do their homework whilst sharing gossip about the boys they fancied. They were just on their way out when Tristan arrived, bundled up against the cold, concern etched across his face.

'Lola what's up?' he asked as he swept through the café, eyes darting over her. 'Are you OK?'

'Yes, I'm sorry, it's just something I need to talk to someone about, someone who is wise but who I also trust,' she said as she loaded the empty hot chocolate cups onto a tray and carried them towards the counter.

'Honoured, though I think Alf might be a better candidate on the wise front.'

Lola grimaced. 'I'm a bit worried it's about Alf.'

Tristan's face flashed with concern. 'Is he all right? I thought he's been walking a bit slower since the cold weather's arrived.'

'I saw that too, but he won't like us fussing. Sit down and I'll explain. I have some Victoria sponge that needs finishing off if you want to join me?'

Tristan grinned. 'Like I could ever say no to you, Lola. Looking lovely and festive in here,' he said as he removed his coat and hung it over the back of a chair. 'That gingerbread bunting is quite cute.'

Lola smiled. 'Sadly, I didn't make it, but it is rather adorable. Freya and I decorated this afternoon. Can you flick the sign to "Closed" if you don't mind, I'm almost out of most things and I need a sit-down.'

Tristan did as he was told with the sign and settled himself into the window seat. Lola brought the tray over and laid out the cups and saucers, a pot of Earl Grey tea and the remains of the cake sliced into two large portions.

'I don't care what Alf says, there's nothing like a nice refreshing cup of Earl Grey.' Tristan lifted the teapot and poured out the tea. 'These little dainty cups remind me of my grandmother. She always used to get hers out on special occasions.' Tristan held one up, the cup adorably small in his large hands.

Lola pushed a generous slice of cake across to him. 'What? It won't be as good in the morning and I'm sure we've both earned a little afternoon indulgence.'

Tristan took a bite of the cake and smiled with pleasure. 'I can always run it off in the morning.'

'Very brave of you, going running in this cold,' Lola said. As she sipped her tea she began to relax. There was something wonderfully easy about sitting with Tristan and having a chat over tea and cake. He never judged, he always paused before answering and he was warm, comforting company. He was the first man Lola had met with whom she didn't have to put on any sort of act or mask. She didn't care to dwell on what this said about her previous relationship with Jared, other than it wasn't all she'd cracked it up to be.

'How was your day?' Lola asked to buy herself some time.

'I spent most of it sorting out the Christmas trees that have been stored for the annual Christmas tree festival. Sadly, church budget doesn't stretch to buying new ones. They're a bit tatty looking so I'm hoping fairy lights and tinsel will help disguise that. Would you like to decorate a tree?'

'Of course! Is there a theme?'

'No, no theme. I tried to come up with one but in my experience no one sticks to it. You can't ask a bunch of primary school kids to do deep and meaningful hand-made decorations, can you? I just want it to be fun.'

'Fun, I can do fun.' Their eyes met for a moment. Something shifted inside her making her suddenly nervous.

Tristan smiled almost shyly at her before signalling to the cake with his fork. 'This is delicious. How on earth do you decide what to make every day?'

Lola paused before confessing, 'Part of it is my sixth sense, I get a sort of idea what people might be after with the weather. Also, there's the favourites that always go down well.' She signalled to the Victoria sponge. 'No one ever says no to a classic. I'm thinking of doing ginger cake and mini strudels.'

'A strudel would be an excellent post-run treat.' Tristan smiled at her, their eyes meeting again and Lola felt safe, knowing she was with someone she could trust with anything.

Taking this as her cue, she said, 'Tristan, there was something I wanted your advice on.'

'Of course, you can ask me anything, Lola, in any capacity, friend or vicar.'

Lola nodded. 'Bear with, I just need to fetch something.' She darted up and headed into the kitchen to grab her handbag before returning to the table. 'Did I ever tell you why I came here?'

'You said you needed a new start after a break-up. That and all the stuff about being drawn here on the wind.' He winked.

'Yes, well remembered. Actually, I know I joke about it, but the wind thing isn't too far from the truth, but I feel a bit silly saying it. I found a postcard tucked inside my grandmother's recipe book last Christmas. I was so down, so lost, that I took a chance, coming here because I felt I was called to. I don't know if that sounds silly.'

'Not at all, my calling was to the Church. It was something I felt deep inside me rather than being a job I searched for in a newspaper.' He smiled encouragingly at Lola.

'I knew you'd understand. Well, my Nannie Ruby led me here. We were very close, very similar. Mum once told me she was jealous of our bond, which is one of the saddest things I've ever heard. Anyway, when Ruby died she left a lot of money to me to make my wish of opening my own café come true. I don't think Mum was properly happy with how the will was split, it caused a bit of tension. My grandmother also left me this.' Lola put the recipe book on the table 'Her recipe book.'

Tristan reached forward to touch it before stopping. 'Can I?'

'Go ahead, but you won't find the secret ingredient, that's kept under lock and key,' she teased, watching as Tristan carefully turned the pages, like he was holding a sacred text, which Lola supposed in a way he was. When he reached the page with the scone recipe on it, Lola leaned across and pointed. 'See what's written there?'

'Polcarrow?' He glanced up at her for clarification.

Lola nodded. 'Last year, when I was feeling very alone, I saw that word and, with the postcard, I don't know, something just spoke to me. I googled Polcarrow and saw this charming little village and felt the pull to come here. And, well . . .'

'The rest is history,' Tristan finished for her. 'But not the whole story?'

'Well, it was, until I got a delivery yesterday. A box full of things Ruby had hidden away in her house. There was a ring I'd never seen her wear, no idea who gave it to her, and other bits and bobs, and this. Her diary.' Lola reached into her bag and placed the small notebook on top of the closed recipe book. 'It's OK, you can open it. I guess it's not private anymore.'

Tristan smiled as he read the first entry. 'When did she write this?'

'The year she came to Cornwall!'

'Have you read it all yet?' He paused as he lifted the cover.

Lola shook her head. 'Not all of it. I was tempted to stay up all night, but I feel a bit nervous about what I might uncover. I wanted to start at the beginning, it's all about her life in Enfield, a side of her I never knew. There was a bunch of letters all tied together that Ruby had been sent. I've not dared open them either. I could tell from the writing they weren't from my grandfather.' Lola paused. 'And there was this.'

Holding her breath, she pushed the cream envelope across the table, watching as Tristan carefully lifted the flap and pulled out the photograph. He studied it in silence for a few moments, time slowing right down, before looking at Lola and placing the photo on the table between them. Sitting back he let out a breath. 'Is that . . . ?'

Chapter Five

'Alf?' She pointed at the man with the fairer hair. 'That's what I wanted to ask you, if you think it's him?'

They both leaned in close over the photo, heads almost touching, to give it more consideration, studying the faces as they came to the same conclusion.

'Lola, I think it is, that's definitely the same grin he gives whenever he's up to mischief now. Did you think it was him?'

Lola nodded and sat back, relieved. 'I did!' She picked up the photo and studied it, lost for words, trying to get her head around the fact that her grandmother had spent a summer in the same place Lola now called home and that she knew Alf.

'Are you OK, Lola?' Tristan asked softly when she'd been silent for a while.

Lola nodded. 'Yes, I think so. It's a lot to think about. It feels rather mad.'

'You had no idea your grandmother came here?'

'I only knew that she knew the name from the recipe book. I just assumed she'd come here on holiday with Grandad or something. We used to come to Cornwall on holiday as kids but never as far down as this. Ruby always just said she liked Cornwall because it was beautiful, like another world, but wouldn't say anything else. As a child I thought that just meant it was really far away, because, well, it is. I never thought it might have been a different world for her in another sense.'

'And you think she knew Alf?'

'If it's him in the photo, it seems that way.' Lola looked at the photo. Ruby wasn't turned towards Alf, but to the other young man, something silent passed between them, captured on film for all eternity. 'But who's the other man? He seems to be the one Ruby's interested in. Look how close they are.'

Tristan picked the photo up again. 'No idea. I take it it's not your grandad or another boyfriend you know of?'

Lola shook her head. 'It's certainly not Grandad. He looks sort of at home, like he's a local or something.'

They both studied him, his features slightly blurred as he turned towards Ruby. From what Lola could make out, he was tall with a thatch of fair hair, his skin sun-kissed. 'Do you reckon he's still alive somewhere? Does he look a bit local?'

Tristan picked up the photo, brought it close to his face, before passing it to Lola. 'I don't know. Maybe he does a bit. Looks like he's used to being outdoors. Alf would probably know him.'

Lola took the photo from Tristan. 'Maybe, but he's so reluctant to talk about the past that I don't feel right just slapping it down in front of him and asking, "Is that you and did you know my nan?". I can't, can I?'

Tristan laughed. 'No, but . . .' His face darkened.

'What?'

'No, it's just a thought.'

'Oh, you can't leave it like that!'

Tristan poured some more tea for them both. 'Remember those young men who died at sea. Remember Alf's brother was one of them. After the memorial I read up about it in a local history book. Terrible tragedy. They were warned not to go out, but they went all the same. No one knows why. They never came back. Maybe . . .'

Lola was silent for a moment as she absorbed Tristan's suggestion but it was too big for her to get her head around. 'I wonder if that's why Alf is so focused on looking forward. Too much sadness in the past. What if this is one of the lads who was lost at sea? Oh my gosh! Imagine if it was Alf's brother! And what if something happened between him and Ruby?' Lola gasped, tapping at the man next to Ruby. 'Maybe we should go and ask Alf?'

Tristan considered this, his eyes catching hers. 'Lola, the answer is likely to be in the diary. Maybe you should read it first? What if it's nothing? We shouldn't risk upsetting Alf, should we?'

'You're right, I'm getting carried away. But . . . I feel it here—' Lola tapped her heart '—that there's something more going on. But I'm a bit scared of finding out just what.' She glanced down at the faded red cloth cover, at the secrets that were still contained in it.

'Ruby was clearly very special to you and if you need anything, to talk or just a friendly listening ear, then I'm here for you,' he said in a low voice, in a way that hinted at more than digging up the past.

'Thank you, that would be wonderful, if you don't have too much else on, what with Christmas kind of being your big event and all that.'

Tristan reached across the table and gave her hand a squeeze. 'Nothing's ever too much for you, Lola.'

The connection and the weight of the unspoken meaning behind those words melted something in Lola. Glancing at their hands, she felt as if she never wanted to let go.

Chapter Six

Saturday, 2nd September, 1950

Dear Diary,

I'm writing this while I'm on the train. We left Paddington first thing and I feel like we've been travelling forever. We've played four rounds of rummy, eaten our sandwiches and now Ida is telling us all about how she wants her wedding dress to look. Jack hasn't even proposed yet, although, I'm sure it doesn't hurt for a girl to be prepared. Joan is asking all the right questions, she's much more interested in settling down than I am, although she's not sweet on any of the men trying to court her. I'm keeping my cards close to my chest where Ernest is concerned, even though they keep asking. He's nice and all that, the dependable sort, but I want more than nice and dependable. I daren't say it out loud to anyone in case they think I have foolish notions, but I want love, grand sweeping fairy-tale love, the sort that knocks your socks off. And he must be dashing. Now that does sound silly.

Later ...

Cornwall is magnificent! Very much worth sitting on the train all day for! Oh my! It's like nowhere I could ever have imagined. Everything is so clear and bright, the sky is cloudless and blue and the sea, I had no idea the sea could be so clear! It sparkles! The air is sweet, I keep taking big deep breaths of it like it's going to clean the London smog from my lungs. The house is gorgeous, like a palace, although Ida and I downplayed our excitement because Joan didn't seem all that wild about the house. Then again she came here as a child. But it's huge! There's a chequerboard floor, a sweeping staircase and we each have our own room. There's a housekeeper, not that we've seen her, but someone had left us some provisions. Joan has the master bedroom at the front of the house even though both Ida and I would've liked it. We're at the back. If I push the window open I can hear the sea. The village is called Polcarrow. It's built on a very steep hill, we're right at the top as if we're presiding over everyone else like lords of the manor.

Lola gasped. There it was, written in blue ink in Ruby's own handwriting, the confirmation that Ruby had been here in Polcarrow, that her link to the village was more than just a name beside a recipe or a holiday destination visited briefly. Lola hugged the book to her chest and exhaled, a sense of connection travelling from the pages to Lola's heart. Excitement bubbling in her veins, Lola lifted the book and finished the entry.

I wonder what the locals think of Joan's uncle building this big house at the top of the hill so he can keep watch. I'm not sure I'd like it if I was one of them. It's tranquil, picturesque, though. I wish I could capture the colour of the sea so that I could show everyone back home what it's like because I don't think they'll believe me.

Hmm . . . a house on a steep hill? No way? Could it be Bayview? Lola couldn't help but laugh at the coincidence. There was only one house she knew of that had a sweeping staircase and a chequerboard floor. The coincidences were scary but delightful. Snapping the book shut and slipping it back into her handbag, Lola gave the café its end-of-the-day clean, put the remaining cakes away and locked the door.

Retreating into the kitchen, Lola swapped her floral apron for a special Christmas print one she'd bought for the sole purpose of making Christmas cakes. With December approaching like an out of control snowball, she knew she had to get on with the first batch. Flicking the radio on, she danced around the kitchen, pulling various bowls and chopping boards out of the cupboards, when a sharp knock at the kitchen door made her jump out of her skin.

After turning the radio down, Lola cautiously approached the door where a tall shadow loomed through the glass. Slowly Lola opened the door, half wondering if she should have kept hold of one of her kitchen knives just in case it was an intruder. Relief washed through her when she saw Tristan, black coat zipped up against the cold November air. She hadn't seen him since the previous afternoon when they'd studied the photo together. Lola brushed away the thought that she'd missed him.

'What a relief!' Lola sighed. 'I thought you might be a burglar or something.'

Alarm flashed across Tristan's face. 'I'm sorry, I didn't mean to scare you, but the front door was locked and . . .'

Lola couldn't help but laugh. 'Don't worry, but I usually find teenage girls hanging around the back door wanting their palms read, rather than vicars on secret missions. I'm assuming this is a secret mission, what with the black clothes and the sneaking about?'

Tristan laughed. 'I guess it is, yes. Do you really read palms at the back door?' he said, glancing down at his own palm, looking at the lines there, amazed that they might mean something.

'Sometimes. Come inside, you're letting all the warmth out, and I'll show you.' Lola stepped back to let Tristan in.

'Ah, the inner sanctum,' he said reverently as he looked around the kitchen.

Lola watched him as he took everything in with the sort of awe people usually only used when admiring grand works of art. The shelves were all neatly stacked with bags of ingredients and boxes of eggs from the local farm. Spare teapots and crockery sat on the top shelves. His eyes took it all in until they fell back on Lola as if she was the most amazing thing in the room.

'Take your coat off if you're staying,' Lola said, holding her hand out for it. Once Tristan had unzipped it and extracted himself from his scarf, he passed them to Lola, who hung them on a peg by the door. 'Now, sit on that stool.' She signalled towards a slightly rickety stool, which she had painted red with white dots especially for this venture.

Tristan sat down and held out his hands expectantly. Lola's heart melted a bit more to see how adorably out of his comfort zone he was. She pulled a second stool over to him and sat down, knee to knee. 'Which hand do you write with?' For a second she felt as if she should know this.

'This one.' Tristan waggled his right.

Reaching out, Lola took his hand in both of hers and gently began to trace the lines, smiling to herself as the contact sent a jolt through Tristan. 'Sorry, I'll be gentle,' she said, her mind going momentarily blank as she thought of where holding hands like this could lead. 'Erm . . . here is your, erm, lifeline. Congratulations, you're going to live to a ripe old age, you might even give Alf a run for his money. I can't see any major health issues, maybe back pain as you get older, and you need to be careful with your knees if you want to keep running,' she forewarned with a smile, catching his eye. 'Your faith shows up as strong, which shouldn't be a surprise given your job!'

Tristan laughed. 'What a relief! Imagine if it said I was meant to be a footballer or an accountant or something.'

'Well, I can see you were good at sports as a child and had a well-supported childhood and were given a lot of freedom to pursue your own path in life. Did you lose someone when you were about ten?'

'My grandfather when I was nine. Does that show up?' Tristan asked with amazement.

Lola nodded. 'Yes, this little cross here, it shows trauma, but I'm glad to report you don't have many of those. Things seem to have been quite plain sailing, which is nice. I'm happy for you about that. Some people have had awful tragedies.'

'What do you do if you see something bad predicted? Do you tell them?'

Lola paused. 'It depends. I mean, I might hint at hardship, but really, does anyone come to have their palm read to hear about the bad things? No. They want to know if they'll find true love or their fortune.'

'What about my true love or fortune?' Tristan asked, leaning in, his voice curling around her.

Glancing up, Lola met his eyes, which sparkled flirtatiously. 'Ah, the question everyone wants the answer to.' She winked before turning back to his palm, slowly tracing her finger along his heart line, enjoying the way she sensed him holding his breath. Its path was so intricately entwined with her own. Could she tell him? She flicked a glance at him, meeting his blue eyes, which crackled with a fire that set her soul alight. She resisted the overwhelming temptation to bring his palm to her lips and kiss it.

'Lola?' He leaned forward a fraction more and all her senses were scrambled as she breathed in the scent of him, earthy but gentle, everything about him deliciously subtle.

Foreheads almost touching, Lola leaned into the magnetic pull of him. There was a pause, a fraction where everything was held in one frozen moment. The desire to kiss him buzzed through her but terrified by what might happen if she stepped over the friendship boundary, Lola pulled back, breaking the spell.

'Yes, there's love, there's always love,' she whispered. 'Not very far away now. In fact, it might be why you've, erm, come here,' she laughed nervously. 'Anything else will ruin the surprise,' she said, passing his hand back to him, as if his touch was burning her.

Before she could say anything else, before he could reach her, Lola slipped off her stool, putting some distance between them. Tristan watched her, puzzled and full of a frustration she recognised. It was a distance she immediately regretted. Lola liked him more than she wanted to admit, but watching him from across her kitchen, the thought of giving in to those feelings sent fear coursing through her veins. He was so perfect, so kind and gentle, she ached to take his hand back, pull him close, see what would happen, but she was frozen to the spot with fear. Her heart beat a frantic tattoo as if to warn her of the danger of getting involved romantically with him. *Friends*, she repeated to herself, *best to remain as friends*.

'So,' she fished for something to say, 'I take it a palm reading isn't why you really came here tonight . . .'

Tristan was looking at his palm as if puzzled by what had made Lola back away. Composing himself, he stood up and walked towards her. 'No. It wasn't, but it's been entertaining. Sorry, that sounds as if I'm dismissing your skills, I'm not . . .' He stopped himself from blabbering on any further. 'I came here to tell you that I've been investigating the fishing disaster.'

'Oh! Go on.' Lola tightened her apron strings as if to secure herself against making a move on Tristan.

Tristan paused as he took in the bags of dried fruit and bowls on the kitchen island. 'What's all this? I'm not interrupting anything, am I?'

'Of course you're not. I'm going to prep the fruit for the Christmas cakes. I need to soak it overnight in brandy so that I can start getting the cakes baked tomorrow. I've had thirty orders already, can you believe it? It's only been one week.' She felt safer back on home turf.

'Wow, that's a lot of cake.' Tristan looked impressed.

'I'm in for a long night,' Lola sighed.

'Well, would you like some help?'

Lola sized him up. 'You mean it? You don't have any pressing parish business to attend to?'

He gave her his gorgeous lopsided smile. 'No, anyway, there can't be anything more pressing than helping provide Polcarrow with cake, which I secretly think is the most important job.'

Lola clapped her hands together in delight. 'Excellent, as long as you don't mind a bit of Christmas music to get us, erm, in the mood.'

'Not at all. It's November, I think Christmas music is now acceptable,' he said as he followed her instructions to wash his hands.

Lola laughed and rifled through the aprons on the back of the door. Slightly relieved they'd returned to their easy chatter. 'Let's get you kitted up. Then you can tell me what you've found out.' She passed him a faded blue and white striped apron and watched as he put it over his head and attempted to fasten the ties. After a few moments of struggling, Lola stepped forward and, giggling, offered, 'Let me help.'

Before she could even think about what she was doing Lola reached around Tristan's waist to grab the apron strings. Her breath caught. There was something nice and solid about him, dependable, that made her want to keep her arms wrapped around him and never let go. As he glanced down, she looked up and knew he'd always protect her. Despite her earlier reservations, the urge to snuggle in against him was strong. She quickly looped the strings and tied them in a bow.

Having secured his apron, Lola stepped back, flustered; at this rate she would need to open the windows to cool off for more than just the baking. She risked a glance back at Tristan. He was watching her, the same look in his eyes from when they'd been perched on the stools. Breaking the tension, she grabbed an industrial-size tub of glacé cherries and passed them to him.

'I need you to weigh these out and then chop them up. Quarters will be fine. It'll be sticky work, so roll your sleeves up.' She peered at her recipe. 'Actually, on second thoughts just do the whole lot.'

Tristan prised the lid off and looked at the glistening, sticky cherries and she wondered if he'd changed his mind. Instead, he announced, 'I loved these as a child. I'd sneak them out of the cupboard along with those little jelly sugared diamond things you used to get.'

'Oh yes, I remember them! I'll have to investigate and see if I can get them, they'd look cute on fairy cakes.' A wave of affection washed over her as they set about their tasks in companiable silence. She watched Tristan concentrating as he carefully cut up the cherries.

'Actually, this is fun, I've not baked anything since school. We made pineapple upside down cake.'

'I love pineapple upside down cake!' Lola gasped. 'I've not had one of those in years! I'll have to add it to the New Year menu.'

Tristan smiled at her then a thought occurred to him. 'Don't. I'll have a go at baking one, one day, when I get time.'

Lola laughed. 'Seriously?'

'Yes, seriously, it'll be good to try something different, have a challenge. You're always willing to help others, Lola, it's time to let someone do something for you.'

The gentle kindness in his voice caught in Lola's heart. Kindness had been lacking in her life for so long she'd hardly noticed its absence until she arrived in Polcarrow, where it has been bestowed on her by Alf, Tristan and Sue as they welcomed her into their fold. Taking a moment to compose herself, she reached into the cupboard and lifted down two bottles of brandy. 'Thank you, I'll look forward to it,' was all she said, her feelings for Tristan blooming a little bit more. 'So, what have you dug up?' she asked before cringing at the phrase.

'I was looking into those who were involved in the fishing accident. Actually, I was trying to see if there's any photos, see if I could identify any of the young men in your photo with Ruby. It was only a few months after Ruby was here.'

A chill crept down Lola's back. 'Did you find anything?'

Tristan shook his head. 'No, sadly not, which is a shame, it'd be nice to honour the men properly, give them a place in local history. It's almost as if someone has tried to wipe it clean. We know Charles, Alf's older brother, was on the boat. With him were four other young men. They went out to fish and the weather turned in a freak storm and they were all lost. Their bodies were never recovered, which is why there's the communal memorial in the churchyard. I cannot imagine what that would have been like. All of those young lads with their lives ahead of them. One left a young widow, but the others don't appear to have married yet,' Tristan said sadly.

'Oh gosh,' Lola whispered, 'that's heart-breaking. I can't imagine what it must have been like for the village.'

'A tragedy for the entire community. It looks like the steady decline of the fishing trade happened afterwards. It must have been so hard for Alf to go out to sea after that.'

'He is made of very hardy stuff, but now he seems a lot hardier than I ever thought. No wonder he's always keen to look to the future and doesn't dwell on things.' Lola paused before asking, 'I keep toying with asking him how he knew Ruby. Because he clearly did. But at the same time I don't want to upset him.' She paused. 'I'm savouring her diary, I've only got as far as her coming to Cornwall, but the entry I've just read confirms she came here. Even more bizarre is that I think she stayed at Bayview!'

Tristan stopped his cherry chopping. 'Lola, that's amazing, surreal, but amazing.' He paused, 'I have to ask, how come you are reading it bit by bit? If it was me I'd have raced through it. Or skipped to the end,' he admitted.

'Tristan!' Lola gasped. 'you cannot skip to the end! Please don't tell me you're one of those heathens who reads the end of a book first?'

He looked slightly guilty. 'Erm . . . maybe . . . but go on, why haven't you skipped to the end?'

Lola opened her mouth, closed it before sighing. 'It sounds silly.'

'Nothing you say could ever sound silly to me,' Tristian said gently.

Lola studied him and seeing that he meant it began, 'It's just, well, Nannie Ruby and I had such a close relationship. She looked after me, maybe raised me more than my mum did. I grew up with one version of her and now this diary feels like her, but also a different person. It's hard to read how dismissive she was of Grandad. He was really good to her, gave her a nice life. I know they had a long, happy relationship, but . . . it's a different Ruby. One I never knew anything about. I wonder if I should even be reading the diary.'

Tristan considered this before asking, 'What are you afraid of?'

'Afraid of?' Lola stepped back from the question, wondering how on earth he could read her so well, before giving in. 'I'm afraid to find out my grandmother was the baddie in the story. There's the ring. What if she broke someone's heart? I've worshipped her for so long but now I realise there is so much I didn't know about her, about her youth, and it seems so strange to think she was here, that Alf might have known her.'

Tristan retreated into a contemplative silence. 'Your grandmother will always be special to you, Lola, the version of her you knew is the one that is correct. You grew up with her so the Ruby you knew and loved, who taught you all you know, is more real and true than the young woman in the diary. I think maybe the Ruby in the diary was young, not fully formed and the version you remember is the truer, complete version. You don't have to do anything with that photo, Lola, you don't need to ask Alf anything. You can leave it forever, or just leave it until the time is right. Not everything is a mystery to be solved, you know. I'm here for you, Lola, as a friend and vicar, if you need any counsel on this subject.'

Lola let his words sink in, surprised at how deeply they touched her. Blinking back tears at his kind words, she nodded before reaching across to squeeze his rather sticky hand. 'Thank you, Tristan.'

His eyes met hers and Lola had the strangest sensation that time slowed right down. It might even have gone as far as stopping. She floundered for something to say but words failed her, instead she pulled her hand away and went back to sorting out the fruit. How could one evening contain so many moments she was unwilling to grasp? Pre-Jared Lola would have been all over Tristan in a flash. Was that the problem? Tristan was not the sort of man you threw yourself at in a fit of passion, but more the sort you allowed yourself to grow closer to, slowly uncovering him layer by layer. That terrified Lola.

'So, is this a family recipe we're all being treated to? Are you going to have to kill me if I find out the secret ingredient?' Tristan asked to lighten the mood.

Lola laughed. 'No, not at all! There's no secret ingredient unless you count love? Cakes need to be baked with love.' She snipped open the top of a bag of sultanas and tipped them into the largest mixing bowl Tristan had ever seen. 'Of course this is a family recipe, it's Ruby's in fact. Soaking the fruit in brandy keeps the cake from drying out and should placate all those folk from sea-faring stock who are concerned I might try and pass a teetotal cake off on them.'

'I'm looking forward to trying it. That brandy smells delightful. What was a family Christmas like for you growing up?'

A shadow passed across Lola's face. 'Honestly? Not great. My parents weren't into Christmas at all. We'd just have a bit of dinner, then Dad would start on the brandy, watch the Queen's speech. It was celebrated more because it was on the calendar rather than because my parents had any inclination. Ruby was always popping in on Christmas morning and after Grandad died, Ruby would spend Christmas with us. Mum and Ruby never quite saw eye to eye so it was always a bit tense. Dad kept out of the way. But I love Christmas,' Lola told him, her face lighting up. 'The fairy lights, the baubles, the way everyone is enthusiastic and tries to find the joy. I left home at eighteen and no matter where I've been I've tried to make Christmas special.'

Tristan smiled at her. 'Does this mean we get to keep you here for Christmas? Or are you heading off to see family?'

Lola shook her head. 'No, my parents spend the winter in Spain now, Mum can't stand the cold. And my brother has lived in Australia for the past twenty years, so, yeah, we're all rather fragmented. I tried to go to

Spain in my twenties but it wasn't the same, the cold always makes me feel festive, you know? Wrapping a coat around a too thin party frock, waiting for a taxi while your feet freeze.' Lola sighed with the memories. 'So, you get to have an extra sparkly Lola Christmas.' She flashed him a winning smile. 'What about you? What were your Christmases like?'

'Less freezing in a party frock and a bit more on the religious side. My family have always been involved with the Church, so it featured heavily in our Christmases. None of them were surprised when they found out I'd decided to join the Church. It might not have been a popular thing to admit as a teenager but I loved midnight mass. The cold church, the candlelight, how solemn it was compared to the carol services. We always had a big Christmas Day dinner with my grandparents and cousins. Lots of presents and games.'

'Sounds wonderful,' Lola replied wistfully, quelling a stab of envy at the cosy family Christmas he described. 'Are you going back this year? Or does duty call?'

'Duty calls, I'm afraid. Midnight mass, Christmas Day service, it's a busy time to be a vicar.' He winked. 'I'll video-call my parents. My sister has three kids so no doubt they'll be busy and won't miss me. I'll take some time off in the New Year and visit them.' Tristan glanced down at his sleeve, which was starting to unwind and heading perilously close to the sticky cherry juice.

'Don't worry, I've got it.' Lola scooted around and carefully rolled the sleeve back up his arm. Tristan looked down at her, the energy shifting between them again. Lola gave his arm a pat and stepped back. 'All sorted now.'

'Ah, yes, thank you. No doubt I'll be inundated with invites for Christmas dinner, well, at least I hope I will!' He grinned at her.

Lola's face lit up as an idea sparked inside her head. 'Why don't you come here? I'll hold a big Christmas dinner for all of us! You, me, Alf, we're all on our own, I'll get some extra sausages for Scruff. I can ask Angelo and Freya to join us. I'm not sure Freya is all that keen on taking Angelo home to Bedford yet. There'll be wine, we can sing songs, it'll be wonderful!'

Tristan shook his head. 'We can't ask that of you, Lola, you need at least one day off.'

'Nope, I'd go stir-crazy. Cooking and feeding people is what I love. I'll get a turkey, a ham and I make pretty amazing roast potatoes. It'll be perfect. No protests, Vicar, I won't hear them.' Lola wagged a finger at him. 'I've only just thought about it but I'm already looking forward to it.'

Seeing him shake his head, she calmed her voice down to convince him. 'Honestly, Tristan, I'd enjoy hosting dinner for us all, you're not allowed to say no.'

A slow smile spread affectionately across Tristan's face. 'I'm pretty sure, Lola, that no one could possibly say no to you.'

Chapter Seven

Sunday, 3rd September, 1950

Dear Diary,

    The village is built on a hill, the house is at the top and we have a very steep walk back up from the beach. There was a long debate about what to do on our first day here. Ida and Joan are keen to go and see the artists in St Ives but after the train journey down I've had enough of travelling. When I got into bed last night I felt like I was still moving! Anyway, we decided to spend the day exploring the village, not that there's much to see but it's very pretty. There's a pub, a small shop and post office but that's about it. All the buildings are painted white, some have hanging baskets of flowers and the beach is covered in fishing boats. We went for a swim, well, a paddle for me, I'm not brave enough to fully submerge myself. The water was almost warm. We were eating our sandwiches when the fishermen came in with their catch, followed by flocks of pesky seagulls. I'd never seen anything quite like *it. I can't imagine what it would be like going out on the sea in all weathers, I'm worried about it when it's calm. Still, it does sound a lot more exciting than typing up dull letters about insurance all day. We watched them with their nets and catch, transfixed by the way they moved, strong arms, tanned skin, completely different from the men we know back home. I must have been staring for too long because Joan pulled me away, a disapproving look on her face.*

'Are you sure I can't convince you to come here for Christmas?' Bridget asked, 'it'll be warm and sunny.'

Lola sighed. Every year her mum tried to convince her to jet out to the Costa del Sol for Christmas, every year Lola declined. 'Thanks, Mum, but I can't leave the café. You know I can't do a warm Christmas anyway.'

'I don't like to think of you all alone,' she sighed.

Lola being alone for the other three hundred and sixty-four days of the year didn't seem to bother her mum as much. 'I'll be fine, I'll have my friends here in Polcarrow to spend it with. I'm already making plans for us all to have Christmas lunch together.' Plus the thought of spending Boxing Day with her feet up and a box of Quality Street was absolute heaven.

'If you're sure.' But the argument already seemed to be gone from her voice.

'Perfectly sure,' Lola said, scribbling 'Organise a Polcarrow Christmas' on her crowded to-do pad. She hesitated before asking, 'Mum, did Nannie ever mention coming to Cornwall before she married Grandad?'

'No. Why?' Bridget asked.

Lola hesitated before sharing. 'I had a package delivered to me. It was some letters and diaries the new owners found hidden in Nannie's house. Nannie came to Cornwall it seems after the war but before she married Grandad.' She didn't elaborate on the fact that Ruby had visited Polcarrow or that there'd been a ring tucked away in the package.

'Did you? So that's what it was. No, she never talked much about her younger days to me. I know she did like spending time in Cornwall, though, and we went there when I was a child. I better go, your dad's just come in from his golf club. Remember, there'll always be a place for you at the table, Lola.' Bridget rang off before Lola could say goodbye.

With a sigh, Lola slipped her phone into her bag and pulled her to-do list closer. With her cakes baking and maturing, and the decorations going up around the café, Lola wasn't the only one busy making Christmas plans. As leader of the village committee, Sue was stuck into her vision to create a perfect Polcarrow Christmas, culminating with the Festive Festival. The lobster pot tree, she had decided, was going to be the focal point. Sue had been very persuasive in recruiting Tristan and Angelo to help with creating and assembling it, along with Steve who ran the pub. There had been no notion of them even turning the opportunity down. Even Alf had been roped in to oversee proceedings.

Sue's plans gave Lola the perfect opportunity to raise her own. Ever since she'd hatched her idea of a Polcarrow Christmas, Lola had been itching to share the invitation with the people who now meant the most to her. Upon seeing that the local farm shop had turkeys for order when collecting her eggs, Lola decided that before she got too carried away and placed an order, she better check who was going to be around. No point ordering a large turkey if it ended up just being three of them, even though she knew Scruff would rise to the challenge and help polish it off.

It was still early on the morning that they were scheduled to create the lobster pot tree and Lola was making sure that the 'workers' were fuelled with a decent breakfast. Once Tristan, Alf, Freya and Angelo were nestled at the window table, mugs of tea and stacks of toast in front of them, Lola interrupted their speculations about how they were meant to make a tree out of lobster pots. The general feeling was that Sue didn't have any practical suggestions, just the photo she'd found online which she'd waved about enthusiastically.

'Now I have you all gathered, I have something to ask.' Lola exchanged a glance with Tristan. Lola had managed to avoid mentioning he'd been her kitchen helper when it came to the first batch of Christmas cakes. She knew everyone had been speculating about their relationship since the summer and wasn't ready for the inquisition – mostly because they were still very firmly in the friend zone. 'What are you all doing on Christmas Day?' she asked.

'Same as every year,' Alf replied, 'trying not to share my sausages with this rascal.' He gave Scruff a scratch under his chin before slipping him a crust of toast.

Freya and Angelo exchanged some form of silent communication that included a raised eyebrow which no one else was able to interpret. 'We don't have any plans . . . yet,' Freya began slowly. 'Mum has been going on about us going up to Bedford or them coming here. I've been putting her off. As soon as they got wind of Angelo and Bayview they've been threatening to come down. Why?'

Lola clapped her hands together. 'Well, Tristan and I were talking the other day about Christmas and I had a brainwave. Since Tristan, Alf and myself are all going to be alone, I've decided to host Christmas Day for us. Of course, do say if you have better plans, Alf.'

'What a splendid idea. I always get invited to other people's houses, but I think this invite tops them all. Make sure you get extra pigs in blankets, they're Scruff's favourite.' The old sheepdog barked in agreement.

'What will the vet say?' Tristan, ever the voice of reason, asked.

Alf made a face. 'He won't say nothing if I don't tell him, will he?' Turning to Lola he said with concern, 'As long as it's not going to be too much work for you.'

'Nonsense, of course it's not. If anything I think I'll enjoy it.' She turned to Freya and Angelo. 'Obviously I understand if you want to go home for Christmas. But also, if your family want to come to Cornwall, the more the merrier. I'd be happy to include them too.'

Freya considered this. 'Are you sure? If you are I'll text Mum and invite them down.'

'But the house?' Panic flashed across Angelo's face.

Bayview House was pretty much a building site, with various jobs started but not finished. Lola had to bite her tongue from spilling out that Ruby had stayed there. She was starting to realise that the more she read of the diary, the more people she'd want to share the story with. She wasn't quite ready for that.

Freya shrugged. 'They can stay at the pub. Come on, it'll be fun. I take it Tristan has already agreed to this plan?' she asked mischievously. 'Considering you cooked it up together.'

'I have and I also tried to tell Lola it was too much work.'

'It is not too much work!' she insisted as she buttered another slice of toast. 'I've decided it all. I'm going to use the café kitchen and we can all dine in here. Push the tables together, get some wine and crackers, it'll be brilliant. I'm looking forward to it. Honestly, it's been years since I've spent Christmas with a group of people I love or had a Christmas Day with all the trimmings.' Another idea flashed through her brain. 'Why don't we make a Christmas pudding? We can all have a stir and make a wish. Like I used to do when I was growing up. My Nannie Ruby always insisted on making wishes and I have her magic stirring spoon.'

Out of the corner of her eye Lola saw Alf freeze at the mention of the name Ruby, as if a memory had surfaced that he didn't quite care for. She sipped her tea and tried extremely hard not to watch him. Tristan threw her a questioning glance. It was on the tip of her tongue to tell everyone Ruby had spent time in Polcarrow, just to see if he reacted further. However, before she could say anything, Alf spoke and the moment was gone.

'That sounds like a splendid idea, Lola,' he said before turning to Freya and Angelo to ask, 'I don't suppose either of you fancy giving Scruff a walk do you? I think he needs to work off all that toast he's managed to thieve off us. Tire him out a bit before the grand lobster pot tree making. A tree made of lobster pots, whatever next,' he chuckled to himself. 'Where do people get these ideas from?'

Scruff rubbed his face against Freya's leg, making her groan at the thought of being chosen to take him out. Tucking her phone into her pocket, she stood up and, looking straight at Angelo, said, 'You're the one who wants to include – how many was it? – three dogs into our future, so you can come and give me a hand.'

Angelo took Scruff's lead and with a quick whistle caught his attention. He then led the dog out of the door and across the road to the beach. Freya tightened her scarf, mumbled something incomprehensible and followed them out.

'I miss being able to walk him like I used to,' Alf sighed. 'He needs more than just an amble down here and back, even if that's enough for me. I'm very grateful that Angelo is keen to get a dog, but I'm not sure he understands how much hard work it is. Not that I'd change Scruff for anything.'

Wondering if this was another chance to lure Alf into a conversation about the past, Lola exchanged a glance with Tristan, who, reading her mind, asked, 'Did you always have a dog?'

'Oh yes, grew up with them. There's always been one around. Great companions. I know it's probably not the same as a human companion, but I've always had a deep understanding with my dogs. Very loyal and they have a better sense about things than most of us. You two ever had any pets?'

Tristan shook his head. 'My sister had a hamster though.'

'Only a couple of guinea pigs when I was a girl. My brother Antony and I were meant to share them but I think Mum ended up doing most of the work, which she resented. When they died we weren't allowed any more. Probably for the best.' Lola gave him a smile to reassure him she wasn't at all sad about her lack of pets. 'I travelled too much afterwards but I always made friends with the local cats and dogs.'

'I could see you with a cat,' Alf said.

'What? Because of all the mystic stuff?' Lola laughed.

Alf shrugged. 'Maybe.' Taking a sip of his tea, his shoulders relaxed as he watched Scruff give Angelo the run around on the beach across the road.

Lola and Tristan exchanged glances. Could this be their moment to ask Alf more about the fishing tragedy? All she knew was that he was happy to talk about the olden days in a general sense, he'd go off on a tangent about stealing boats for secret treasure hunts as a boy but was less keen on delving into his personal life.

'So, you were never tempted to leave Polcarrow and find your fortune elsewhere?' Tristan gently persisted.

If Alf was surprised by the question, he didn't show it. 'Never. What more treasure is there than that?' He signalled out of the window towards the sea. 'Too many people go in search of their fortune and it rarely does them good. I've seen it with the young'uns who head off to the city and years later they're coming back. Cornwall is in my blood, it's in my roots, and anyway, I had a sense of duty to my family. Even if I had wanted to leave, I couldn't have done.' A shadow passed across his face as he said this.

'How come?' Lola asked, whilst all the hairs on her neck pricked up in anticipation. Beside her Tristan sat up taller, the expectation radiating off him.

'Water under the bridge now, some things from the past don't do with being dug up. I don't get all this harking back to the past, life moves on and changes, usually for the best.' He chuckled, giving them both a glance as if he knew what they were up to. 'There's a lot more to look forward to you know, like this Festive Festival Sue's organising.' His face lit up at the thought. 'I'm very much looking forward to seeing what it's all like, never had anything like it here before.'

'I'm sure it's going to be grand.' Lola beamed at him but inside her heart sank slightly. Standing up and leaving Tristan explaining the Christmas tree festival to Alf, Lola began to clear away the plates, satisfied that she'd managed to get her Christmas Day plans all tied up with a big bow, which went a little way to make up for her disappointment that Alf was still reluctant to discuss the past. Ruby's fate was clearly only to be discovered in her diary.

Or the letters. Lola hadn't touched the letters yet. She felt they were the final chapter of the story. Perhaps she should read everything before jumping ahead and quizzing Alf. Maybe it would turn out that he was right, that the past was better left alone.

Chapter Eight

Monday, 4th September, 1950

Dear Diary,

I got up early today and sneaked out of the house down to the sea. The sunrise was so bright and pink, it was beautiful. I've never seen anything like it. Everything is slower here, more gentle. I don't think I'll ever want to go home. At the beach I went for a paddle in the water, right up to my knees! It was freezing but thrilling. It felt marvellous to know I'd done something small and secret like this. Afterwards I sat and watched the boats go out. One of the men kept looking at me. I was a bit far away to see what he looked like, but he was tall and nicely built. I am curious. Something about the day felt different, like a page had turned. I'm not sure if that sounds silly or not. Joan would say it does. I rather fancy a trip on one of the boats myself, but I know the men are working and not here to take girls out sailing, but I can hope. Or better than hope, I can ask. Yes, I'll ask, after all,

Mum usually says I'm not backwards about coming forwards.

Despite the fact the sky looked as if it was about to chuck it down at any moment, Lola and Freya stood in the doorway of the café watching, as further up the harbour road, on the paved area in front of the pub, Tristan, Angelo and Steve were attempting to fix together an assortment of lobster pots. Alf was perched on a rickety stool, supervising, Scruff curled at his feet. The men were trying to listen to Sue as she flapped about, waving the photo she'd printed off under their noses. Tristan eventually placated her panicking as Angelo rubbed his head with frustration.

Freya stifled a giggle. 'It looks like a case of too many cooks spoiling the broth.'

Lola grimaced as the pot Tristan had tried to position toppled off. 'I'm not sure Tristan really knows what he's doing.'

'At least Angelo knows a bit about sticking unusual objects together. Oh dear, if she's not careful I think Steve might tip Sue into the harbour.'

They watched as Alf stood up, hands out in a placating way. Sue put down the life ring she'd been holding and took a step back. Realising the best approach would be to remove Sue from the operation and let the men get on with the task, Lola called her name and waved her over. The men stopped work and watched as Sue retreated towards the café, only taking up tools when

Lola had pulled her inside and given them a thumbs up to confirm it was safe for them to continue.

'Come on, let's have a cuppa, leave them to it. I've got some shortbread fresh from the oven,' Lola said as she closed the café door behind them.

'Sounds scrummy,' Sue admitted, with a glance over her shoulder towards the café's door, 'but I'm a bit worried they won't do it right.'

'Angelo knows what he's doing,' Freya reassured her. 'He used to be a sculptor so making things comes naturally to him.' Freya looked at Lola. Neither of them felt it needed mentioning that Angelo's art was obscure structures made out of metal. Sue wanted a Michelangelo, not a Picasso of a lobster pot tree.

Sue looked rather embarrassed. 'Yes, I'm sure you're right. It'll all be fine. Who would have thought organising Christmas in a small village would be so stressful?'

'It's just because you want to do it well.' Lola smiled at Sue as she passed her a steaming mug of tea.

'Maybe I should've listened to Cathy and just had a normal, real tree or just done the light switch on, like we've done in the past. I think the success of the Fisherman's Fair this summer has got me a bit carried away.'

'Nonsense!' Lola exclaimed. 'I won't hear it. I think the lobster pot tree is a fabulous idea, in keeping with our seafaring past. You just need to trust the menfolk to do it their way.' She pushed the plate of biscuits across the table, encouraging Sue to take another. 'I also love the idea of the Festive Festival, we've had lots of people pick up leaflets and say they'll pop along.' Rather than reassuring Sue, this made her face blanch.

'No pressure then!' She laughed nervously as she reached for another biscuit.

While Sue was distracted with tea and biscuits and quizzing Freya about Angelo's artistic credentials, Lola took the opportunity to take hot drinks out to the workers, which they fell upon.

Steve tipped three sugars into his tea and shook his head. 'This is madness, I don't know why we couldn't just have a proper tree.' He gave the lower layer of pots a kick. They wobbled slightly.

'You have to admit it does look rather nice,' Tristan placated. 'I rather like how it links to our fishing past.'

Alf chuckled. 'I thought it was a bit mad to begin with but I actually like it.' He held on to the photo Sue had left with them. 'After all, the pots are just lying around, might as well use them.'

Angelo said nothing but was rubbing his chin thoughtfully as he prowled around the base several times, sizing it up, making mental calculations, his hair whipped wild by the wind that was getting up. This was quite clearly the distraction from the house he needed. He knocked back his coffee and passed the cup back to Lola.

'It's OK, boys. Freya is keeping Sue distracted in the café, so I reckon you have at least forty minutes to make a go of it.' Lola told them. Scruff barked encouragingly. 'I'll make some bacon sandwiches when you're done,' was her parting shot in the hope it'd help speed things up.

Before she headed back into the café, Lola cast a glance over her shoulder, pleased to see that now caffein-ated and with Sue out of the way, the men had quickly organised themselves and were working on the best way to stack and secure the pots. Lola didn't feel the need to tell Sue that Angelo had dismantled the entire thing and was now directing proceedings. She'd distract her with knitting pattern talk instead.

An hour later, Lola's phone beeped with a text from Tristan to let her know it was all done. 'Ladies, shall we pop along and see how it's turned out?' she asked.

Sue was up and out in a flash, leaving Freya and Lola to stick a note to the café door saying they'd be back in five minutes, and lock up.

In the middle of the harbour they found a pyramid of lobster pots which Tristan and Steve were decorating with various bits of fishing paraphernalia, including the life ring Sue had been clutching on to at the start of the project. Angelo was making sure the structure was secure.

'Oh wow! That's marvellous! You've all done a super job; I was silly to doubt you.' Sue clapped her hands together. 'It's a lot taller than I expected. Do you have all the lights?'

'We're just fixing them,' Tristan said, picking up the tangled mess of lights. 'We couldn't have done this with-out Angelo's direction. He's the only one of us who's ever built anything.'

Angelo ignored the praise as he jumped down from the top of the tree. 'It's sturdy enough and shouldn't blow away, even in a gale.' To demonstrate, he gave it a little shake, which made Sue gasp.

Alf chuckled to himself. 'I should hope not. Cathy would be onto us with all her health and safety stuff.' Everyone laughed. Cathy was known for trying to disrupt the peace in village proceedings.

'It's best to be safe, Alf,' Sue reminded him. 'Thank you, Angelo, for showing me the tree is secure. Let's all hope we don't get any horrific winter storms.'

Alf made a non-committal noise. 'Can you turn the lights on?'

'Hang on! They're not all up yet,' Steve called from behind the tree.

Lola and Freya stepped forward to help. Lola made a beeline for Tristan and grabbing one end of the lights, began to work with him to untangle them, their bodies blown close by the breeze.

'That was hard work,' he said in a low voice so that Sue didn't hear. 'I didn't think we'd get it done.'

'But you have and it looks smashing,' she said, glancing down at the lights. It appeared they had tied themselves in more knots. Lola held up her hands. 'Oh dear, I think we better concentrate.' She glanced over her shoulder where everyone was watching them. 'I'm feeling the pressure!'

Once the structure was draped in lights and all the decorations were in place, Tristan said, 'Shall we see if it works?'

Everyone stood back and waited with bated breath while Tristan turned the lights on. The tree sparkled into life and twinkled with all its rustic, seaside beauty. They all stared at it in awe, not quite believing they had managed to pull it off. Lola wiped a tear away; it was truly marvellous.

'It's beautiful!' Sue gushed, giving them a little round of applause. 'You've all done a fantastic job, it's far exceeded my expectations. I was silly to doubt you.'

Freya slipped an arm around Angelo and gave him a congratulatory squeeze.

'It's wonderful,' Lola said from where she stood next to Tristan. 'I love it. Sue, your vision was perfect.'

'It's come out a treat,' Alf said as he took a slow lap around the base, glancing up at the lights and layers. 'I'm almost ninety but there's always something in life left to surprise me. A lobster pot tree, hey,' he chuckled, before grinding to a halt. 'But it's missing something!' Six faces turned to him in bemusement. 'It needs a fairy on the top. Or a star. There used to be one that we put on top of the Christmas tree every year, just some doll and people would take it in turns to sew her a new dress, but we always used to put the fairy on top of the tree before the official switch on.'

'Do you know where she is?' Lola asked.

'No. Vanished years ago, like everything else round here,' Alf said sadly. 'Maybe a seagull made off with her or she ended up in the bin after being pecked one too many times. She had an eye missing, terrified the little ones.'

'I'm sure we can find something,' Sue placated. 'You're right, it does need something on the top.'

'But something modern,' Tristan said, 'as a village we're moving forwards, not back, so this should be a symbol, a beacon of hope for the future.'

Silence fell over the assembled group as they contemplated what to do. Angelo stepped forward and, hands on hips, stared up at the bare top of the tree. Everyone waited. Angelo had sworn off making art when he arrived in Polcarrow. He was adamant that he was here to make a new life with Freya at Bayview, not to start painting or sculpting. However, it didn't take a genius to notice something had shifted in him, as if he was listening to a call no one else could hear. Lola glanced at Freya, who was looking at her boyfriend with nervous excitement.

'You're right, it does need something modern,' he said before lapsing into silence for a few more moments, running his hand down the side of the tree. Angelo's silence was broken only by the squawks of some curious gulls who came to give the tree their approval.

'I could make something.' Angelo seemed as surprised by his words as everyone else did. Sue and Alf's faces lit up at the suggestion. 'I am supposed to be on sabbatical . . . but . . . I don't know . . . I feel it calling to me.'

Tristan turned to Angelo. 'Are you sure? There's no pressure but I do agree this tree needs to be finished with something a little extra special.'

Angelo simply gave a quick, tight nod in response. 'Leave it with me.'

Chapter Nine

Monday, 4th (later on)

Dear Diary

Everything is so different here but in a way that I love. I feel like I could stretch my arms out and gather it all in. The sun, the sea air, the calmness fill me in a way I didn't think anything could. I think Ida and Joan are a little bored now they've been for a swim, looked at everything in the shop and sampled the local cider in the pub. They're talking about taking the bus to St Ives or Penzance but I'm perfectly content to stay here. At home it's such a struggle to get up when my alarm goes off, but not here, it's almost as if the sun creeping over the horizon is teasing me awake. This morning I threw on whatever clothes came to hand and, after grabbing an apple, I went down to the beach again to see the fishermen. I'd waded into the sea, almost in up to my knees before I heard a commotion behind me. I watched as the men came out, pushing their boat towards the sea. There were six of them, all sorts of ages, some wizened by the sun and sea, others young, not yet tainted by their work. My gaze was fixed on the one at the back, the same tall one from yesterday with the strong muscular forearms. When he looked at me I swear my heart skipped a beat. We kept looking at each other as he went out to sea. I wonder who he is. I'm determined to find out.

Lola reclined in post-work bliss. It had been a successful day what with her invitation for Christmas dinner having been gladly received and the lobster pot tree standing proud on the seafront waiting for the big switch on at the weekend. The added bonus had been that the Polcarrow residents had picked up gingerbread lattes on their way to inspect the tree.

Having indulged in a long soak in the bath, topped off with all her favourite lotions and potions, Lola was ensconced in her living room, the television flickering a nature programme in the background, sound turned down, a glass of Baileys on hand, whilst she concentrated on her next project: knitting Alf and Scruff's Christmas jumpers. Knitting was another skill Ruby had taught her. Lola smiled to recall how wonky her first attempts at a scarf had been, a deep red one she'd knitted in secret for Ruby for Christmas – red being her favourite colour because it matched her namesake. It had been misshapen, there had been dropped stitches and even a couple of tiny holes. Lola smiled as she remembered Ruby wearing it proudly, telling everyone on the bus how talented her granddaughter was.

Reaching for her phone, Lola texted Tristan the latest update in the Ruby saga:

Ruby's 100% got her eyes on a fisherman! She's swooning in her diary.

The sunshine-filled pages had been a balm after the freezing day they'd spent on the harbour side

His reply was almost instant:

Are you sure it's not Alf? Imagine if it was?!

I don't think so. Says he's tall. Alf isn't that tall. I think it's another one of the lads.

Argh! Just read it and put us both out of our misery!

Smiling to herself, Lola quickly tapped back:

Don't they say patience is a virtue?

The door being unlocked and slammed back into place by the wind made Lola jump, her phone skittering onto the floor. She listened. One set of footsteps. As much as she adored Angelo, it had been a long time since she and Freya had had the chance for a catch-up.

'Lola?' Freya called.

'In the front room. No Angelo?'

Freya pushed open the door and headed straight to the fire to warm her hands. 'It's turned really chilly out there. No, he's downed the wallpaper scraper and has retreated into the shed, which I reckon is a health hazard with its rotten roof, muttering something about angels and mermaids.' Freya shrugged. 'I think that means he might be working on something for the tree.'

'Ooh, that would be wonderful, but I hope we didn't put too much pressure on him.' Angelo had a slightly tetchy relationship with his artistic side.

'No, it'll do him good. He was a bit distracted when I turned up which means he's on to something. Now I can get up early and get on with my next painting.'

'How's it going?'

Freya made a face. 'I hate it. But I think all artists need to go through a hating their work stage. I found it exciting displaying my work in the St Ives gallery but now I think I'd prefer to paint smaller pictures again. Sell them online. I'm not sure I like them taking all that commission . . .' She trailed off as if wrestling with the dilemma.

'I'd be happy to display them in the café again. Especially next summer,' Lola suggested, quickly warming to the idea, 'bill it as a sort of artist in residence. I know the gallery has been a fantastic opportunity but you're not beholden to them, you can sell your work wherever you like and I'm happy for you to use the café.'

Freya was silent for a while as she took this in. 'Thanks, Lola. Angelo said the same. There's been so much pressure to get the painting done and it's been stressing me out. I think we should get Christmas out of the way and then I can make some decisions in the New Year. So much has happened this year what with coming here, meeting Angelo, him buying Bayview. I'd like to have some time to just digest it all. Also, Mum said yes to coming to Christmas. She's already booked into the pub B. & B., so, no going back now!'

'As if I would! I don't know why everyone is so worried about me hosting Christmas dinner. I volunteered, after all. If people want to muck in and peel potatoes then they can.'

Freya reached for the bottle of Baileys and poured a glass. She took a sip and studied the creamy liquid. 'I never know why I don't drink this other than just at Christmas. What are you making?' she asked as she settled back on the sofa.

'A Christmas jumper for Alf.' Lola held up her knitting. 'I'm going to make a matching one for Scruff.'

Freya laughed. 'That is too adorable! I've ordered one online for Angelo and I'm going to surprise him with it on Christmas Day.' She fixed Lola with a mischievous look. 'Come on, Lola, it's not just Christmas that's coming up is it?'

Lola laughed. 'No, it isn't!'

'What do you want to do? It's not every year you turn forty,' Freya pointed out.

Lola continued to knit and gave a little shrug. 'I've not really thought about it.'

'Liar!' Freya exclaimed. 'You love a party, so I don't believe that for one second.'

Putting her knitting aside, Lola sat forwards. 'OK, OK, of course I've thought about it! But it's a funny time of year to have a birthday. There's always so much going on.' Lola sighed and admitted, 'A party would be nice, lots of fizz and balloons and a disco. No Christmas tunes,' she stipulated. 'And cake, a nice sponge cake to offset all that rich fruit cake.'

'So, no, you've not thought about it at all.'

Lola couldn't help but laugh. 'I thought about having it at the pub but I've not had a chance to catch Steve to ask him about hosting.'

Freya topped up their glasses. 'No, Lola, I'll ask him. I'll plan it for you.'

Lola froze. She was the planner, the one who had everything under control. 'You don't have to do that.'

'But I want to.' Freya shrugged. 'Anyway, what more do I need to do than get Steve to agree, get some balloons and bake a cake.' Freya paused and revised this, 'Or buy a cake as we know my baking skills are no match for yours. Or I might rope Mum into helping. I'm digging a hole here, aren't I?'

'Yes, and honestly, I can make the cake.'

'No! You cannot make your own birthday cake. You spend all your time baking. I'll sort it, trust me.'

The urge to fight Freya over the baking was strong, but the stern stare her friend was giving her made Lola back down. 'All right then, I relinquish control of the cake into your mum's capable hands. I'm sure by then I'll be up to my eyeballs with Christmas cakes anyway.'

'So what's going on with Tristan?' Freya wiggled her eyebrows.

'Tristan? What do you mean?' Lola feigned innocence and picked up her knitting again.

'Come on, Lola, are you sure nothing is going on with you two? You were making heart-shaped eyes at each other as you untangled those lights earlier. He clearly adores you. You might not see it, but he cannot take his eyes off you.'

Resisting the urge to ask more about how he looked at her, Lola simply said, 'Nothing, nothing's going on. I didn't come here for romance, Freya. I came here to concentrate on making a life for me, man free and uncomplicated. Tristan and I are friends. He's been a great support to me, but that's it.' She wondered who she was trying to convince.

'I don't get the issue,' Freya said as she sat down. 'Tristan is probably the world's least complicated man. And any relationship would be pretty rubbish if you weren't friends as well so that card doesn't play well.'

'I don't want to ruin what we have. It's that simple. For the first time in my life, I feel settled and content. I'm happy with the way things are, Freya, honestly,' Lola said, knowing it was true. 'I have more than I ever expected to have here. I don't need to add any complications.'

For a moment it looked as if Freya was going to argue the point but instead she just shrugged and peeled herself up off the sofa. 'Fair enough, if you say so. But I think you'd be so much happier with him. Don't deny yourself love, Lola. Right, shall we get the cottage decorated for Christmas?'

'Ooh yes, let me just finish this bit off,' Lola said, turning her attention back to her knitting, flustered that Freya had used a leaf out of her own book to push her point about Tristan. Holding the jumper out at arm's length to check how the pattern was going, Lola tried to ignore the feeling that was unfurling inside her. She couldn't ignore the fact that she kept thinking about the golden sunshine of Tristan's smile, and thoughts of more than simple friendship. Shaking the idea away, Lola got up and took the Baileys glasses into the kitchen. Switching on the kettle, she reminded herself that after how much of a scoundrel Jared had been, it was Tristan's kind, uncomplicated nature that she liked. Simple friendship. The most important thing to have. Why would anyone want to risk ruining that?

Chapter Ten

Buoyed up by Baileys infused hot chocolates and pleased with how Freya had helped her turn the cottage into a Christmas grotto, Lola slipped into bed, closed her eyes and exhaled. Lola tried to match her breathing to the sound of the waves in an attempt to relax but her mind was whirring. Buzzing with the thought that Ruby had possibly found romance in Polcarrow. The thought of her grandmother indulging in a holiday romance was strangely thrilling. Lola's mind drifted. What was this young man like? He was clearly different to Ernest, who she couldn't help but feel a little put out for, and knowing how the story eventually ended didn't help her mind from speculating what had happened in Polcarrow between Ruby and the fisherman she had her eye on.

Opening her eyes, Lola glanced at the bedside table where the diary sat temptingly on top of a stack of books. An image of Tristan speeding through towards the end came to mind. His impatience to find out what happened seemed completely at odds with the calm, collected persona he presented to the world. This little piece of himself that he had revealed reminded Lola that there was still so much more of him to discover, and she was surprised to realise just how much she wanted to delve beneath his surface. She hadn't been lying when she'd told Freya she valued his friendship above all other possibilities, because it was the truth. However, the other truth was that Lola knew what was brewing between them was something deeper than any fling she'd had before. It had solid foundations. She enjoyed his company and she could no longer deny it to herself that she'd wanted to kiss him when she'd been reading his palm, but she didn't want to rush anything. Life was not a race, she was realising; the journey was as important as the destination.

However, she reasoned, as she sat up, that didn't mean she couldn't sneak another entry from the diary. After all, that was the only way she'd work out who Ruby's summer fling was. Knowing that if she didn't satisfy this curiosity, she'd only lie awake turning it over in her mind, Lola reached for the book and flicked to the next entry.

Tuesday, 5th September, 1950

Dear Diary,
Joan and Ida were miffed I'd been out without them. We've decided to go for a drink in the pub this evening, or at least I've persuaded them to. The afternoon was spent reading books on the beach. I wish I'd brought some with me because all the ones on the shelves are awfully dry. Who wants

to read about ancient history? Not me! Anyway, I put on my favourite dress, the one with the pale green flowers on it, and took extra care applying my makeup. I did not tell them about the beautiful Adonis I saw pushing the boat (maybe I'm not so bored by ancient history or myths as I think!). Anyway, it was wonderful to be in the pub. We were sitting in the garden overlooking the sea, pretending to enjoy our cider, when a group of young men turned up. I saw the man from the beach at the back, our eyes met and I hoped Ida and Joan would blame the sun for the flush on my face. They got their drinks and came over to us, the thrill of seeing three girls as exciting to them as they were to us. We got chatting, I was careful not to make a beeline for my favourite. Charlie is his name. We spoke a bit. There's something gentle about him, something kind. Maybe I do read too many novels? It might sound daft, and I'd never tell the other two this, but even as we spoke about the weather, what we'd been up to, it was as if our souls were having a different conversation.

Charlie? Lola's brow furrowed before a chill ran down her spine. She reached for her phone, about to message Tristan but saw it was almost eleven. Hadn't Alf's brother been called Charles? Could it be the same person? What were the chances of there being two men with similar names of similar ages? Lola read on.

We've had a success! All the sitting on the beach enjoying the sunshine has piqued the interest of the young fishermen, the ones we met at the pub. They've offered to take us out on their boat for a sail around the bay. Ida went a bit green at the thought, apparently she was a bit seasick just going around the local boating lake, so I reckon she'll sit this out. Charlie did the asking. Afterwards Joan made a comment about him being sweet on me and although I was absolutely thrilled by this, I pretended that I hadn't noticed. Joan can be the jealous type. Charlie is lovely though, his eyes are as blue as the sea and I fear I might drown in them, but oh, what a lovely way to go!

'Oh gosh', Lola whispered to herself, 'Ruby had it bad.' Her eyes fell on the stack of letters sitting on her dressing table, the urge to untie the ribbon that had kept them together for over seventy years was strong. They must be from Charlie. Charlie who was Alf's brother. Lola exhaled, tried to breathe through the emotions that were rising in her chest like a squally sea. Who cared if it was late, she grabbed her phone and texted Tristan:

I have to talk to you about something, come round the back of the café tomorrow morning, don't let Alf see you!

Chapter Eleven

'Lola, what's up?' Tristan asked as he threw open the kitchen door early the following morning, his eyes skittering across her face searchingly. 'Are you OK? Sorry, I've just seen your text. I was out like a light last night.'

The flash of concern in his eyes hit Lola right in the centre of her chest, causing her words to dry up and her hands to pause in the middle of mixing a batch of scones. They stared at each other across the kitchen as Tristan caught his breath and Lola regained her composure. She shivered as the cold air curled around her, causing Tristan to close the door and step inside.

'Yes, I'm fine, all good,' Lola said as she left the mixing bowl and went to wash her hands. 'Cup of tea?' she asked to bide her time as she flicked the kettle on.

'Is this going to need tea?' A wary look crossed his face as he unzipped his coat.

'Everything needs tea, Vicar.' She gave him a saucy wink before faltering – this probably wasn't the right moment for flirtation. 'It's about Nannie Ruby,' she explained.

Tristan's exhale of relief did not go unnoticed. The fact that he'd been worried that something had happened to her scrambled Lola's thoughts.

He pushed his hands through his hair. 'Yes, go on. What have you found?'

'The diary is in my handbag. Go on, get it out – I've put a bookmark in – and have a look yourself.'

Tristan hesitated before reaching into Lola's bag and pulling out the book. He perched on the stool by the back door and began to read whilst Lola made the tea. Sneaking glances over at him, she took in his reactions to the words as the truth came to light on the pages.

'Charlie?' he asked with disbelief, his eyes moving from the book to Lola's and back again. 'It's not . . .'

Lola moved towards him and peered over his shoulder at the words, the scent of his aftershave assailing her, making her head swim. He smelled good. Resisting the temptation to bury her nose in his neck, Lola stepped back at the same time he turned and caught her eyes. 'I wondered the same. Charlie. Charles.' She shrugged. 'Or am I jumping to wild conclusions?'

Tristan flicked forward a few pages before remembering it wasn't his place to look. Passing the book back to Lola, he said gently, 'I don't think they're too wild, it could be the same person.'

Lola's stomach plummeted. She knew what fate had befallen Charles. Alf's words at the memorial service swam back up and stung her. Something about needing money for a woman.

'You remember what Alf said . . . I don't think he approved.' She chose her words carefully, trying not to speculate. 'We need to know what Charlie looked like. Need to see if he's the same guy in the photo with Ruby.'

Tristan considered this. 'I can have another look, see if there's anything in the local history books or parish records. There's some old photo albums in the office that I've never looked at. I could try them?'

'Could you?' She slipped the book back into the safety of her handbag. 'It's just, I'm worried Ruby might have been the woman Alf said Charles needed money to run away with and we all know how that ended . . .'

Heartbreak, loss, grief. For a split second Lola thought Tristan was about to reach out to her but he caught himself just in time. Her face felt the ghost of his almost touch.

'Anything for you, Lola,' he said softly, the words like a caress.

'Thank you.' She passed him his tea. 'It's that or ask Alf and I'm not ready, not yet. I've still got so much left to read.'

Tristan nodded his understanding. 'I'll have a look this morning. Are you coming to decorate your tree for the festival later?'

'Oh! Yes! Of course,' Lola bluffed. She'd half forgotten about it. 'Three o'clock? I'll ask Freya to cover.'

'Perfect.' He smiled. 'I can't wait to see what your tree will look like.'

'Me too,' she laughed, 'and I look forward to seeing what's in those dusty old albums.'

Their eyes caught and slowly their gazes explored each other's face, searching without quite snagging on the moment. Lola settled into Tristan's calming presence and was warmed by the idea that if they tore down the boundaries they were pretending to defend, every morning could be like this, intimate in its simple ordinariness. Tea and chatter. Lola felt as if she had been presented with what she had been searching for. Peace and companionship. Friendship that flirted around the edges of love.

Chapter Twelve

The prospect of having to decorate a total of three Christmas trees, and to keep them all sparkling with individuality would daunt most people, but Lola, loving anything that could be considered the icing on the cake, was ready to rise to the challenge. In her opinion, Christmas trees were one area of life where the old adage of 'less is more' went out the window. Having warmed up by decking out the cottage, childlike joy surged through Lola as she approached the tree that had been allocated to her in the church.

Lola hummed festive tunes as she stood in the rather chilly church, hanging glistening baubles on the tiny tree and festooning it with more tinsel than was strictly necessary. Memories of attending her annual Christingle service as a child stirred inside her – the sharp tang of the oranges and cloves, the perilous flickering candles. The church smell was almost the same: damp stone, an ancient mustiness with a slight chill. Yet here the sea air crept under the ill-fitting door and mingled with the smell of newly polished pews.

Having decided to quit with the tinsel while she was ahead, Lola stepped back and studied the tree she'd spent the past twenty minutes decorating. She was just making some tweaks when her attention was caught by the church office door opening and from the corner of her eye, she saw Tristan emerge.

Lola readjusted a piece of pink tinsel and turned to Tristan. 'Ta-da!'

'Looks good,' he said as he joined her.

They both regarded the tree, decked out in sparkly gold baubles, pink and blue tinsel with a wonky angel stuck on the stop.

'Think she's been on the sherry.' Tristan nodded at the fairy and Lola tried to straighten her out as he asked, 'No handmade decorations?'

Lola sighed. 'No. I wanted to crochet some but I didn't quite have the time. Maybe next year. Anyway, if it's a competition then I think it's only fair the Scouts or the school win. I went a bit mad in the pound shop. But I like it, it reminds me of when I was little and my brother and I decorated the tree. No taste, no colour scheme, just throwing on whatever glittered.'

'So it has sentimental value?' he asked and when Lola nodded he continued thoughtfully, 'Isn't that really what Christmas is all about? Rediscovering our joy? People put far too much pressure on themselves to have a perfect Christmas when really, what is it about? Spending time with people you love.'

He slipped a glance at Lola as he said this and, slightly lost for words, she smiled back before saying, 'You're right. All the other trees look lovely. I can't wait to see them with all their lights turned on, it's going to be absolutely magical. Freya and I decorated the cottage last night. If you think there's too much tinsel on this tree, then you should see my living room!'

'Sounds wonderful. My tree is still in its box,' Tristan confessed. 'I don't normally put it up until the first of December.'

'But that's only a few days away! You can't have people come round and there be no tree!'

'The nativity set is out, if that helps?' he offered.

Lola narrowed her eyes. 'Well, as you're a vicar, I'll let you off. You are more responsible for the baby Jesus side of things. But we need to fix this tree situation.'

'Well, if you've got nothing better to do right now, fancy giving me a hand?'

Lola made a show of pretending to wrestle with other plans. One tree was enough for one day, but Tristan looked adorable as he asked her. 'Oh, go on, you've twisted my arm.'

Following him out of the church she stopped and pointed to a tree still in its box. 'What's that one for?'

'It's a spare. It's a lot bigger than the others and I'm not sure what to do with it. It was in storage, but I decided not to give it to anyone to decorate, didn't want to be accused of favouritism. I'll probably just stick it back in the cupboard.'

The box was dusty and held together with yellowed Sellotape. It contained a six-foot tree rather than the three-foot ones that were dotted about in the window alcoves. An idea began to form. 'Why don't we do a collective tree? Get everyone to put a decoration on it that means something to them. Or a gratitude or hope tree. Make some little cards and get everyone to write something on them and then hang them on the tree? It'll be a community event.'

'That's a fantastic idea, Lola! I'm sure lots of people have things to be grateful for this year, what with the festival and that wonderful mural celebrating our fishing heritage, and life in Polcarrow looking to be on the up. I'd certainly put tea and toast at Lola's on mine.' Tristan grinned.

'You charmer.' Lola swatted the compliment away, her heart warmed by Tristan admitting her café was what he was most grateful for as she waited for him to grab his coat. 'So, did you find anything about our mysterious Charlie?'

'Sadly not much,' he said as he zipped up his coat. 'I'm sorry to disappoint you. I was hoping there'd be a photo or something but all I could find was his entry in the baptism records. Born 1928, which would have made him twenty-two at the time Ruby visited.'

'Twenty-two,' Lola echoed, 'that seems so young now. Maybe . . . No.'

'What?'

Lola sighed. 'Maybe I should just ask Alf?'

They walked in silence contemplating this.

'You could,' Tristan ventured. 'What's stopping you?'

'It's a big thing for me to get my head around, to think Ruby actually came here, that she knew Alf and fancied

111

his brother. Or who we assume is his brother. I know it doesn't end well because Charlie died. Maybe it was just a summer fling,' Lola sighed.

Sensing there was more Tristan supplied, 'But?'

'The letters.'

'You've still not read them?'

Lola shook her head. 'Part of it still feels like I'm trespassing. I keep thinking of how Alf tells everyone to not dwell on the past and here I am raking it all up. The box was hidden so maybe none of us were meant to know. And here I am going through it like it's a romance novel. My grandmother had a lovely long life, she was happily married to Ernest in the end, but I can't help my curiosity.'

'That's understandable. I'm here for you whatever you decide and whenever you want to talk about it. You don't have to do any of this alone,' he said as he unlocked his front door and held it open for her.

'Thank you. I think I might take a break from reading the diary for a while,' Lola said, pausing slightly before stepping over the threshold. 'I can't believe I've not been in here before,' she said, taking in the slightly outdated décor in the hallway.

'You'll be the only one. When I first arrived there was a steady stream of callers bearing cakes, biscuits and words of advice about the village.'

'What did Alf tell you?'

'To not to listen to everyone else. Miserable lot, he called them, all stuck in their ways.'

Lola laughed. 'Sounds like Alf. I wonder if what happened with his brother is why he's so against looking at the past? Once upon a time I would've gone in all guns blazing, tossed the photo on the table and asked him to tell me everything.'

'I'm sure he'd be willing to talk to you, but I understand your concerns. Shipwrecks and storms were commonplace in seafaring communities, but it was also a long time ago. Maybe Alf would find it comforting to remember his youth?' Tristan took Lola's coat and scarf and hung them on the rack by the front door. 'We do have a tendency to romanticise the past. Oh, I didn't mean anything about you, of course,' he blustered as he spied Lola's 1950s style dress.

'No offence taken,' she said, laying a reassuring hand on his arm. 'I know what you mean. I like the style but I'm not sure I would've liked to live in those times. I probably wouldn't have been allowed to run my own business.'

Lola took in the hallway; the telephone table with an ancient landline plugged in. 'Does that go straight to God?' she asked, picking up the receiver.

Tristan took it from her. 'Only I have his number and I'm not at liberty to dish it out. Go through.' He indicated to the living room.

'Spoilsport.' Lola pretended to sulk as she walked up the hall into the living room. It was homely, decorated more for the previous, older resident. Dark green armchairs and sofa, an electric fire and paintings of the countryside on the walls. 'Didn't they redecorate for you?'

'There wasn't much time. It's OK, I'm used to it. It gives the villagers something stable, unchanged to feel at peace with. Tea or coffee?'

'Tea please.'

Tristan disappeared into the kitchen leaving Lola to have a little nose about the living area, searching for something, anything personal, but there was nothing other than a few early Christmas cards and some photos of people Lola assumed were Tristan's sister's children. Photos of them were dotted around the place and an adorable one tugged at Lola's heart. Tristan and the three children were hanging from a set of monkey bars in an autumnal park. Lola picked it up off the shelf for a closer look, her heart melting a little. Tristan was a bit younger, his golden hair still gloriously getting in his eyes, which were alight with humour from messing about with the children, who had been captured with big, laughing grins on their faces. Lola turned, photo still in hand, as Tristan entered.

'I hope it's up to standard,' he said as he passed a mug to her. 'Ah, that's my niece and nephews. Harriet, Oliver and Sam. They're generally really well behaved – too well behaved in fact for three under tens, so I like to go and ruffle their feathers, as much to annoy my sister as anything else.'

'They're very cute. How come they've not visited?' Lola asked as she replaced the photo.

'Busy lives,' Tristan explained, but not before he'd taken a longing look at the photo. 'My brother-in-law started a new job and ended up not being able to take

114

the leave they'd hoped for. My sister hates driving long distances and can you imagine navigating that lot on the train?' Tristan chuckled, but Lola noticed the sadness in his eyes. He clearly missed them. 'Still, I'll go and visit in the New Year, and they've already got a holiday cottage booked for the two-week Easter holiday. I do miss them.'

'Lucky them having an uncle by the sea.'

'Yes, they can't wait to go surfing. I don't know how to tell them that it's not my cup of tea.'

'Oh, we'll send Freya out with them, she's dying to give it a try.'

Tristan smiled his gratitude. 'I'll remember that. So, shall we get on with this tree then? Two pairs of hands will be quicker than one.'

Lola suspected that the plastic tree and decorations had been inherited with the rectory. They smelled rather musty and the baubles had lost a bit of their shine, but once on the tree along with well-placed fairy lights and tinsel the tree would sparkle.

'It needs to go by the window—' Lola intercepted Tristan as he went to position it by the fireplace '—so people can see it as they walk past.'

Following her advice, Tristan moved the tree to the space in front of the window. Lola stepped forward and fluffed up the branches, evening it out. 'Now, that's a lot better. Can you pass me the decorations.

'Thank God you're here to supervise,' he said as he brought the box over to Lola, watching as she rummaged through the red and gold baubles and tinsel.

Smiling up at him she said, 'Decorating a tree is always more fun with two people. Here, can you check the lights actually work?'

Once he'd confirmed the lights did work, Tristan put on a Christmas music playlist and they bopped around as they hung the baubles and Lola wrapped tinsel around the mirror and mantelpiece, before draping some around her own neck and then Tristan's. Two pairs of hands made quick work of the tree. Lola reached into the box and handed Tristan the star. 'It's your tree, you do the honours.'

Tristan reached up and carefully placed the golden star on the top. 'Do you think Angelo is going to make something for the lobster pot tree? I worry I put him on the spot.'

'Freya seems confident he's working on something. He wouldn't have volunteered unless he wanted to do it. He takes his artistic integrity quite seriously, so I wouldn't worry too much.'

They lapsed into silence as they studied the tree, checking it over, making sure it was all perfect. Lola swapped a couple of baubles round then stepped back.

'Do you think it's ready?' Tristan asked as he straightened up the star on the top.

Lola gave the tree a final once-over. 'Yes, I think it's perfect, anything else would just spoil it.'

Tristan smiled at her. 'Close your eyes and I'll do the honours with the lights.'

Lola nodded and uncoiled a length of tinsel she'd been wearing like a red sparkly feather boa. Closing her eyes, she felt him move across the room, heard the switch and the room was plunged into a darkness full of anticipation. Lola felt it prickle at her neck, the dryness at the back of her tongue.

'No peeking,' Tristan instructed from somewhere to her right.

Lola heard the click of the switch being flicked, felt the darkness recede and as Tristan took his place beside her, everything about the moment felt right, comforting.

'Open your eyes, Lola,' he instructed, his voice as soft as a kiss.

Slowly, savouring the moment, Lola opened her eyes and gasped. The tree was glorious, the golden lights sparkled like a hundred little wishes. 'It's beautiful,' she said, risking a glance at Tristan.

He was watching her reaction, a look of tenderness on his face laying bare his feelings, as if she was the most beautiful thing in the room, not the tree. Overwhelmed, Lola turned back to the tree, and later she couldn't say if she imagined it or not, but she swore she felt the briefest glance of his fingers against hers, sparking something inside her.

'We make a good team,' he said. His eyes met hers and something warm began to unfurl inside Lola, something that felt very much like coming home.

Chapter Thirteen

The Saturday of the Festive Festival dawned clear and bright, promising one of those perfect blue-skied winter days, where sitting wrapped up on the beach with a takeaway coffee would feel like a treat. As she unlocked the café, for what she knew would be a very brisk day of trade, Lola praised the fact the weather gods had seen fit to bless Polcarrow for the event. With a yawn, she set herself up for the day, turning on the fairy lights she and Freya had hung from the shelves and giving the Christmas tree a little bit of a touch up. Freya arrived and shrugged off her coat, an air of sleepiness still hanging around her. They'd been working late the previous night to get the café looking shipshape for the festival. Lola was pleased with her bunting and the little Christmas tree they'd managed to perch rather precariously on the countertop in front of the till.

Sue flew through the café door about fifteen minutes after opening, panicking that everything wasn't quite ready, making Lola wonder if she needed a shot of brandy, not gingerbread syrup, in her coffee.

'It will all be fine,' Lola reassured her as she passed her the frothy drink. 'You've got a perfect day for it and you know the lobster pot tree has been all anyone can talk about. I can't wait to see it all lit up properly.'

Sue sipped her drink. 'I was hoping we'd have the topper by now,' she said with a glance in Freya's direction. 'It was supposed to be delivered this morning ready for when the festival starts.'

Panic flashed across Freya's face. 'I'm sure it's all in hand, you know what Angelo's like.' She gave a nervous laugh before realising Sue didn't know. 'He's a perfectionist. Don't worry, I bet he's just making last-minute tweaks.'

Sue's phone started ringing and stopped any further questions about Angelo's whereabouts. Juggling her coffee and her bags, Sue waved at them and made her way out of the café.

Lola turned to Freya and asked, 'It is all OK with Angelo, isn't it?'

Freya exhaled. 'I don't know. I hope so. He's been a bit secretive about the project. I've not seen the topper yet but I know he is working on it. I wasn't going to tell Sue but I'm a bit worried that he's not finished it.'

'Do you want to go and check on him?'

Freya shook her head. 'That's the last thing he'd want. We'll just have to trust he'll turn up in time.'

'You all right if I take these up to the church?' Lola asked as she emerged from the kitchen later that morning, her arms laden with the boxes of mince pies Sue and Tristan had ordered.

Freya's eyes popped out at the sight of them. 'How many mince pies do you think people are going to eat? You know what, we should've had a mince pie eating contest. I bet Alf would've been up for that.' She picked up her phone, scrolled, then put it down again.

Lola laughed. 'He'd probably cheat and get Scruff to help.' Noticing Freya was acting a bit twitchy she asked, 'You sure you're OK? You can take these if you want to have a break and I'll man the counter?'

'I'm fine. I may have had one coffee too many and I'm worried about Angelo. There's still no news about the tree topper. Nothing. I'm a bit concerned that if it's not up to scratch he won't bring it,' Freya confessed. 'I thought he'd have been here by now and he's not replied to any of my texts or calls.'

'Oh, Freya, I'm sure he won't let Polcarrow down,' Lola placated. 'I'll be back as quickly as I can then you can go and check on him. Call me if there's any sort of cake-related emergency.'

Freya rolled her eyes and signalled to the counter with its piles of festive-themed bakes. 'I think it's highly unlikely. We'll be eating snowman cupcakes all week. I've already had two,' she announced almost proudly.

Chapter Fourteen

As Lola made her way up to the church she could see that the Festive Festival was proving to be a success. Carol singers were standing on the harbour front singing. What they lacked in talent they made up for with enthusiasm and they had attracted a small audience. Children bundled up against the cold and wearing an assortment of Christmas hats ran around on the beach and people were pausing to admire the lobster pot tree. Lola pushed open the door to the church and gasped with surprise at the sight that greeted her. Inside, the church twinkled like a grotto with all the tree lights switched on and gentle carols were playing on an old CD player. There had been a performance from the primary school and locals hovered around the refreshment table, where Lola deposited the boxes of mince pies to a very grateful-looking Jan and Sue.

'So far so good,' Sue said as she opened one of the boxes.

'Do either of you need a break or a hand?' Lola asked.

Both women shook their heads, 'No, Cathy's going to come in a bit,' Jan said. 'You've been working in the café so go and have five minutes and look at the trees, some of them are lovely.'

Lola glanced around, finding the way the church glittered magical. Wondering where to start, she noticed people were gathered around the gratitude tree reading the cards and adding their own thoughts to the branches. A surprised smile spread across her face. Although she'd suggested the idea to Tristan, Lola had no idea he'd actually decided to set it up. Heading to the tree, she began to read the messages. Some brought tears to her eyes, but then Alf's made her chuckle. She glanced around, trying to find him and spotted Steve sitting in Santa's grotto, dressed in a rather thread-bare Santa outfit, handing out small gifts to the local children and listening to their earnest little wishes. Even Scruff was in on the action, wearing a set of ant-lers with a level of obedience Lola would never have imagined he possessed.

Alf was sitting outside the grotto, an elf hat on his head. 'Think I'm a bit old to be an elf,' he grumbled when Lola took him a mince pie, 'but it was the only way to get a seat for the duration, plus, I'm looking after the reindeer.' He slipped Scruff a bit of pie crust. 'Tristan's done a good job, but he did tell me that tree of hope, or gratitude, was your idea. Everyone has been writing something down.'

'Thanks for mentioning on yours that you're grateful for my baking.'

'Well, I am! Been a long time since I had a scone that good, reminded me a bit of the ones my mum used to make. Aggie, the previous owner, tried her best, but bought in scones could never be up to your standards.'

Lola was very tempted to blurt out that maybe they tasted like the ones his mum had made because quite possibly it was his mum Ruby had got the recipe from. Instead, she dropped a kiss on Alf's head. 'Always my biggest fan, but I think I better go and circulate. Find Tristan.'

'When you circle back this way you couldn't bring me another pie and a cuppa, could you?'

'Of course.'

Lola made her way around the church, stopping to admire each tree. The one from the primary school was adorned with salt dough candy canes, all painted in a variety of lurid colours by enthusiastic children. The Women's Institute had chosen white and silver, producing an elegant tree, but the effect was rather spoiled by it being next to the pub tree. Steve had clearly run out of inspiration and had hole-punched several beer mats and attached them alongside some precarious-looking fairy lights. Various other clubs had made a good show of their trees but the gratitude tree had the most people buzzing about it.

'Think that's been a success, don't you?' Tristan sidled up to her.

Lola turned at the sound of his voice. 'Yes, it has been. I didn't realise you'd actually implemented my idea. Alf's admitted to being grateful for my baking.'

Tristan chuckled. 'He's not the only one, and not just your baking either. The tree was very inspired, Lola, the perfect suggestion. I wanted it to be a bit of a surprise.' Their eyes met and Tristan faltered. 'When I came to Polcarrow I wasn't expecting much, OK, maybe the usual villagers who are stuck in their ways, the odd few who want to modernise. The sort of teething problems any new vicar might have. I admit I was expecting Polcarrow to be a stopgap on the way to wherever else I was called, but I've fallen in love with the place and all the unexpected things that have come in this year.'

Lola smiled up at him, warmth spreading through her at how his sentiments mirrored her own. They glanced around at the mural, which was partly obscured by the gratitude tree but still garnered a lot of attention. Lola anticipated Angelo's next big reveal and despite Freya's apprehension, knew it would be a treat.

'Yes, it has all been a bit unexpected, but the best things usually are,' Lola eventually said. 'I'm glad Sue is determined to put the village on the map; it'd be a shame if the likes of Cathy allowed it to fade away. I understand the need to preserve the traditional, but we have something here people want as well. I do hope the press turn up and make Sue's dream of Polcarrow stardom come true. She's worked so hard on this and the Fisherman's Fair.'

Tristan agreed. 'I'm going to encourage people to continue to add to the gratitude tree.' He paused before asking, 'I know church isn't really your thing, but I would very much like it if you came along to the carol service we'll be holding later this month.'

Lola glanced up, her eyes meeting with Tristan's. He gazed down at her, full of affection and she couldn't help but smile. 'Of course, I'll be there, although you might regret it when you actually hear me sing.'

Tristan laughed. 'So there is an end to your many talents? I don't think I believe it.'

'You're only saying that to make me prove it to you, which is a slightly underhand way to get me to come along to the service. I better go and take Alf another mince pie and a cup of tea. Are you heading to the pub after the lobster pot tree unveiling?'

'If you're there then I wouldn't miss it for the world,' he said, making Lola's heart skip a beat.

Chapter Fifteen

'Is your idea that if my hands are full I won't be able to eat them?' Freya asked as Lola passed her some boxes of mince pies to take to the tree switch on. Dusk had fallen and the café had been tidied up and closed down ready for the evening. 'Also, how many pies did you make? You took just as many to the church earlier.'

'Honestly? I lost count. Tristan ordered some for the church and Sue ordered some for the switch on. It's only just December and I'm a little bit sick of the sight of mince pies, which doesn't bode well,' Lola said as she followed Freya out of the café and locked up. 'Have you heard anything from Angelo?'

Freya's face blanched as she shook her head.

'Nothing?'

'No.' Freya sighed. 'But I've got everything crossed he'll be there when we arrive and I've been worrying for nothing.'

They made their way along the seafront towards the lobster pot tree where a crowd was gathering. A local sea shanty choir had been booked to perform before the switch on. Their deep, melodious voices were singing Christmas songs, in a stirring way that brought a tear to Lola's eye. The Polcarrow streets twinkled with white fairy lights and a sense of togetherness washed through the village. Lola and Freya set the boxes of pies on the table where Cathy was running a raffle. Sue was busy with an urn of non-alcoholic mulled punch, the smell fragrant on the cold air. Sue pointed a finger in the direction of a woman with wild curly hair in a black coat and mouthed, 'Press.' Lola gave Sue a thumbs up. Mission accomplished.

Lola wrapped a mince pie in a napkin and took it over to Alf, who was the only person sitting down. 'Hello, love, I feel like king of the village here, not that I need to sit but Tristan and Sue insisted and I'm not one to create more of a fuss, that's more his job.' Alf gave Scruff a scratch behind the ear. 'Thanks for this. I've lost track of how many of these I've had today,' he said as he took the pie from her, then seeing Freya, asked, 'Where's your young man? The tree is still without its fairy.' Alf gestured to the top of the stack of lobster pots.

Despite it being almost dark, Lola saw the blood run from Freya's face.

'I was hoping he'd be here with it,' she said, her voice shaking. Freya threw a panicked glance at Lola.

'I'm sure he's just being a perfectionist.' Lola tried to reassure Freya but her own nerves were suddenly on edge. Surely Angelo wouldn't let everyone down.

Freya surreptitiously checked her phone – nothing. 'Maybe he's just running late,' she suggested with faked brightness. 'I'll give him a call.'

Alf shook his head at Lola. 'Maybe he's got wind there's press here?' Alf pointed to the woman who was busy chatting to Tristan and scribbling something in her notebook.

Alf and Lola exchanged a glance. Press would definitely be problematic to Angelo, who had become a self-imposed artistic recluse following a very public breakdown at an art auction earlier in the year, which had been one of the reasons he'd ran away to Polcarrow. Freya pulled her phone out of her pocket and rang Angelo, walking away from the crowd so no one could listen in. Lola threw her a questioning look, which she answered with a shrug and tried him again. Lola tried to catch Tristan's eye to stall him but he was too busy talking to the reporter. No one seemed to realise the tree topper wasn't in place.

Any further discussion was stopped by Tristan stepping onto a small platform that consisted of two rather rickety-looking crates and, due to lack of a microphone, shouting, 'Good evening, everyone! Can you hear me? Good. Now, welcome to the Christmas tree light switch on. As you can all see we've gone for something a little less traditional this year, which is still in keeping with the local customs. A lobster pot tree!'

There were a lot of appreciative sounds, but Lola saw the moment Tristan realised something was missing. He threw a glance at Freya who was forced to shake her head when Tristan mouthed, 'Where's Angelo?' It was long past the time when the lights were due to be switched on, it was growing darker and colder and Lola saw the moment Tristan decided they'd just have to go on without the topper.

'I'm not one for big speeches, plus it's getting cold.' Tristan rubbed his hands together to demonstrate. 'I'd like to thank you all for coming and, without further ado, to welcome Alf, our local superstar, to come and do the honours.'

'Look after Scruff, will you?' Alf asked Lola as he made a big show of standing up and ambling over to Tristan. Just as he reached the platform a loud cry of 'Stop!' sounded through the crowd.

The whole of Polcarrow turned as one as Angelo loped out of the shadows, cradling something wrapped preciously in an old rug in his arms. Alf and Tristan looked at him. Angelo glanced around the assembled villagers until his eyes met with Freya's. Lola saw the relief wash through her followed by a quick nod of encouragement. Lola felt the apprehension buzzing in the air ahead of the big reveal.

'Sorry I'm late—' Angelo stepped forward '—I completely lost track of time. I hope you weren't thinking I'd forgotten all about the tree topper.' He glanced around the crowd. 'I went to bring it down and it needed one last tweak and maybe I got carried away trying to make it even more special, but here it is. I wanted to do something to reflect a village that is trying to rise again, something that entwined the old seafaring past with the hope of the future. The village is on the cusp of rediscovering itself, it's having a renaissance, and as sad as it might be that we can't find the old fairy, I think it's fitting that we have a new one. Except,' Angelo admitted, 'it's not quite a fairy, but . . .' He whipped off the old blanket.

'A mermaid!' Alf gasped as Angelo held aloft a figure made of wire and metal.

'I know it's not traditional . . .'

'But it's perfect.' Sue stepped forward and placed a hand on his arm. 'You are right, we have to move forward and this is just what we need. Someone get a ladder so we can pop it on the top of the lobster pots.'

There was a bit of commotion as Steve rushed to the pub to retrieve a ladder. It stood a bit rickety on the pavement but along with Tristan and Steve holding it firm, Angelo made his way up, step by careful step, to secure the mermaid on top of the tree, rearranging some of the lights so that they would shine on her. He scampered back down to a round of applause, which he bashfully took, before finding Freya and pulling her to him. Lola and Tristan exchanged relieved glances.

'That is amazing, I'm so proud of you.' Freya kissed him. 'Although I have to confess, I was getting a bit worried you wouldn't show up.'

'Kept you on your toes.' He kissed her back, his eyes glittering. 'Did you really think I'd let everyone down?'

Freya squeezed his hand. 'No. Not at all. I think it's fantastic, so does everyone else.'

Lola watched as Angelo surveyed the rapt crowd, all eyes trained on the lobster pot tree.

'OK, take two!' Tristan announced as Alf flicked the switch on the lights.

Chapter Sixteen

Following the success of the light switch on and a little time spent watching them sparkle against the night sky, the residents of Polcarrow decamped to the pub to warm up. Bar owner Steve was pleased that frosty fingers reached for his potent mulled wine and Lola was in no doubt that there'd be a few sore heads the following morning. She'd taken one sip of it and secreted her glass away, hoping he wasn't expecting his cake to match it for alcohol content. Everyone buzzed around Angelo, who took the praise with an awkward smile whilst clutching his beer and sending 'help me' glances in Freya's direction. She only rescued him when she spied a local journalist trying to corner him.

Tiredness swooped in and after a long day on her feet Lola began to flag. She stayed for one more drink, but didn't dare brave the mulled wine again. She wanted to be up early to get the Christmas pudding mixed together ready for everyone to give it a stir. Desperate for sleep, she said her farewells. Lola kissed Freya and Angelo goodnight, who clearly were ready for bed themselves, although, from the way they buzzed around each other, clearly not to sleep. Stepping out of the pub Lola took in a deep breath of the cool night air, her gaze following the line of the harbour towards where the lobster pot tree twinkled. She hoped Sue was proud of what she'd managed to achieve, the day had been a complete delight.

The sound of the pub door opening behind her caught Lola's attention and she turned towards it expecting to see Freya and Angelo but instead Tristan stepped out, all wrapped up in a black puffer jacket and pulling on thick fleecy gloves.

'Anyone would think you're heading off on an Arctic expedition,' Lola remarked, 'not heading home along Polcarrow's seafront.'

'It's always good to be prepared. Are you heading off or just getting a bit of fresh air?'

'Heading off,' she said with a yawn. 'I've had a long day baking more mince pies than one village strictly should eat and it's only the start of December.'

'Come on, I'll walk you home.'

'Oh, you don't need to do that, I'm perfectly safe,' she said whilst trying to not remember some of her more dicey solo late-night walks home.

Tristan held out his arm. 'I don't, but I'd very much like to.'

Having no reason to protest further, Lola slipped her arm through his and they made their way slowly towards the tree and paused to watch it twinkle.

'I did think Sue was a bit crazy when she suggested lobster pots,' Tristan admitted, 'not to mention when we bravely battled to make it, but now, I think it looks very jolly. I like it. And Angelo's mermaid. I was worried he wasn't going to turn up.'

Lola grimaced. 'It was a bit hairy there for a moment. Freya was worried too, but Angelo is a man with integrity, if he says he's going to do something, he does it. He just has a rather lax approach to timekeeping. I can't wait to get a better look at her in the daylight.'

Meandering along the seafront, Lola tugged on Tristan's arm, signalling him to stop. 'Listen,' she whispered, making them both pause, the sound of the waves whooshing against the shore. 'Isn't it beautiful? There's absolutely nothing better than the sound of the sea. I love how peaceful it is here, no cars, no planes, almost like the modern world is tucked away out of sight.' Lola tipped her head back, there was very little light pollution in Polcarrow and the stars were scattered across the dark sky like diamonds. 'I used to be able to identify the constellations once upon a time,' she sighed.

Tristan craned his neck. 'You know when I first came here I was amazed at just how many stars I could see, especially after being in a city. I bought myself a little telescope and a constellations book.'

'Did you?' Lola gasped. 'That's very exciting.'

'Well, it would be if I'd got the telescope out of its box and done more than flick through the book,' he admitted.

Lola laughed. 'Well, there's a new year coming up, always a good time to add a hobby to the list.'

Tristan was silent for a while before speaking. 'Lola, I know where we can go and properly watch the stars. There's a little cove accessible if you're not afraid of clambering down some rickety steps and the light pollution there is even less. We could go stargazing one night.'

Lola stared at him. 'Stargazing?' she repeated, her brain scrambling to work out if this would be a date or just an outing for two friends.

Tristan took her pause the wrong way. 'Only if you want to, that is,' he tried to backtrack.

'No! I'd love to. It sounds . . .' She couldn't say romantic so she settled on, 'Wonderful. Wonderful and enchanting.'

'Great.' Tristan gathered himself together. 'Well, we need a clear night, so I'll look at the calendar and the weather and work out when would be best to go. You'll have to wrap up warm though, I reckon it could get chilly.'

Lola resisted the urge to suggest he could keep her warm. Ever since she'd helped him decorate the tree she had been wondering how to cross the friendship barrier she'd put up. The one Freya was encouraging her to dismantle. Maybe this was it? Stargazing had date stamped all over it. She stole a glance at Tristan. With his kind, open face and his affable nature, she found it difficult to subscribe wholeheartedly to her mantra that men just made life more complicated. A voice inside her whispered that he'd make it so much easier, if she just gave him a chance.

'Thank you, I will certainly dig out some extra layers,' she told him. 'Ooh how exciting, a midnight picnic on the beach. Let me know what I can bring.'

Placing a hand on her arm, he stopped her. 'Lola, you bring nothing, let me look after you for once.'

Lola dissolved at the way he said those words. No one had ever offered to look after her before.

Chapter Seventeen

'Don't forget we're making the Christmas pudding this morning!' Lola banged on Freya's door bright and early the following day, excitement at the task buzzing through her. Having eschewed Steve's punch the only thing that had kept sleep at bay was replaying her conversation with Tristan. Had he asked her on a date? As in a romantic date? Lola hoped so.

'Ugh, do we have to?' Lola heard Angelo grumble. 'I don't think I even like Christmas pudding.'

Freya's voice was muffled until she called out, 'Sure, we'll see you there in a bit.'

Satisfied with Freya's response, Lola headed downstairs, wrapped an extra-long rose-pink scarf around her neck and pulled on her green checked coat, without caring that the colours clashed. She loved providing a dash of vibrancy to a dark winter morning. Letting herself out through the front door, she shivered as the cold breeze found its way under the few gaps in her layers.

Straightening her shoulders, head held high, Lola crossed the road to the harbour side and watched the sea swirling grey against the sand, enjoying the way the fresh air cleared her head. She set about doing her daily gratitude ritual, listing off her thanks for the gorgeous sea view she was blessed with every day, having friends who were willing to come together for a communal Christmas, and for how successful the Festive Festival had been. She was sure Sue would be buzzing this morning. Satisfied and looking forward to hearing Sue's festival debrief later, Lola stepped away from the harbour wall and hurried across to the café where she quickly unlocked the door, went inside and craving a few minutes peace, locked it behind her. Once in the kitchen, Lola made herself a breakfast of tea and a toasted teacake, smothered in butter, which she ate whilst planning out that morning's bakes and getting the ingredients ready for the Christmas pudding.

Flicking on the radio, Lola bobbed along with the music as she pulled her Nannie Ruby's battered and stained recipe book off the shelf, holding it to her chest in lieu of being able to hug her grandmother. As she thumbed through the book, passing recipes for rock cakes, scones and trifle, golden tinted happiness washed over her to remember the Saturday afternoons they would spend baking fairy cakes and icing them, leaving sticky pink trails across the countertop. The Christmas pudding recipe was near the back, the pages slightly better preserved as they'd been less used. With a sad smile Lola set the book down and rummaged under the table for her scales.

Her phone bleeped and Lola saw Tristan's name flashing up on the screen. Lola unlocked the phone and read the hurried message:

Sorry, will miss breakfast, got a bit of an emergency.
I'll be there in time for the pudding X.

Lola honed in on the kiss, reading all sorts into it, indulging in a daydream about actually kissing Tristan. He'd be slow and careful as he leaned in towards her. Her toes tingled to think of him picking the right moment. With a sigh she put the thought to the back of her mind. After all, she signed all her texts with oodles of kisses, even once, embarrassingly so, to the farmer after he'd confirmed her order was ready.

As a distraction Lola set about making a fresh batch of scones and a coffee and walnut loaf. While they were baking in the oven, she busied herself weighing out the dried fruit for the pudding, selecting the largest pudding basin she had, figuring that if they were going to make a communal one then it had to be an impressive size.

Engrossed in singing along to the radio and weighing out her ingredients, Lola almost missed the banging at the café door. Lola gave her hands a quick wipe before hurrying out to see Freya, Angelo, Alf and Scruff all huddled in the doorway. Freya was peering through the glass, hand raised ready to knock again.

'Sorry, I was miles away,' Lola apologised as she pulled the door open.

'I forgot my key,' Freya explained.

'Morning, perishing out there,' Alf remarked. 'This pudding better be worth it.'

'Of course it will be! I'm almost done, I've weighed all the stuff out and I'm just about to mix it all together, then you can all have a wish.'

'A wish?' Angelo asked, bemused.

'You all give the mixture a stir and make a wish,' Alf explained. 'I guess it's more for kids but I think it's a nice tradition.'

'We never did anything like that. Christmas was always a bit hybrid, Italian and English. I don't think I've ever had Christmas pudding,' Angelo mused.

Alf's mouth dropped open. 'What? But you've had turkey, yes?'

Angelo laughed. 'I'm half Italian, not half alien. Yes, we had turkey, we just never had Christmas pudding. You know I've not got much of a sweet tooth.'

Alf gave him a long look and shook his head in disbelief. Freya set about making hot drinks and toast, and Lola used a chair to prop the kitchen door ajar so she could listen in on their conversation about Angelo's renovations of Bayview House. Alf was putting him through his paces.

'You see, that house was built when I was a lad, we used to go up there and watch the builders. We'd never seen anything like it, all those big windows, how grand the rooms were, completely different to our little cottages. People didn't approve of the building back then, but the owner helped modernise the roads in the village, which soon stopped people complaining.'

Lola listened from the kitchen. Hmm, she thought, it seemed like Alf was happy to gabble on about the past when it suited him. She toyed with the idea of dropping into the conversation the fact that she thought her grandmother had stayed there one summer. She imagined how their jaws would all drop, that Alf's eyes would light up with surprise and the story would all come tumbling out. Lola imagined it like some sort of reunion, her and Alf united in memory of their lost family members. Then she realised it wouldn't be like that. She knew it would be a shock, there would be a lot to process and unpick.

Freya stuck her head around the kitchen door and asked, 'Where's Tristan?'

'He's had a brief emergency this morning, but he'll be here for a quick stir before morning service,' Lola replied from the kitchen. 'What are you doing after this?'

Freya rolled her eyes. 'Guess? More wallpaper removal. Although I'm tempted to tell him just to paint over it all. I've had enough of steaming and scraping. I can stay and work if you want?'

'That would be great, I need a bit of time to start feeding brandy into the Christmas cakes that are maturing,' she said, as Freya headed out of the kitchen to take a plate of toast to Alf and Angelo.

Lola carried on singing along to the radio and whilst everyone else tucked into breakfast, she finished off the pudding prep and set about icing the coffee and walnut loaf. She heard the door swing open and the sound of Tristan's voice greeting everyone.

'Sorry, have I kept you all waiting?' he asked as he unwrapped his layers, eyes darting straight to Lola, stopping her in her tracks.

'Not at all, perfect timing actually,' she said as she placed the cake on the counter. 'There might be some toast left if Scruff hasn't got to it all.'

The dog barked in protest, but instead of joining them at the table, Tristan came over to the counter and paid for an Earl Grey tea. As Lola made it, he lowered his voice and said, 'I've been checking the forecast and Tuesday looks clear for stargazing, if you're still up for it?'

Lola passed him his tea. Tristan was looking at her as if her answer meant everything. 'Of course I am. Tuesday would be perfect.'

The smile that flashed across his face was like a lightning bolt through Lola.

Once they'd finished their breakfast Freya flicked the latch on the door so that they could have a few moments peace and Alf told Scruff, in a very stern voice, to stay sitting where he was. They all filed into the kitchen where Lola handed out aprons and supervised handwashing, after shutting the door on Scruff despite his whimper at being left out.

Angelo took his apron with a dark look. It was pink with little yellow ducks on it. 'I'm stirring a pudding. I'm pretty sure I can trust myself not to get any down me.'

Freya giggled and slipped hers over her head before rolling her sleeves up. In the middle of the kitchen island sat a huge mixing bowl full of fruity, fragrant pudding mix. 'It smells divine! I love Christmas pudding. We used to help my grandparents make them. I've not had a home-made one for years.' Freya dipped a finger in the mixture, a movement that earned a slap on the wrist from Lola.

'This is my Nannie Ruby's recipe,' she told them, pausing to see if the name registered with Alf. Either it didn't or he'd developed a very good poker face, so she continued, 'I have to confess I've never tried making it myself because it was always her domain, and I've never had the need to whip up a massive pudding. But it smells and looks exactly as I remember, so I think she'd approve.' Lola pulled out a wooden spoon, its handle worn smooth. 'This is her famous stirring spoon. It's what imparts all the magic into my bakes, and you're very honoured to all have a go with it. Who wants to start? Alf?'

'Oh go on.' Alf came forward and seized the spoon and started to stir. 'This is good, takes me back to my childhood. We didn't do much for Christmas then, it wasn't as commercial, just church and gathering together. None of these stacks of presents. We've lost our way with all this commercialism,' he mused as he stirred. 'But I think this is good, being together is the true spirit of Christmas. I'm looking forward to Christmas Day, us all being together. I don't really need to wish for anything else.'

'What would you usually do at Christmas?' Tristan asked.

Alf relinquished the spoon and shrugged. 'Mostly just me and Scruff. I get invited by all sorts of people to join their Christmases, which is lovely, but I'm not one for imposing or big celebrations. At least not with the wrong people. I might be alone but I've never felt lonely.' Scruff started to whine in the café, put out that he wasn't being included. Alf rolled his eyes. 'In fact, I never get a moments peace with that one!'

Everyone laughed and Freya stepped forward to take up the spoon. Lola watched her stir the gooey pudding mixture with focus, turning it over as she mentally sent out her wishes. Resisting the urge to give an Alf-style monologue she simply said, 'I'm looking forward to it too, especially all the lead-up to Christmas.'

'Are you not missing London?' Alf asked.

Freya shook her head. 'No, I was mostly working at Christmas when I was there, which can be fun, but it's also exhausting. I always felt like I was part of the party but not properly in it. I'm much happier here with all of you. Christmas is what you make it.' She passed the spoon to Angelo, who looked a bit puzzled.

'Erm, I've never done this before, so, here goes.' He gave the mixture a tentative stir before finding his rhythm. 'Actually, this is quite fun. But I'm not telling any of you what I'm wishing for, even though I basically have everything I need right here. I'm properly contented for the first time in my life.'

'But you'd like some house-decorating fairies to turn up, yes?' Freya teased.

Angelo grinned. 'Ssh, I'm not meant to divulge anything.' He stopped stirring and stepped back to let Tristan take his turn.

'In all the years I've been a vicar I've never felt as welcome as I do here. I might have comforted the bereaved or counselled the lost but I've never stirred a Christmas pudding with a group of people who have become friends I love. This has been a wonderful village to join and although there was some resistance when I arrived because I was young and new, I've enjoyed the challenges. You're all so passionate about life here, you make my job so much easier,' Tristan said.

'I think you're preaching to the converted,' Alf pointed out, 'we're all on your side anyway, but it's a lovely sentiment.'

Tristan stirred in silence for a while longer, concentrating on the hypnotic way the mixture folded and turned in on itself, the festive aroma filling the air. When he'd done enough he held the spoon out to Lola.

'I've already had my wish, it'd be greedy to have another one.'

Tristan took her hand and pulled her over to the bowl, transferring the spoon into her hand. 'There will never be enough wishes for the woman who makes all the magic happen.'

Face flushed, Lola took the spoon from him, their fingers brushing, gazes lingering. Slowly she began to stir. Aware that everyone was watching them, Lola broke her gaze from Tristan's and concentrated on stirring the pudding, trying to ignore the way her stomach had flipped at the touch of his hand, her excitement for Tuesday blooming even more.

'Happy thoughts and love—' she smiled warmly at her friends 'are what really make the world go round. And I have both in spades here with you all.'

Chapter Eighteen

Wednesday, 6th September, 1950

Dear Diary,

   What a wonderful day it's been! Ida and Joan went into St Ives but I pretended to have a headache so I could meet with Charlie without them spoiling it with being all disapproving. Charlie rowed us out to a secret cove. Just the two of us, his brother wasn't best pleased to have been left behind. The water was crystal clear and Charlie was patient enough with my attempts at swimming. I thought he'd laugh at my doggy paddle, but he didn't, which made me like him even more. He even showed me how to swim properly and I did a few strokes, but I'm not a natural. Charlie is, but then again if you grow up by the sea you should be good at all sea-based things. He showed me how to row but I took us around in circles. We laughed so much. Anyway, I much preferred the view when he was rowing. He's strong, tanned and very kind. We swapped all sorts of stories about our lives. He is only working as a fisherman because it's what's expected of him but he has such grand plans, he wants to study, better himself, fishing is the work of the past. He asked me so many questions about what it's like to live near London, how we coped with the war. We were both too young to do our bit so we lamented this but agreed we can play our part in shaping the future. Charlie gets me, understands that I want more than to just become a housewife, although I did try to persuade him that Cornwall is a lot nicer than anywhere else I've ever seen, which to be truthful, isn't many places. Charlie listened to me and I was secretly very pleased I didn't have to share him with anyone else. Ida and Joan were not best pleased to find out I'd been out with Charlie, but I don't give two figs about what they think!

Fizzing with excitement at her date with Tristan, Lola stood in front of her wardrobe wondering what on earth to wear, musing on whether or not Ruby faced the same dilemma when she met up with Charlie. Lola rummaged around looking for some things to layer up, pulling out an old striped jumper she'd not worn for ages and a cardigan that complemented it. Freya was up at Bayview again with Angelo, working on putting the newly delivered bed together, and most likely giving it a test run. So there was no chance of a proper pre-date panic. In fact, Lola hadn't even told Freya she was going on a date with Tristan. She wanted to keep it to herself for a while longer, allow things to develop without anyone else sticking their oar in. The air of secrecy, of sneaking out on an adventure conjured up images of Ruby going out on Charlie's boat. Ruby must have felt the same; giddy and nervous, balancing on the brink of change.

Tristan's instruction for her not to bring anything had pushed Lola out of her comfort zone, her hands felt light and empty. Looking after people was how Lola felt in control and she rarely relinquished this to anyone, but . . . Tristan, she trusted him. The realisation stopped her in her tracks as she paced up and down the hallway. Lola tallied up all the men she had dated before and not a single one of them had made her feel as safe as Tristan did.

Tonight her nerves were like the bubbles in a glass of champagne, something celebratory and glorious, no twinge of anxiety, just anticipation at the night ahead. Even her longest relationship with Jared, who she had been so head over heels for that she'd allowed his glamour to blind her to his faults, hadn't been like this. Lola suspected that she'd overcompensated in that relationship with her cocktail-making skills and flirty banter. Sometimes, looking back, she wondered how much of it had been love and how much of it had just been down to the potent gin cocktails she'd mixed them.

A knock on the door made her jump. Lola composed herself before reaching for the door handle. She had the strangest sensation that this was the moment before everything changed. A smile spread across her face when she saw Tristan standing there, bundled up against the cold, the keenest, sweetest look on his face. A look that told her he sought only to make her happy. Lola swallowed that notion back as they drank each other in. He was wearing an expensive-looking winter coat, the type that comes from a hiking shop, a black beanie hat pulled low over his ears, and he carried both a backpack and another bag.

'Where are we going? Antarctica? You look like a pack horse, let me help with one of those.' Lola held out a hand.

Tristan laughed. 'Not quite, but you will need this,' he said as he passed her a torch. 'We're going down to the cove; I've checked the tide times and the sea is out at the moment. It's the least light polluted place I can think of so best for seeing the stars.'

'And the most treacherous,' Lola reminded him with a raised eyebrow.

'Erm, yes, but we'll be fine, I tried it out the other night and I'm still intact.' He gave himself a satisfied pat on the stomach to prove the point.

'Good, my first aid is a bit rusty.' She took the torch and stuffed it into her pocket. 'What's in all the bags?'

'Provisions. And stuff to keep us warm.'

Lola smiled at him as a thought about other ways they could keep each other warm raced unbidden through her mind. She quickly wiped it away. 'Lead on!'

Tristan waited as she locked up, then handed her the bag containing the blanket and the whisky. 'The most important part,' he instructed, 'look after them.'

They made their way along the harbour front like two fugitives, climbing up to the headland and stopping briefly to look back at the village, which twinkled with festive joy.

'Doesn't it look magical,' Lola whispered. 'Everyone tucked up in their houses while we're off on an adventure.'

'Yes, it's all so peaceful. I like coming up here to clear my head. I look back, hoping I'm doing the right thing for everyone. It's hard sometimes to know if I am. I thought a village would be easier to manage, but the challenges are just different. More petty grievances,' he sighed.

Lola gave his arm a reassuring pat. 'Well, I think you're doing a splendid job.'

Tristan smiled at her. 'That's high praise from someone who's never been to a service.'

Lola's cheeks flushed. 'I'm sorry I've not been, it's not really my thing. Does that matter?'

Tristan considered this and shook his head. 'Probably not. God can be found anywhere. If he's supposed to have made the sea, the flowers, the beach, then why should people not worship in their own way or in the way that brings them comfort?'

'That's very progressive of you.'

'I've had to be. I wanted to become a vicar so that I could help people, provide them with guidance and support, somewhere to go in their time of need. Need doesn't just occur for an hour on a Sunday morning.'

Lola studied him. 'No, it doesn't. It comes in the night sometimes, or with the dawn. It can be resolved over a cup of tea and a slice of cake.'

Tristan laughed. 'Of course. We're really not so different, are we?' he said gently.

Lola smiled at the tinge of hope in his voice. 'No, no we're not.'

They fished out their torches and Tristan led the way down some slightly rickety steps, his hand held out should Lola need it. The path would have been slightly treacherous in daylight but night-time added an extra frisson of danger. They lapsed into silence as they concentrated on getting down safely, Tristan occasionally warning Lola if the steps were worn out or steeper than the previous one. Lola picked her way down and was slightly relieved, but exhilarated, to land on the soft sand at the bottom, the sounds of the waves swooshing through the dark mysteriously.

'I feel like a smuggler,' she said, following Tristan over to the middle of the beach.

He laughed. 'I do too a bit. I think here is fine.' He dropped his bag and then began to remove some of the contents. 'What's next with Ruby and Charlie?'

'I was thinking about them before I came out,' Lola said as she smoothed the blanket over the sand, 'of them sneaking off on his boat away from everyone. Her friends weren't best impressed so I don't blame her not telling them much. This feels very much in the spirit of Ruby and Charlie.' She signalled around them.

'Moonlight picnics on the beach? Yes, it is terribly romantic.' Tristan cast a glance at her as he assembled his portable fire bowl.

'Is there anything I can do to help?' she asked, feeling slightly at a loss.

'Nope, just sit and relax, you do enough looking after me every morning.'

Lola shrugged but found she was actually enjoying the novel sensation of someone doing things for her and she started to relax. She swallowed back the shame that accompanied any realisation of how awful her previous relationship had actually been, how she had done all the work for no reward. Not to mention how upset she had been when it ended. Still, she reminded herself as she smothered the anger, she was in a much better place now and her life was everything she'd ever dreamed of; who wouldn't want to be living by the sea and running a café? Lola couldn't imagine anything better. To distract herself from any more thoughts of Jared, she pulled out the bottle of whisky from the bag, and sank its bottom into the damp sand. She watched as Tristan set to work filling the fire bowl with logs he'd collected before lighting it, the orange flames slowly starting to lick away at the darkness.

'Won't that spoil our view of the stars?'

'Maybe a bit, but it'll keep us warm. I can't have you freezing to death, Alf would never forgive me for depriving him of the best scones he's ever eaten.'

Lola laughed. 'I never really paid much attention to the word Polcarrow written next to Nannie's recipe, but now, it feels, I don't know, like fate, perhaps? It's easy to think Ruby got the recipe when she visited here. What if she got it from Alf and Charlie's mum? Imagine that! Maybe that's why he likes them so much? Maybe I'm just being fanciful . . .'

'It's not fanciful if it could be the truth. I think they're pretty special, although I've not eaten quite as many as he has,' Tristan said to her as he set up a camping gas stove and popped a tiny little kettle on top of it. 'For tea.'

'This is all very Boy Scout,' Lola remarked, affection creeping into her voice, touched by the effort he'd gone to.

'Well, I was a Boy Scout,' Tristan confessed. 'You name it, I did it – Scouts, Duke of Edinburgh, summer camps.'

'It all sounds very wholesome. I don't think I've ever met anyone who was in the Scouts before. That said, the sort of people I used to hang out with would never have admitted to it even if they had been. Thanks.' She accepted a cup of tea.

'I don't have milk, that's why the whisky is there, keep us warm.'

Lola tipped in a slug before passing the bottle to Tristan. 'You're very prepared. Do you do a lot of camping?'

He joined her on the blanket. 'Yes, we used to have camping holidays when I was small. The only reason they stopped was because my sister decided she'd had enough of roughing it and not being able to use her hair straighteners,' he laughed. 'I've always enjoyed the outdoors, camping, walking. I keep thinking of taking myself off wild camping for a night but even in the wilds out here I bet someone would find me.'

Lola laughed at the thought of someone tracking him down in the wilds of Cornwall to complain about something trivial. 'I've not properly camped for years. It was never my parents sort of thing but I tried it with friends in my late teens and loved it, the freedom, being under the stars with a bonfire. What? Don't look at me like that! Just because I can execute the perfect eyeliner flick doesn't mean I don't like to camp. I was on the road for years remember. Camper vans though, so a little more luxury.'

'Do you miss travelling?'

Lola sat and gazed out in the direction of the sea and sighed. 'Maybe a bit, but mostly because it was what I was used to. If something went wrong, I just packed up and moved on. Now, that's not so easy. Also, as a coping strategy it's probably just classified as running away. Now if I make a mistake I have to fix it. I miss the people, but they all moved on too. I guess part of me found it exciting – meeting people from different walks of life, trying different jobs. Now it seems like it happened to a different Lola. The permanence of being here is a bit scary sometimes, but mostly I like it. It's given me a chance to relax, to just be.'

'Would you ever go back?' Tristan's question was asked lightly but Lola sensed the weight behind it.

'No,' she said firmly. 'No. There's nothing for me there anymore. The people I knew have all moved on, evolved, and settled down. I was the last to go. I miss it in a rose-tinted, nostalgic way, like pining for my youth. It is hard work constantly packing up, moving on, never knowing who you're going to see at the next destination. I used to alternate between helping friends at festivals and finding temporary work in bars, cafés and kitchens. There was always a pub that needed someone to bash out desserts at the end of service and I made sure to keep my food hygiene certificate up to date.'

'Was food always your passion?'

'Cake was,' Lola corrected him. 'I love that people use cake to both celebrate and commiserate. Birthday cakes for children, tea, cake and sympathy when something goes wrong. Baking cakes is my duty. I, erm, sidelined this dream for years, which was foolish really.'

'What made you decide to come back to it? Or open a café even, that's quite a big thing to do.'

'It was Ruby really. When she died I realised I needed to sort my life out, I couldn't keep flitting about. She always wanted to see me settled somewhere, see me happy. If I couldn't do it in her lifetime, then it felt right to do it in her memory. After she died she left me an inheritance and instantly I knew what I wanted to do with it. At the time I was with a guy called Jared, he was a musician and a magician, he could put on these really enchanting shows. We'd sit up, a bit like this this, with a bonfire, talking about the future. I had this crazy notion of opening a magic-themed café. I'd do cakes, cocktails, afternoon teas and he'd do tricks.' Lola laughed at the idea of it all. 'Thank God I decided to take an extended stay at my grandmother's after she died. It gave him time to find someone else and show his true colours.'

'Oh, Lola, that sounds awful, I'm so sorry.'

'Don't be! I was devastated at the time, mostly because I had no idea what to do next and I wasn't one to normally be out of ideas. He met someone else. I think he rather fancied getting some of my inheritance and keeping this young woman on the side. Honestly, Tristan, the scales dropped from my eyes and I saw what he was really like, but it was just a knife in the wound of losing Ruby.' She sipped her tea and wondered if there was any chance of having just a tot more whisky. Tristan seemed to read her mind and added an extra dash.

'Thank you. So, anyway, we don't want to give Jared any more time than he deserves. I cried my tears over him long ago. Last Christmas, being in a little village in Oxfordshire really helped heal my broken heart. I decided I'd resurrect my café dream. I never planned to come to Cornwall, but I found the name Polcarrow next to the recipe in Ruby's book and I just had this feeling I had to come here.' Lola shrugged. 'And the rest is history. I honestly never thought I'd end up by the sea, but it's been very healing. It just felt right to stay here.'

'You've had quite the time of it, Lola. I'm sorry to hear Jared couldn't treat you the way you deserve.'

'Thank you. I honestly think if I had stayed with him, my grandmother would've come back and haunted me until I dumped him . . . so . . . maybe it was for the best. It's strange how all these things that feel awful at the time work out in the end.' Lola took a swig of her whisky-laced tea. 'What about you? Any hidden heartbreaks?'

Tristan laughed. 'Not at all. I was seeing someone at my old parish, Anna. She was, let's just say, rather keen on becoming a vicar's wife. I thought that was what I wanted for a while too. We were well matched but I wasn't ready for her at the time. We ended amicably, or as amicably as it's possible to end things when one person has high romantic hopes. I did feel I'd let her down, but I'd also not promised anything.' He glanced into his cup.

'I'm sure you did the right thing and did it well,' Lola told him. 'You're always very considerate. How long were you together?'

'Two years, so long enough for people to start asking questions, including myself, but I was completely burnt out by my old parish and needed to recharge.' Tristan sipped his tea and changed the subject. 'Speaking of doomed love affairs, have you read the letters yet?'

Lola shook her head. 'No, they feel like they really are the end of things. I'm a bit scared to open them. I've been reading about this love affair that made Ruby so

158

happy and we all know Charlie died and Ruby married my Grandad Ernest, so there's clearly not the happy ending anyone had been thinking of. I'm just enjoying being swept away to that glorious post-war summer where they were all full of youthful hope. Ruby was happy with my grandad later and it's easy to forget that while digging up the past.'

Tristan was silent for a long while before saying, 'How did you become so wise, Lola?'

'Me, wise? I just watch people, listen to them. When people come to me for a palm reading or the tarot cards, I know they're after solace or guidance. They feel lost and it's quite easy to make them feel better.'

'Do you ever tell people if you see something awful?'

Lola shook her head. 'Never. Because what if it doesn't come to pass? Especially with the tarot cards, it's all suggestive. I know there's this wonderful, romantic notion of fate – that our lives are all plotted and planned out, and yes, to some extent, I really believe that we are led down certain paths and have chance meetings. But there are always forks in the road, so if something doesn't work out you'll be magically redirected towards something that will. Those choices determine where we end up.'

'Like us both being here,' Tristan said, his voice carefully light.

Lola swallowed back the thought of fate drawing them together, down to the very tip of the country, at the same time. 'Yes, exactly,' she said as their eyes caught, the firelight making Tristan's eyes burn like two blue flames. 'I'm glad it brought us both here. All of us, actually. Think of it. Angelo and Freya. Sometimes it's too mad to think of all these chance encounters and how they all turn up. Even I can't get my head around it.'

'Well, you don't need to figure it out just yet,' Tristan told her, before reaching to pull his bag over to him. 'I have something special for you.'

Lola's eyes lit up. 'What? I'm intrigued!' She leaned forward eagerly to watch what he'd do next.

Tristan delved into his rucksack and pulled out a box. Lifting the lid, he shone his torch onto a perfectly baked pineapple upside down cake.

'No way! For me?' Lola's voice caught, remembering the conversation they'd had when prepping for the Christmas cakes. 'No one has ever baked for me before.'

'Probably because they wouldn't dare. I'm pretty proud of how it turned out though, but I know looks are only one part. Do you want to try it?'

'Yes please!' She clapped her hands together in delight.

'Sorry I couldn't bring any custard,' he said as he cut generous slices of the cake and passed one to her.

Lola took the slice from him. 'I'm sure I'll forgive you. Would've been a bit messy.' She took a bite. The sweetness of the pineapple had soaked into the light sponge, the taste bringing back school day memories; wet lunch breaks where they kicked around the corridors, the smell of chalk on the blackboard, the cookery classes that had been her favourite because she'd excelled. 'Oh my God, this is amazing, you really made it?'

Tristan laughed. 'Yes, and I'm guessing that's your seal of approval.'

'It's delicious. I think if I were to freeze to death out here you'd be able to keep the café going. Do you think I could add this to the menu?'

'I don't see why not, but I'm not coming round every morning to bake one for you.'

Lola pouted. 'Shame. I could do it in the new year – retro bakes to cheer everyone up. Everyone's always so depressed in January but I see it as a fresh start.' She finished off the cake and confessed, 'This has been a real treat, it's been a long time since someone has made me sit back and relax. Thank you.'

Tristan took her hand and gave it a squeeze. 'You don't have to do anything alone any longer, Lola, you have me. There's Freya and Alf and even Angelo. You have us.'

Lola squeezed his hand back. There was a pause, a moment when the thought of leaning forward and kissing him assailed her. He'd taste of tea and whisky and sweet pineapple. Lola sat back, befuddled, reminding herself it was the whisky and the surprise cake that was getting her all carried away . 'Thank you. I feel so safe here, so at peace. I don't think I'll ever want to leave.'

'That's good to hear because I for one don't want you to leave.' Tristan pulled himself up and before Lola could register what he'd said, he'd changed the subject. 'Now, how about some more tea and we do a bit of stargazing. I brought my portable telescope and the book about the constellations.'

He passed the book to Lola, who began to flick through it. 'When's your birthday?'

'Sixth of March, why? Are you going to do my birth chart because I'm not sure I'm meant to wholly believe being a vicar and all that?'

'No, I'm not actually that good at birth charts, so you're safe. I was just curious.'

'Hmm. When's yours?'

'Has Freya not cornered you yet? It's Christmas Eve!'

'What? Really?'

'Yes! Freya is determined to organise a party for me. I'm guessing since you have no idea about it that the party planning hasn't got very far. She was adamant that I'm not allowed to plan my own birthday party.'

'She's said nothing.' Tristan looked horrified.

'You'll have to have words with her. I think she was going to host it in the pub. Ask Steve, I bet she's not done that either! Maybe I will have to take it upon myself.'

Tristan put a hand on Lola's arm as if to physically hold her back from marching back up the steps and straight to the pub. 'I'll chat to Freya. I'll talk to Steve. She's right, you can't organise your own birthday party.'

'Maybe you'll have to be on cake-baking duty after tonight?' Lola suggested.

'Ah. A birthday cake might be a bit of a challenge, but I could be up for it. So, what would your ideal birthday party be like?'

'Definitely cake, so no pressure there, but also lots of sparkles and no Christmas music. Growing up I always hated how my birthday was commandeered by Christmas. I should have an unofficial birthday in June, make the most of the long nights and the lack of Christmas tat. I'm a bit worried that if I have a party no one will come, what with it being Christmas Eve.'

'Nonsense, I'm sure everyone will come, or at least those that matter will. It'll likely just give everyone a chance for an extra glass of sherry.'

'Sherry! I'm turning forty, not ninety,' she said before she realized she had rather hoped to keep her age a little bit under wraps.

'Forty? Even more reason for a party, Lola,' Tristan convinced.

'Thank you. Turning forty is a bit scary,' she confessed to him, 'especially as a woman, there's always this notion that things should have been different. I think there's some hard-wiring in us that even if we don't desperately want marriage and babies, there feels a loss of sorts. Oh gosh . . . don't mind me . . . I don't mean to get all maudlin, not when we're having such a lovely time.'

'It's OK, Lola, I understand. You can talk about it if you want, but if not, we can just sit back and watch the stars and finish off that cake.'

Lola studied him and her heart melted slightly. He really was such a good, kind soul. 'You really mean we can finish it off?'

Tristan held the box out to her. 'I'm sure it won't be as nice in the morning.'

Lola pretended to wrestle with the idea before reaching in for another slice. 'Thank you, it is scrummy, and actually it is OK to talk about the big things.' Since they were outside with the whole Universe spread across the sky, it felt like the right time to talk about the deeper stuff. 'What do you want from life, Tristan?'

'It sounds like a massive cliché, but really, I just want to be happy.'

'Are you happy?'

Tristan snuck a glance at her. 'Right now, yes, very happy. I'm very happy in Polcarrow. I'm in one of the most beautiful places on earth, I'm here with you, there's a fire, there's cake and we have whisky. I have nothing to complain about.'

'Does your belief make it easier to be happy?' Lola wondered aloud.

Tristan thought about the answer for a long time. 'I think it does, yes. Awful, terrible things will always happen, but having a greater power to believe in will always provide comfort. Surely you understand that,' he said softly.

'I do. The feeling that there's something bigger than us. Looking up at all those stars is very humbling. It amazes me to think these same stars shone down on all our ancestors and they'll carry on sparkling for years to come.'

'You're quite the romantic underneath it all, aren't you?'

Lola exhaled, 'I've never thought about it like that.'

'You want to dish up happy-ever-afters with your cakes, that's why you care so much about Alf and Ruby, or Charlie and Ruby. Angelo and Freya. What about your own happy ending? What do you want, Lola?'

'Oi! I asked you first,' she said to deflect, 'and you never properly answered.'

Tristan stared off into the distance. 'I want to settle down with someone I love. If I'm lucky enough to be blessed with children, then that would be a wonderful thing, if not I know there's other ways to parent. Maybe a dog. I know they're the simple things but really it's the simple things that matter, that make people feel most at peace.'

Lola had closed her eyes whilst he spoke, allowing herself to wander through the sun-drenched rooms of his dreams. 'It sounds absolutely wonderful. You're right, the simple things are what matter the most. I've been all sorts of places, seen all sorts of things, but it's only since I've been here that I've realised that the simple life is a happy life.'

Tristan was quiet for a while. 'So what does Lola's future look like? What do you want to find?'

Lola paused, there was a weight to his question, as if her answer mattered more than anything on earth. The answer caught in her throat, its truth making her feel foolish, silly, like a girl believing in a fairy-tale notion, not an almost forty-year-old woman with responsibilities. 'I want true love,' she said, 'love with someone who'll never let me down. The rest would all be sprinkles on the top of the cake.'

Tristan glanced back at her, the firelight flickering over him. His gaze caught hers and held it. Even though she was huddled up in three layers of knitwear, she had never felt as exposed as she did in that moment. Had never allowed anyone to see so deeply into her soul. Rather than feeling fragile, as if any wrong move would fracture her, Lola had the notion that Tristan was about to wrap her up in bubble wrap and look after her. She didn't know if she was ready for this, it was as overwhelming as it was beautiful.

Somehow she found her voice but it wobbled as she spoke. 'Tristan, the stars,' she reminded him, passing the book back to him, before lying back on the blanket, eyes trained on the heavens. She felt him lie back down beside her and briefly wondered what would happen if she reached out her hand to his, but it never became anything more than a thought, a possibility she was not quite ready for.

Chapter Nineteen

They spent another hour or so on the beach, burning away the rest of logs, shining the torch onto the pages of the constellation book before peering up into the blackness of the night, trying to figure out what shapes were twinkling above them. Even the portable telescope didn't help.

'I don't think stargazing is going to be my new hobby,' Tristan admitted as he doused the fire and began to pack up.

Lola pulled herself up, slightly stiff from the cold and blurred around the edges from the whisky. Shaking the sand off the blanket, she bundled it up and shoved it into the bag with a yawn.

'Oh dear, we better get you home,' Tristan said, holding out a hand to her.

Lola hesitated before taking it, slipping her gloved palm into his, relaxing into his hold. Sleepiness washed over her and the desire to curl into him was strong. Instead, she stifled another yawn and said, 'Lead on.'

Tristan paused before shouldering his bag and making his way across the sand, slowing his stride so that Lola could keep up with him. They ascended the steps in companionable silence, torches lighting the way, the sound of the waves bidding them farewell. Contentment settled over Lola like a snuggly blanket, as she followed Tristan up, listening to his instruction, falling for him a little bit more with each step. As she reached the top, Tristan offered Lola his hand to help her up over the final step. She took it without hesitation, sucking in a breath at how natural the contact felt.

Lola drew to a stop next to him, catching her breath as she studied Polcarrow, a reminder of reality, their lives and responsibilities spread out before them. On the beach it had felt as if they were the only two people enveloped in the star-spangled darkness. Tristan paused, as if he too wanted to prolong the magic. Lola squeezed his hand, snuck a glance up at him, her heart tumbling over and over as he glanced down at her. Shyness swept through Lola, an unusual feeling for her, but one that told her whatever happened next with Tristan mattered.

Hand in hand, they meandered home in a silence that fizzed with whatever was coming. Lola wracked her brain for something to say, anything, but she didn't want to break the spell. Walking next to Tristan was grounding, there was no pressure, she trusted him not only to take care of her, but to do all the right things. Lola couldn't remember the last time she'd met a man she could truly let her guard down with. The sensation was terrifying but thrilling.

Although their steps had felt slow, they arrived at her cottage far too quickly. 'It's like we're the only two people in Polcarrow,' she whispered, entwining her fingers through his, giving his hands a little tug.

Tristan glanced up the street. 'It is, but I like it.'

There was a pause, a shift as he stepped slightly closer, his eyes locking with hers before dropping briefly to her lips and back up again. Lola's breath caught, her brain scrambled and her body swayed forward.

'I've had a really lovely time,' he said. 'Would you like to do more of . . . this?'

'Was this a date?' Lola asked, every part of her on edge waiting for his reply.

Tristan let out a nervous laugh. 'Yes, I think, yes, it was a date, Lola. You must know how I feel about you.'

Knowing she had the slight upper hand, and wanting to hear him say it out loud, Lola teased, 'I think you should tell me.'

Tristan leaned forward and kissed her on the cheek. 'I like you very much, Lola. Why do you think I've come for breakfast every morning and let Alf make fun of my tea choices?'

'Because I have good marmalade?'

Tristan's arm came around her waist. 'Well, that too, it is very good marmalade,' he said as he pulled her to him, his face growing serious.

Everything stopped, it was as if they were the only two people on earth, let alone in Polcarrow. Lola relaxed into him. Slowly she reached up and pushed the locks of hair that always flopped forward off his forehead. 'I've always wanted to do that.' Her voice caught.

'And I've always wanted to do this,' he said as he bowed his head and kissed her, ever so gently, but ever so perfectly, on the lips.

As she kissed him back it was as if all the stars they'd been trying to spot on the beach collided.

Chapter Twenty

Closing the door behind her, Lola's hands flew to her lips as if to cram all the happiness that was bubbling up back in.

Tristan had kissed her!

Not only that, he'd been wanting to kiss her for a long time. And what a kiss it had been! Lola swooned at the memory of his lips on hers, the way she'd melted against him.

Happy dancing into the kitchen, Lola removed her scarf and gloves, scattering her outer layers along the hallway as she replayed the moment in her mind. The sweetly seductive way he'd leaned in, the fact that he'd been waiting for the moment to come. It had been the perfect end of a first date kiss, full of gentle intent. There had been all sorts of passionate clinches in Lola's life, but nothing had ever felt quite as good, or as right, as being kissed by Tristan. She had the distinct feeling that she had been kissed in the way she had always meant to be.

Lola poured a glass of water and concentrated on drinking it in an attempt to calm herself down before heading upstairs to bed, knowing full well she was unlikely to get any sleep that night whilst still buzzing from the date.

As she got ready for bed, she relived all her favourite moments. The cake had quite possibly been the most adorable thing anyone had ever done for her, and also, exceptionally brave. Ten out of ten to Tristan. Licking her lips, Lola imagined she could still taste the sweetness of the pineapple, the smokiness of the whisky. It had been utterly perfect.

Makeup removed, her hair smelling slightly of the bonfire and the salty sea, Lola sat on her bed going back over the stories they had shared, snippets of each other lives ready to be woven together. They had spent the best part of the year sharing morning pleasantries over tea and toast, checking in on each other as they found their feet in a new home and became firm friends. Lola may have had huge reservations about crossing the friendship barrier but tonight had left her in no doubt that it had totally been worth the risk.

Lola mused about how both she and Ruby had come to Polcarrow and found love. Love? Lola flushed at the thought – was it too early? They had known each other all year, they were friends but something had always been burning beneath the surface, but love, it felt too soon, like a gift that needed to stay wrapped up just a little longer. She picked up her grandmother's diary, ran her fingers over the cover, but did not open it. She didn't want the sadness of Ruby parting with Charlie to seep into her own evening. She gave the book a kiss brimming with gratitude that her grandmother had led her here, to Polcarrow, to a place she could put down roots.

Could those roots now include Tristan? The starlight had tipped them over the friendship edge and although her brain issued a warning that they needed to proceed with caution, her heart was drumming a full speed ahead tattoo. Tonight, it had come together, the whole package had been delivered bundled up against the cold. It was like Lola's birthday and Christmas had been rolled into one and arrived early. No more wavering, no more worrying about ruining the friendship, she knew this was exactly what she wanted.

With a wistful smile Lola thought back over all her previous relationships. They had started with a bang, with what she believed was a burst of love at first sight. Burning fast and bright, these romances had been peppered with arguments and accusations, tears and tantrums. Lola cringed as she recalled that what she had believed were passionate affairs had, in fact, been immature connections, full of desperation and distrust. Lola recalled the one time Ruby had met Jared. She hadn't liked him; she'd made this clear and now Lola wondered why on earth she hadn't paid her grandmother's advice any heed.

Lola knew Ruby would approve of Tristan, she'd have seen all along that he was a good man, the sort of person you'd want at your side whilst you traversed through life. Lola reached for her tarot cards and began to shuffle them, more out of habit and comfort than wanting an answer. Did she want the future revealed in a spread of cards? She paused. Or did she want to see it play out like a surprise?

Lola restacked the cards. She didn't need to know anything yet, she wanted to just enjoy it, the possibility of the future fizzing on her tongue like sherbet. She tingled with it, the idea of new love, and the twinkling joy of discovering that Tristan felt the same. Polcarrow liked to gossip but Lola wanted to keep everything between herself and Tristan while it was fragile and new, and enjoy it just for what it was – friendship blooming into something more.

Chapter Twenty-One

Thursday, 7th September, 1950

Dear Diary,

It seems to have become a thing me sneaking out of the house to meet Charlie. I must confess it's absolutely thrilling, like something from a book. His face always lights up when he sees me and that makes me happier than I could ever imagine being. This morning we sat on the beach eating some scones his mum had made. They were divine. I made so much fuss about them that he's going to ask his mum to teach me the recipe so I can make them when I get home as a memory of Cornwall. Cornwall and Charlie being nothing more than a memory was like a black cloud across my sun. I told him that and he was silent for a moment, then he turned to me, looked me in the eyes, like he was properly seeing me, and after a deep breath he suggested that if we wanted, we could make this more than a holiday. I didn't know what to say so instead I kissed him and he had to go off on the boat, but when I see him next

I'm going to tell him yes, let's make this more than a holiday romance.

So, there it was, written in black and white in Ruby's hurried, girlish writing, confirmation that the scone recipe had come full circle back to its home in Polcarrow. Lola tried, but failed, to comprehend the strange, almost magical set of circumstances that had led to this twist of fate.

She carried out a fresh batch of scones and put them in pride of place on the counter. She then made her way to the window, pulling up the blinds, as if waking the café up for the day. Lola gazed out of the window at the flat grey sea. As much as Polcarrow buzzed in the summertime she was fond of an out-of-season seaside town, it was like a showgirl minus the makeup. She glanced around the café, all decked out for Christmas and took a sip of her gingerbread latte. Unable to sleep following her date with Tristan, she was up early and had already baked a batch of gingerbread men, a chocolate cake and the orange and cranberry scones, which had been going down a treat.

Glancing at her to-do list, Lola crossed off the bakes and quickly scrawled down her daily gratitude list, making sure that Tristan didn't take up all three points. She'd washed the scent of the bonfire out of her hair that morning, but as the memory of cosying up around the flames filled her mind, an idea began to form, one she sat back and let brew whilst she watched the seagulls soaring outside as she finished her coffee. The sea was always instantly calming, a reminder that nature was a bigger force than any human and that the world would roll on and on long after she was gone. The thought was huge but strangely comforting.

Putting down her mug, Lola picked up her pen to write, but paused, not quite ready to commit the slowly forming idea to paper. There was a yearning in her to do something special, something different, something Polcarrow probably hadn't seen before. She wanted to show them something from her world, something a bit deeper than gingham bunting and a perfectly risen Victoria sponge. All the buzz surrounding the lobster pot tree made her think the village wanted new and different experiences. Lola leaned into the comfort of her idea. Now that it was growing, she knew she wouldn't be able to let it go.

As much as she loved the bright promise of a rose-tinted, never-ending summer's day, there was something about the short dark winter months that appealed to Lola's more pagan side. Something about the winter solstice always stirred her, a chance to reflect on the year that had passed, to put it to bed before the Christmas celebrations kicked off. An opportunity to give thanks for everything she had been blessed with. A way of welcoming in the coming light. Lola had always performed her own ritual – lighting candles, meditating and purifying herself and her surroundings with sage – but what if she offered the people of Polcarrow the chance to do the same, to partake in the ritual together? A bonfire on the beach to say goodbye to the old year.

She chuckled to herself imagining Cathy's horrified face. The village stalwart was hugely opposed to change. Still, if no one wanted to join in, she'd do it alone. That would give everyone something to gossip about. It was important to Lola that she did something to honour her first year in Polcarrow, to give thanks for all she had achieved and the friends she had made. Ruby would definitely approve. She had always enjoyed listening to Lola's tales of partaking in fire walks, forest retreats and dawn yoga sessions. Gosh, she hadn't done yoga in years, she realised. So many parts of her old life had been parcelled up and packed away, but now Lola wondered if it was time to pull out the hairpins and unleash that side of her, provide an antidote to the ever-encroaching commercialism of the season.

Lola quickly added 'Plan Solstice Ritual' to her list and vowed to run the idea past Tristan, to see what he thought and, hopefully, if he gave it his seal of approval, the rest of the village would too. Some had raised eyebrows at her offering tea and tarot but many had been intrigued enough to have their cards read so she felt confident that enough people would be interested in celebrating the solstice as well.

Tristan and Alf arrived at the same time, just after opening, and Lola was surprised that Alf didn't suspect anything had shifted between her and Tristan with the matching smiles that spread across their faces. Lola didn't get a chance to speak to Tristan properly as Alf had commandeered his attention and then the early morning coffee rush began. It was only when he came to pay for his breakfast that Tristan cast a quick glance over his shoulder and asked in a low voice, 'Are you doing anything tomorrow night?'

Lola pretended to think about it. 'I guess I could fit you in.'

Tristan laughed. 'Great, I'll pick you up at seven.'

'It's a date,' Lola said, grinning at the cheesy line and realising it was true.

In lieu of a kiss, Tristan gave her hand the briefest squeeze.

The following evening, they were ensconced in very cosy, rustic pub in a village further down the coast, famous for its fish pie and local ales. Lola had decided to try both. Glancing around whilst Tristan placed their order at the bar, she admired the way the establishment was decked out in all sorts of seafaring paraphernalia and entwined with fairy lights. Sea-shanty-style Christmas carols were playing in the background. Lola relaxed into the vibe.

'This place is gorgeous,' she said as she chinked her glass against Tristan's. 'How did you discover it?'

'I was looking for somewhere nice to take you and this place had such a good write-up. Plus, it's away from home, so we won't have anyone eavesdropping into our conversation.' Tristan rubbed his face. 'Being a vicar means you're considered public property and honestly,

I could sometimes do with a break from Cathy popping around to complain about the hymns I've chosen or telling me which bits of my sermon she didn't like. I don't think she's ever forgiven me for being under seventy and having all my own teeth.'

Lola laughed. 'Well, I'm very glad you're under seventy and have all your own teeth. All those old vicars must have been young once,' she mused.

'Some people just struggle with change,' he said diplomatically. 'I understand it, life's constants are what keep us feeling safe. Cathy had the ear of the old vicar. It gave her status in the community so I can understand why she doesn't like me coming in and changing things. I've had to use a lot of compassion and tact.'

Lola considered this for a while. 'You are very wise. I guess it comes with the job?'

'Something like that—' he smiled '—but it's more that I've allowed myself time to observe people. I see them at their happiest at weddings and christenings and then at their lowest at funerals and grief counselling. It teaches you a lot about humanity. It's taught me a lot about myself too. I guess you find that as well with your alternative therapies?'

'"Alternative therapies", I like that.' Lola sipped her drink and considered this. 'Yes, I do. People mainly want reassurance, they normally know the answers but just need a little help finding them.'

'So can you predict the future?' Tristan asked with genuine curiosity.

Lola considered this before replying, 'I don't know if it's so much that I can predict the future but more I get a hunch or a vision or a sense that something will happen. Like Freya and Angelo. I had a feeling there was a reason for them both to come here. I read Freya's cards and got an image of a dark man. I felt the calling to come here too and well, look . . .' With a smile she signalled at him. 'It's all turned out very well, although, I didn't get a premonition of all this, just a sense that I had to move, that there was something about the name Ruby had written in her diary and, well, it turns out there was.'

'Does that not scare you a bit?'

Lola studied him, realising that she could be completely open and honest with him. 'Yes, it does. I would always have found my way here eventually, Ruby's diary would have tempted me had I not already been here. Now I can't think of being anywhere else. How did you feel about coming here?'

'Relieved, mostly. The city had been tough. The constant deprivation, the problems, I needed some space to recharge, to stop myself questioning everything. It's hard to tell people that it's all in God's plan when they're really suffering. I learned not to use that line pretty quickly. I experienced a bit of a crisis of faith before I decided my role was to be there as a guide, a listener and that helps a lot more than anything. Not just for me, but for the people who depend on me.' He took a sip of his drink. 'I didn't expect to be here long. I thought I'd get bored, but I've grown to love Cornwall and the people I've found here. It's been very healing, more so than I expected. It's definitely where I want to put down roots.'

Lola reached for his hand. 'It does feel like magic to think how many of us have been drawn here and plan to stay. It feels like some sort of divine alignment.'

Conversation stalled as their food arrived and they tucked in. Lola could see why the fish pie was scoring so high on the online ratings.

'That was amazing,' she said as she put down her knife and fork. 'Thank you so much for this.'

'It's been my pleasure. Any space for dessert?'

Lola made a show of pretending to be too full but still perusing the menu she asked, 'What would you go for?'

Tristan studied the options. 'It feels really indulgent on top of that, but probably a sticky toffee pudding.'

'That's my favourite,' Lola gasped, catching the glint in his eye before suggesting, 'While we're here I think it'd be rude not to try it, I mean, it says recommended.'

'You've twisted my arm, Lola, shall we share it?'

'Yes, I think if I have a whole one, you'll be rolling me home! I'm so full already!'

Tristan pulled a serious face as he leaned across the table. 'But the most important question is: custard or ice cream?'

Lola squirmed as if it was a trick before declaring, 'Ice cream because I like the way it melts in with the hot toffee sauce.' She waited with bated breath and Tristan pretended to consider his answer. 'Go on, stop it! Put me out my misery!'

'OK.' He leaned even closer, dropping his voice to a whisper. 'I'd be going for the ice cream too.'

Lola let out a sigh of relief. 'Phew! That settles it then.' She turned to the waiter who had come over to their table and with a beaming smile ordered one sticky toffee pudding, with ice cream, to share.

While they waited for their dessert, they linked hands over the table. Lola liked the way they fitted together, how Tristan made her feel anchored in a way no one else ever had. The silence that fell between them was companionable, like a blanket to sink into, a peacefulness Lola hadn't realised she'd been craving.

'This is wonderful,' she said, 'I'm always on the go, always doing something, it's nice to just . . . be.' She smoothed her thumb over his knuckles. 'There is something I'm thinking of doing and want your opinion on it.'

'Go on.'

'All this Christmas stuff has got me thinking about the other side of the season, the more pagan side. I've always marked the solstice with a little ritual. Candles, incense, meditation, and I'd like to do something like that for Polcarrow, get anyone who wants to come along involved.'

'Do you want my seal of approval?'

Lola nodded.

'What are you planning on doing for it?'

Lola shrugged. 'The ideas are vague but a big bonfire for us all to gather around. I'll do a meditation and we can have a bit of a social afterwards.'

'Sounds like it would be a great opportunity to take a break from all the crazy last-minute shopping.'

'Is that your seal of approval?'

'Do you really need it?' he asked softly.

Lola thought about this. 'No, but it's nice to have it.'

Tristan placed his other hand on top of their linked ones. 'Consider this my official blessing.'

Laughter burst out of Lola. The waiter appeared and laid the bowl of sticky toffee pudding down between them, along with two spoons. Lola picked hers up and gave the ice cream a little prod. It slipped around on the sauce as it melted.

'It looks very good,' Tristan said as he let go of her hand. 'I wonder if it'll be as good as everything you make.'

Lola leaned across as if to impart a secret. 'I suspect my enjoyment of this will be heightened by the fact I didn't have to make it and I don't have to wash up afterwards.' With that she swiped up a spoonful of pudding and ice cream and popped it into her mouth, sighing at the heavenly flavours. Tristan's eyes went from Lola to the pudding and back again as if he didn't know which one he wanted the most.

Chapter Twenty-Two

Friday, 8th September, 1950

Dear Diary,

    It has happened so quickly, almost so quickly that I didn't see it coming. After lots of early morning picnics and walks on the beach, lots of whispered plans, I have fallen head over heels in love with Charlie. This is what love is like, what I've been looking for. He is the sun in my sky, the person who understands me the most. Isn't it strange to think someone you've known a handful of days can understand you more than people who've known you half your life? I tell him I want to come to Cornwall, that I love not just him but the sand and the blue skies. He tells me there is no future in Cornwall, which I find hard to believe, that he wants to come to the city, find a way to make his fortune there. That is the only sticking point between us: money, or the lack of it. I'd quite happily stay here, not board the train back home, but Charlie has promised to write every day, so have I. We have to save as much money as we can so we can marry (I can hardly believe it and am going to keep this to myself) and set up a home.

'Hello, earth to Lola,' Freya's voice sounded, breaking through Lola's thoughts of the previous night with Tristan, comparing and contrasting their budding relationship with the love Ruby and Charlie had found. Marry! Ruby had wanted to marry Charlie. That was going to take some digesting. Lola spared a thought for her grandfather, the solid dependable sort. Had Charlie given Ruby that ring she'd found?

'Hmmm, you called?' Lola turned to see Freya standing in the kitchen doorway.

Freya put down the tray of cups she was carrying before opening the dishwasher. 'Yes, I did, about five times.'

'Oh, what's up?' Lola glanced around as if something untoward had happened.

'Tristan's come back.'

'Has he?' Lola sprang into action, smoothing her hair and crossing the kitchen.

'Got you! No, just this from the postman.' Freya placed a stack of mail on the counter. 'I knew something was going on.' A triumphant smile spread across Freya's face. 'The pair of you have been wrapped up in each other even more than usual. Come on, spill!' Freya demanded as the look on Lola's face gave everything away.

Lola glanced through the kitchen door to check there were no customers waiting. 'OK, so we went on a date,' she said, 'well, maybe more than one date. Maybe we're actually dating, but we've not had any conversations about being exclusive or whatever it is. He's kissed me, several times, he's a very nice kisser.'

'Oh my God!' Freya squealed and did a little jump for joy. 'He kissed you! Come on, what happened, where did you go? I need to know everything.'

'He took me stargazing on the beach. How adorable is that? He made me a cake!' Lola couldn't keep the swoon out of her voice as she melted at the memory.

Freya's mouth hung open. 'What? He made you a cake. That's a very brave man.'

'I know! And it was delicious, really well cooked. Pineapple upside down cake,' she reminisced, still able to conjure the taste in her mind. 'Freya, he's just so lovely, so different from anyone I've met before, but that's kind of scary.'

'How do you mean?'

'Well, he's so easy to be with. I like him as a person, his company, the conversation and I fancy him. I've never had the two. I always thought Jared was the big love of my life but now I'm doubting that even more.' Lola sighed. 'It was fun being with Jared, he was the life of the party, but for every evening he was fun, he'd have another one where he was moody and I was always treading on eggshells, but I thought that was what love was: wild, unpredictable.'

'But it's not, is it?' Freya made a face as she thought about it. 'Well, I can hardly talk what with Angelo, but his heart is in the right place. So, Tristan, is he the one?'

Lola's face flushed. 'I don't know,' she said, all the while hoping that maybe he was. 'It's too early to say, or is it? But it's nice, I'm liking what's happening . . .' She trailed off and for a moment considered telling Freya about Ruby but it didn't feel right for anyone else to know until Alf did.

'So what happens now? Are you official? Are you announcing it to the village? Can we finally rejoice that the pair of you have seen sense and realise you belong together?'

'Slow down, Freya, so many questions! We want to keep it to ourselves for a bit, so we can figure out dating each other or this change from friends to . . .' She shrugged before turning serious. 'Freya, he's so lovely, so kind, so caring, he's everything I've never had and never knew I needed. I like him, really like him, and he really likes me, so we're taking it slowly, or as slowly as we can.' She couldn't help but smile at the thought of seeing Tristan later. 'I don't want anything to ruin it and I don't want people to be sticking their noses into our business. You know what it can be like.'

Freya nodded. 'Yes, but it bothered Angelo more than it bothered me to be honest. Can I at least tell him? It's not like he goes around gossiping, is it?'

Lola smiled. 'No, quite the opposite. Of course you can.'

'This is amazing,' Freya said before wondering out loud, 'Does it mean you'll end up living at the vicarage?'

'Freya! I told you we're taking it slowly!' Lola pretended to be outraged to cover up the fact she'd been lying in bed the previous night having the exact same thoughts. Whilst mentally decorating the tired old house. That magnolia paint would definitely have to go and those dull chintzy curtains were only fit for the bin. For Tristan to have survived so long in an interior design time warp she was sure he wouldn't object to her colour schemes and mood boards, putting her own homely, vintage spin on things. Nope, she hadn't thought about it at all.

Chapter Twenty-Three

Tristan had sent her a text as she was locking up, inviting her over for dinner. Within seconds of her accepting he responded to tell her not to expect too much. Lola didn't care. She'd been on her feet all day and the thought of someone else cooking for her, even if it was just a frozen pizza, was complete heaven. Remembering the delicious pineapple upside down cake, Lola suspected Tristan would have skills that far extended beyond sticking a pizza in the oven.

Back at the cottage, Lola sorted through the post, mostly circulars and bills plus a couple of Christmas cards, made herself a cup of tea and then headed up to the bathroom. She had a couple of hours until she was due at Tristan's and decided to fill that time with a long, luxurious bath, full of bubbles. Lola sank beneath the bubbles, allowing the hot water to unwind all her muscles, and somehow managed to switch her brain off from her ever-growing Christmas to-do list. At least Alf's Christmas jumper was almost finished. She just needed to work out what size to knit for Scruff by looking at him. Whipping out a tape measure in the café would likely give the surprise away.

Once the water had cooled, Lola got out of the bath and wrapped herself up in several towels and then slipped into her bathrobe before padding into her bedroom. Flicking on the lights, she meant to head straight for the wardrobe to figure out what to wear. Part of her wanted to knock Tristan's socks off, but the other part knew that he fancied her having seen her wearing all sorts throughout the year. Not knowing how warm the vicarage would be at night, she pulled out a cream knitted jumper and a pair of dark green checked trousers. The outfit was cute, casual and Christmassy.

As she settled onto the bed, Lola's eyes caught sight of Ruby's box and her heart twinged for the passionate young woman who had been in love with Charlie. Lola couldn't help but wonder what life would have been like if Ruby had run away to Cornwall and put down roots by the sea. It almost blew her mind to think that Alf would have been a sort of grand-uncle. Maybe this was why they felt so comfortable with each other? Why they'd been drawn together. It was as if their souls knew they were linked before their minds and hearts did.

Lola pulled the box over to her and flicked through the diary. It ended abruptly after a lot of agonizing about whether Ruby should move to Cornwall or if Charlie would come to London. Slowly, as time moved on, the pages became sparser and Ruby had written daily observations; a new dress she'd seen, how one of the girls at work had suddenly left, cinema trips and dances, usual daily life things. Until there was nothing. Just a date and written under it in blotchy black ink:

19th November, 1950

The most awful news today. I can't even bear to write it down.

Lola didn't need to be a super sleuth to figure out the date was very close to that of the fishing tragedy that had taken Charlie. Her heart lurched. Were those Ruby's tears running the ink? It must have seemed as if Ruby's whole life was over in that instant. Lola couldn't imagine the loss, the heartache, the sheer gut-wrenching pain that news must have brought. On top of it all, Lola's instincts, along with what Ruby had hinted at, told her that no one had known of her grandmother's dreams and plans to elope with a Cornish fisherman.

Closing the diary, but hungry for more, Lola picked up the bundle of letters, flicking through them, noticing the Cornish postmark, the writing on the envelopes neat, as if the letter writer was trying very hard to make his writing look presentable. Lola untied the old red ribbon that bound them. A treasured stack of love letters, hopes and dreams parcelled up and put away. The letters fell loose across her lap as if to scatter their secrets. Picking the top one up, Lola lifted it to her face, breathing in its aroma, not quite knowing what she was expecting. The scent of the sea perhaps, but there was nothing, just old paper and ink, all that was left of a love story that had ended tragically, a life cut short.

Carefully, Lola extracted the first letter, it was brief but affectionate:

Dearest Ruby,

I'm hoping this letter makes it to London before you do. I'm imagining my words and you having a race across the country. You must let me know who wins! I think of you unlocking your door and finding this waiting for you, or you waking up in the morning to this piece of Cornwall.

I can hardly believe it's only been a week. That I've known you for even less time than that, but everything is altered. I already miss you and you haven't even gone yet. I know you want to come back and live in Cornwall, but there isn't much future here. I want to come to the city, I want to study, better myself, so we can have a nice modern house. I don't want to keep going out to sea. But I don't want to start this letter with any disagreements. I just want to say I love you and I can't wait for our lives to start properly, wherever that may be.

All my love
Charlie

'How sweet,' Lola said to herself, running her eyes back over the words, Charlie's careful, looped writing, the way he so openly admitted his love for Ruby. Lola's heart swelled as she placed the paper back into the envelope and reached for the next letter. The sentiments were similar, interspersed with chatter about their days. There were stacks of them.

Lola toyed with the final envelope, but found she couldn't open it, knowing what had happened, how it had all ended. She didn't want to read the neatly written words of a boy who was lost to the sea on her own. Retying the ribbon, Lola knew there was one person she wanted to share the letters with, the only person she felt was equipped enough to hold her hand through the family tragedies she was uncovering. The one person who'd provide her with the guidance and counsel for what to do next and help her weather the storm that was threatening to blow through an old man's peace.

Chapter Twenty-Four

'Lola, what's up?' Tristan's brow furrowed with concern upon opening the door. 'Come in, come in,' he ushered, holding the door open. 'You look like you've seen a ghost.'

Lola handed the box to Tristan. 'I've not seen one, but I may have been reading letters from one,' she said as she unbuttoned her coat and unwrapped her scarf.

Tristan looked from the box to Lola's winter clothes.

'Don't worry, I can hang them myself,' she said, looping the scarf over one of the coat hooks, then following it with her coat. 'Something smells yummy.'

Tristan passed the box back to her. 'It's a shepherd's pie.'

Lola's face lit up. 'One of my favourites, especially as the leftovers taste even better.' She followed him through the lounge and into the kitchen. The radio was playing softly.

Tristan held up a bottle of red wine. 'Would you like a glass?'

'Yes please,' she said, sitting down at the kitchen table, placing the box on the placemat in front of her.

As Tristan poured the wine, she took in the rather cosy-looking kitchen. It was a lot more homely than she'd imagined with pale cream cupboards, a fridge freezer with various drawings, notices and reminders kept in place by a collection of magnets from holiday destinations.

Tristan caught her looking at them. 'Ah, I sort of unofficially collect them. A practical token of wherever I've visited. I usually pick the most lurid, hence the bright pink flip-flop from Corfu.'

Lola laughed, they chinked glasses and she took a long sip of the rich, fruity wine.

'Is this about the letters?' He signalled to the box.

Lola pulled the lid off. She'd placed the letters in an old plastic container to protect them. 'Yes. Charlie's letters to Ruby.' She passed him the top one and waited while he read it.

Tristan placed the letter back in the envelope. 'That's very sweet. He clearly adored her.'

'Yes, he did. She must have been heartbroken when he died. Her diary ends with just the mention of some terrible news. I know she was happy in the end with Ernest, he treated her really well and shared her love of dancing. They married quite quickly and she always had happy memories. He was a kind man, my grandfather, the only one who was ever able to rein Ruby in. I have no idea if he knew about Charlie.'

They lapsed into a thoughtful silence, the pile of letters sitting between them.

'What are you really afraid of, Lola?' Tristan eventually asked.

'This is the end of it. All those lives changed,' she said, signalling to the letters.

Tristan placed them back into the box. 'Let's have something to eat, then we can think about what to do.'

Dinner was lovely, the wine helped soothe Lola's worries about the letters and Tristan provided a welcome distraction from everything by telling her about the video-call he'd had earlier with his niece and nephews, all of them bouncing around with the excitement of Christmas and driving their mum slowly mad.

'Would you like your own family?' Lola asked, her edges blurred by the wine.

'Yes, if it happens, it would be delightful, but if not,' Tristan gave a shrug and asked, 'What about you, Lola?'

A jolt down her spine made her wish they'd skipped right onto Charlie's letters. 'I've never really thought about it,' she admitted. 'I guess once upon a time I imagined everything would just fall into place, but now, well, I'm almost forty, I'm not sure time is on my side anymore in that regard. Gosh, that is more sobering than discussing shipwrecks,' she said, trying to lighten the mood.

Tristan squeezed her hand. 'It's OK, Lola. I don't have a checklist for my life and I'm a firm believer in divine timing and whatever will be, will be,' he said as he picked up their plates and stuck them in the sink. Coming back to the table, he kissed her before sitting back down.

Lola picked up her glass. 'A toast to whatever will be.'

Tristan chinked his glass against hers, took a sip and then asked, 'The letters, shall we read the rest of them together?'

Lola nodded and pulled them out of the box. Heads together, they took it in turns to read the missives. Lola imagined Ruby sending Charlie pages and pages of gossip and lovestruck dreams. Charlie's letters were full of romantic longing, descriptions of the sunset and plans for the future.

'That's very sweet,' Tristan said.

'He's smitten, isn't he?'

'And working so hard. Your grandmother must have been really worth it, Lola, this isn't just some summer crush, is it? They really wanted to spend their lives together.'

Lola toyed with one of the envelopes. 'Yes, I guess they did. I've not seen it like that because I know how it ends. I never considered this might be how Ruby expected her life to turn out. I wonder if they'd really have been happy together though. Ernest had a very good job and Ruby had a nice, very comfortable life and I think it may have been different if she'd run away with a Cornish fisherman, even though that's terribly romantic.'

Tristan picked up the next letter and read, '"We don't normally go out this time of year but we've heard there's a large shoal coming in. It should be a good catch. My brother doesn't want to go out, says he thinks it's dangerous this time of year, but myself and some others think it'll be worth it. You're worth the risk Ruby."'

Lola shuddered and caught Tristan's gaze. They both knew what happened next. Had it been worth the risk? Maybe if Charlie had taken it with his love for Ruby in his heart.

'Lola? There's one letter left.'

Lola studied it, the handwriting was different, smaller, more solemn. She picked the letter up and opened it, then paused, her stomach sinking.

Dear Ruby,

It's with regret I write to inform you that Charlie has been lost at sea. I would ask you to respect our family during this time of mourning. Please do not contact us again.

Lola swallowed back her tears; the letter was almost cruel in its preciseness. Lola's mind flicked back to the tear-stained final diary entry. How had Ruby felt to have received this letter, to have the rug pulled from under her feet? For that glorious summer-tinged future to be wiped out in a few harsh words. Even more shocking for Lola was to see the name signed at the bottom. A name of someone she had come to love like a surrogate grandfather, a name that had likely torn her own grandmother's life apart.

Alf.

Chapter Twenty-Five

Every time Alf came into the café, Lola's stomach churned with indecision. She had placed the photo and some of the letters in a protective plastic wallet and slipped them into her handbag, waiting for the right moment to place them in front of Alf and ask him to fill in the missing pieces. However, every time she saw him, with his jovial nature, his interest in her different festive bakes, even if he did proclaim the reindeer cupcakes too sweet and the gingerbread latte 'not bad if you like that sort of thing', she lost more of her nerve. Would it be better to leave Charlie and Ruby to rest? Would it be any comfort for Alf to know Ruby had gone on to live a long, happy life, when Charlie had never seen his twenty-third birthday?

Lola found other ways to occupy her mind. The ticking down of the days towards Christmas meant more people were popping in for treats and Tristan had placed an order of mince pies for the mingling after the carol service. She'd started to plan out how she was going to decorate the Christmas cakes, Alf's jumper was finished and if she got a move on, it wouldn't take long to finish off Scruff's. The solstice ritual was gathering a bit of interest. Lola earmarked an evening in her diary to sit down and plan it out properly, including writing her meditation. She wanted it to be special, reflective of her new life here and hopeful for the future. Lots of old furniture that was beyond repair had been left in Bayview House and Angelo had promised to bring it along to burn. Her Christmas shopping was mostly done, she and Tristan had managed to sneak off for an afternoon of what should have been retail therapy but was more akin to retail hell.

'I hope everyone likes handmade soaps and rum truffles,' Lola had grumbled as she shut the door on Tristan's car and relaxed away from the crowds. 'Every year I say I'll start shopping early and do I? No.'

Tristan, who had managed to remain calm despite the hectic shops, pulled away from the car park and said, 'Well, I think this might deserve a celebratory sticky toffee pudding.'

'Celebratory? More like congratulatory for surviving that. Also, I might not feel so up to sharing this time after that traumatic shopping experience.'

Despite the unsatisfactory shopping trip, Lola was loving having someone to do Christmas with. Jared had never been interested, claimed it was all commercial rubbish, he hated mince pies and thought roast dinners were the devil's work. Again, Lola questioned why she'd spent so long hung up on him. Tristan managed to make all the stressful bits that little bit more fun. Lola was starting to think she might not be able to heed her own judgement and take things slowly. They fitted together like they were meant to be.

As the carol service drew near, Lola's nerves about attending grew into excitement. The mince pies had been delivered around lunchtime with strict instructions to Tristan not to eat them all. Leaving Freya in charge of the café, Lola had gone home to get herself ready, both physically with a gorgeous red velvet dress she'd bought, and mentally. It felt strange to be going to a church service, to be seeing Tristan in action, when she wasn't a believer. The sun set that evening in a hellfire blaze over the sea, which Lola hoped wasn't an omen.

As she made her way up the church path, the windows glowed warmly through the dark night, and Lola thought of how the people of Polcarrow had gathered here on Sunday mornings, and for weddings and funerals. She swallowed back a lump in her throat as she thought of the service that had taken place for Charlie and the other young men who had been lost to the sea. Churches, she realised, contained so much more than prayer books and psalms, they marked the stations of life in a way nothing else did. In that instant, Lola almost envied Tristan his faith.

On stepping through the door she stopped, enchanted. The church was illuminated by a mix of flickering golden candlelight and the artificial twinkle of fairy lights on the trees. Lola gasped at the magic of it all. There was something comforting, primal even, about the low lighting, the hushed darkness that made her think of centuries past and all the things Christmas was really meant to be about. Togetherness, love and the ending of one year's cycle. A surge of comfort enveloped her, of peace. The pews were full of villagers, their voices hushed as they exchanged pleasantries and gossip. The gentle anticipation of what was going to happen.

Then there was Tristan greeting everyone, dressed in his vicar's robes, eyes twinkling and not a hair out of place. The sight of him caused Lola to pause, catch her breath, it was as if she was seeing him anew. Used to seeing him in jumpers, jeans or bundled up for a night-time expedition she was taken aback to see him dressed for his role. He beamed at her, completely comfortable and at home in his rightful place, which reassured Lola. Their eyes met and Lola flushed; he'd been watching her reaction to the church, a look of such adoration on his face that Lola was struck speechless.

'You came.' His voice was soft with wonder and Lola noticed that he just managed to stop himself from reaching out, touching the side of her face. Lola leaned forward instinctively to receive that imaginary blessing. It felt as if they were the only two people in the world.

'Of course I did.' Her voice caught. 'It's the first time I've been to a church service since I was a child.'

'Then I'm honoured you chose mine.' Tristan placed a hand on his heart.

Lola, seeing how much it meant to him, smiled her gratitude. He hadn't put on any pressure, simply extended the invite and left it for her to make her own mind up. 'The church is beautiful all done up like this. I feel, well, I don't know, but I feel something.' She glanced around wondering if church could really become part of her life if things ramped up with Tristan. Lola tried not to quake at the enormity of that thought and recalled Freya telling her she'd make an excellent vicar's wife with her perfect combination of caring and baking skills. Lola pushed the thought away.

'Something is always better than nothing,' he replied gently. He handed her a folded sheet of paper which had the service printed on it. 'I think Alf has saved you a seat.' Then in a lower voice, he added, 'I'll catch up with you later, Lola.'

Lola made her way down the aisle and slid in beside Alf. 'No Scruff?'

'Tone deaf that dog,' Alf chuckled. 'I need a night off, anyway. He'll be fine. I left him a bone to chew, he won't miss me.'

'Oh, Alf, I'm sure he will.' Lola flicked through the service sheet. 'I don't think I'm much of a singer either. Or a believer, but there's something here.'

'You don't have to believe like Tristan does, this is more about community. We came to church every Sunday, it was just the thing we did. As many people came to gather as they did to worship. But I had more conversations with the Lord out on the sea in high winds than I ever did in this building. People need to keep their own beliefs in their own way, trouble only starts when people try inflicting them on others.'

Lola's reply was cut short by the door swinging open as Freya and Angelo burst in at the last minute. Flustered and with Cathy mumbling something about the time, they hurried down to the front and slipped in beside Lola and Alf. Lola noticed that Freya's hair was messed up and she had a smear of white paint on her forehead. Angelo's shirt was misbuttoned. Lola stifled a smirk and Freya elbowed her.

'Stop it, we're in a church, if you don't mind.' Freya dragged her fingers through her hair and rubbed in vain at her forehead.

'Oh, don't I know it.' Lola's eyes were like saucers as Tristan led the procession down the aisle as they opened with 'Once in Royal David's City' and took his place at the front of the church, sneaking Lola a look. Suppressing a giggle, she noticed Freya shake her head in disbelief.

What the congregation of Polcarrow lacked in tune, they made up for in enthusiasm. Lola muddled her way through the carols with Alf singing loudly beside her and she was amused to see even Angelo singing along to 'We Three Kings'. Lola had been prepared to turn up, add to the numbers and show willingness to participate in all aspects of village life. She had not, however, expected to be so moved by the singing, the flickering candlelight and the togetherness she experienced when the village was all tucked up in a common aim.

Her first experience of seeing Tristan in full vicar mode – the robes, the sermon, the leading of the prayers – did not disappoint. The goodness in him shone out through the church and touched Lola. As he spoke about the true meaning of Christmas, the church made Lola feel truly safe. The idea of Tristan looking after her because kindness was etched in his soul was gently seductive. He was not the sort of person to let anyone down, in fact, he was exactly who you would need by your side. Lola only realised she was crying when Alf squeezed her hand and passed her a hankie.

'It gets everyone at some point,' he whispered, his soft Cornish accent comforting.

She squeezed his hand back. 'I never thought it'd get me.' When she glanced back to the front of the church, dabbing at her eyes and thanking the Lord for making waterproof mascara, Tristan was looking at her with such tenderness that it took all her strength not to cry again. He gave her a reassuring wink before carrying on with the service.

Before the closing carol he announced, 'There'll be tea, mulled wine and mince pies in the hall after this. Extra-special ones this year, baked by our very own Lola, rather than the supermarket.'

Amusement echoed around the church as the congregation rose to their feet for the final song. Alf never let go of Lola's hand and she was grateful to him for keeping her tethered. Tristan ended the service and waited by the door to shake everyone's hands as they left. One of the choirboys held a bowl full of chocolates for people to help themselves to on their way out. As they were at the front of the church, Lola and her crew were the last to leave and by then there were only the toffees left.

'Can't have them with my teeth,' Alf pretend-grumbled.

'Here, I think this is a strawberry cream—' Freya passed him a pink-wrapped chocolate '—or a fudge. I like the toffees.'

'Help yourself,' Tristan encouraged, pushing the bowl towards her. 'Actually, take them with you, I just need to slip this robe off and lock up.'

'Do you need a hand?' The words slipped out of Lola's mouth before she could stop them. 'Erm, with the locking up, I mean.'

'I'm sure I'll manage.' Tristan struggled to hide his amusement. 'I'll see you in the hall.'

The night was nippy after the cosiness of the church, stars visible in the sky as they made their way to the hall, Freya unwrapping her toffees and stuffing them in two at a time. Lola and Freya walked ahead whilst Angelo meandered behind with Alf.

'I never had you down as a convert,' she quipped at Lola.

'What? Just because I had a tear in my eye doesn't mean I've got church fever.'

'Vicar fever more like it,' Freya chuckled. 'I'm pretty sure the way you two were making eyes at each other tonight the whole village will be ramping up their gossip by morning.'

'We were not making eyes at each other,' Lola protested, 'Tristan was just looking out for me. It's my first time at church for years.'

'He winked at you in front of everyone,' Freya pointed out. 'But it's cute and I think everyone will give you their blessing. People do like a love story after all and it's almost Christmas, the perfect time for romance.' She passed Lola the now empty bowl as they drew up outside the church hall and turned to Angelo. 'Better fix your buttons. You two go in, we'll see you in a bit.'

Alf and Lola exchanged a smirk as they entered the hall, the bright lights an intrusive bump back to reality after the soft candlelight in the church. Lola glanced around as she placed the empty bowl on top of the piano. Villagers were milling around with paper cups of mulled wine. Sue waved at her from behind the serving table.

'Do you need a hand?' Lola asked as she slipped behind, noticing the plates of mince pies and mini chocolate logs were half gone.

'I think we've got it covered now the initial onslaught is over. I don't know what you put in those pies.' Sue laughed.

'Magic.' Tristan's voice caught her attention as he walked into the hall and over to them. 'Lola bakes with magic.' He winked again as he helped himself to a mince pie, earning himself a scowl from stern village committee member Cathy as she passed him some mulled wine.

'I don't think you should be promoting magic, Vicar,' Cathy pointed out.

Tristan refused to rise to the bait. 'I don't see why not. After all we all need a bit of magic in our lives. I'm also very keen to see what Lola has in store for the solstice ritual.' He put a hand on Lola's shoulder and gently steered her away from Cathy before the older woman could make any complaints about Lola's alternative beliefs.

'You shouldn't antagonise her,' Lola warned him.

'I know I shouldn't but it's just too hard to resist, although I'm pretty sure as a vicar I'm not meant to admit that, but sometimes it gets a bit too much trying to constantly keep the peace.' He took a sip of his punch before turning to Lola and asking, 'So, how did you find it?'

Lola met his eyes and saw genuine interest shining in them, as if after all his years of service it was her opinion that mattered the most. Not quite knowing where to start, or how to articulate just how moved she'd been, Lola took a sip of her drink. 'Honestly? I didn't expect to feel as much as I did. It's been years since I've been to a church service. I've always felt somewhat as if I'm trespassing somewhere I'm not meant to be, but tonight, well, there was something wonderful and cosy about it. I cried a bit,' she admitted with a cringe.

Tristan laughed. 'I hope they weren't tears of boredom.'

'Never! The whole thing just got me here.' She put her hand on her heart.

Tristan's gaze softened. 'I bet you didn't expect that. There is something moving about the church at Christmas, it strips away all the baubles, all the commercialism and reminds you what the season is really about.'

Lola nodded and held back from the temptation to curl herself into him. 'Alf looked after me too. I don't know how I can ask him about Charlie and Ruby. I feel so guilty, after all, he's done so much to make me feel welcome.'

'Maybe you remind him of her?' Tristan ventured.

'Maybe, but from that last letter I don't think he had warm fuzzy feelings towards Ruby, did he?' Lola reminded him, thinking of the curt way the letter had been written. She knew she resembled her grandmother but surely Alf wouldn't remember that much detail, it had only been a week, over seventy years ago. 'Or maybe he's just a warm, kind person who doesn't deserve his painful memories being brought to the surface.'

Tristan considered this before asking, 'Would you be really happy if you never knew?'

After a brief pause Lola replied, 'No. I feel like I need that piece to put Ruby to rest, it's just there's a price to pay.' She finished her drink. 'Every time I see Alf I'm holding back from blurting it out.'

'I'll come with you if you want when you talk to him.'

Lola shook the offer away. 'No, I think it's better I do this myself. If he's upset I wouldn't want you implicated.'

Sensing it was time to change the subject, Tristan asked about the solstice ritual. 'Did you do your planning for it earlier?'

Lola rolled her eyes. 'Of course I didn't, I got distracted trying to figure out Scruff's jumper. I might have to wing it at this rate. I guess all we need is a bonfire. I picked up some sage when we went shopping the other day and I might just instinctively say whatever comes to mind on the evening. Angelo has offered me some things to burn from Bayview.'

'Maybe you should have a whip-round? Ask people to donate their wonky chairs so they can go up in flames.'

'That's not a bad idea, it'd fit in with the theme of togetherness and cleansing of the year,' she mused.

'If you need any help, Lola, let me know.' He touched her elbow. 'I'm really looking forward to it. It's been a while since I've celebrated other people's faiths. I love Polcarrow but sometimes I miss how diverse the city was.' He grew wistful. 'Although I wouldn't trade my run along the coast followed by toast at yours for anything in the world.' They exchanged a long, heated look. Lola pushed away the desire to kiss him.

'I'll stay and help you clear up, if you want?' she said, trying to keep the suggestion of getting him alone out of her voice.

'That would be very kind,' he said before going to take a sip of his drink only to realise it was empty. 'Come on, let's be brave and get a top-up. I suppose I better mingle.'

Chapter Twenty-Six

Lola woke the morning after the carol service knowing she had to talk to Alf about Ruby. Mulling over what to do, thinking about Ruby and Charlie's short-lived love affair, was distracting her from all her other Christmas chores and she knew she'd put ripping the plaster off for long enough now. To stop herself from chickening out, Lola texted Tristan to let him know what she was planning. Tristan responded to say he'd delay coming to the café and that Lola was to call him if she needed anything. Lola slipped her phone into her apron pocket alongside the small bundle of letters. As she opened the café she prayed for the first time for a quiet morning.

'Morning, Lola,' Alf called as he shuffled in with Scruff. 'Enjoy last night?'

'I did!' she replied as she made his tea and slipped a mince pie onto a plate for him to have with his toast. She hesitated before adding another in the hope it'd provide a bit of extra sweetness to her questions. 'It's been a long time since I was in a church, my grandmother, Ruby, was always suspicious of them.' She paused to see if he reacted to her grandmother's name, but he was too busy trying to get Scruff to sit still.

'Where's Tristan?' Alf asked as she placed the breakfast tray on the table. 'Not like him to be late.'

'He's got something that's come up this morning,' Lola said as she sipped her own tea.

Alf chuckled. 'About time you made an honest man out of him, Lola.'

'What?' she spluttered.

'Come on, everyone can see it!' Alf shook his head. 'Ever since you arrived in Polcarrow you've been making doe eyes at each other across the toast rack. The whole village thinks the same.'

Lola paused. Tristan wouldn't mind her telling Alf, would he? No, this was not the morning for it, she'd decided to ask him about Charlie and Ruby, she didn't want any distractions. 'We're just friends,' she said rather lamely.

Alf rolled his eyes. 'Do you not see it? Or feel it? Anyone with eyes and half a brain can tell you're both head over heels for each other.'

Resisting the urge to blurt out all the dates they'd been on, all the romantic moments and secret kisses, Lola just shrugged. Her palms grew sweaty, but Alf was on a roll with his chosen subject. Narrowing her eyes at him, Lola suspected he knew and was enjoying his line of questioning. She sipped her tea to hide the smile that was trying to escape.

'I've watched him all along, he's been into you since you arrived.' Alf shrugged. 'Has that surprised you?

Well, take some time to think about it, Lola, love isn't always that easy to come by and if the years have taught me anything then it's that moments should be seized. Too much thinking, too much worrying about what might go wrong just steals away the happiness.'

Lola was silent for a while as she absorbed his words, taking them as her cue to seize the moment. 'Alf, there's something I need to show you, something I need to ask you. Before I do, I want you to understand I don't mean any harm in this, but there's a reason I came to Polcarrow.' She paused. 'Last Christmas I was alone, my previous relationship had broken down and my beloved grandmother had died. She left me some money with the promise that I'd use it to make my dream of running a café come true. I didn't plan to come to Cornwall but the name Polcarrow was written next to her scone recipe and it felt like a sign. I also found a postcard of the bay. That's why I came to visit and well, the rest, as you know is history.' Lola smiled nervously.

Alf froze as if he wasn't sure he wanted to hear what came next but lacked the power to move away. 'Go on.'

Lola reached into her apron pocket and placed the photograph on the table. 'That's my grandmother; it seems she came here.'

Alf picked up the photo and contemplated it in silence for a long time. Lola tried to give him space but she couldn't help but sneak a glance at him. The emotions that washed over his face surfacing for the first time in over seventy years. The momentary joy of seeing his brother's young face quickly melted away into sadness about what happened next. Alf passed the photo back to her. 'I remember her now. She visited with two friends. It was a good summer. You look like her. I always wondered why you were so familiar.' He spoke cautiously, as if he wasn't sure he wanted to travel any further into the memories.

'Yes, we've always been very much alike, I miss her so much,' she said as she took the photo back from him. 'Alf, that's not the only thing I have. I recently received a box of her belongings that had been hidden away in the attic of her house. Inside were these.' She passed the pile of letters across to him and watched as his face blanched. Instantly she wished she could snatch them back, banish the pain that transformed his features.

Alf picked at the pile, shuffled through the letters but did not remove any from the envelopes. Instead he sat and studied the writing on the front, the black ink rewriting his memories. He carefully piled up the letters and handed them back to Lola, unread. 'This is the past, Lola, and the past is where things should stay.'

'I understand that, but I just want to know more about Ruby's time here,' she pleaded as she tried to push the letters back to him.

Alf refused them. 'When you've lived as long as I have you'll understand how important it is not to dwell on the hurtful or painful things life has delivered us. I can tell you this, Ruby was a ray of sunshine, very much the life and soul of the party like you are, but at my age I'd rather not dig up the dead. Things happened that summer that I'd rather stay buried.' He finished his tea and stood up, whistling for Scruff. 'Please respect that I don't want to drag it all up again. That summer changed everything.'

Lola opened her mouth to plead some more but the words died on her lips as Alf pulled open the door and hurried out of the café. She'd never seen Alf look so old, so fragile, so hurt and the knowledge that she'd caused his pain rocked her. She watched him go, rushing along the seafront as quickly as his legs could carry him in his haste to get away from her, from the reminders of the past, Scruff barking in confusion at the hasty exit. Blinking back tears, she reached for her phone and dialled the number of the one person she relied on above all others.

'I think I made a mistake,' she said.

'I'll be there in two minutes, Lola.' Tristan's voice was hurried and it sounded like he was putting his coat on as he spoke.

Chapter Twenty-Seven

Tristan arrived so quickly that he must have run down the seafront. He pushed open the door, making the bell jingle. Lola glanced up from where she was tidying away Alf's breakfast things and trying not to blame herself for the fact he hadn't finished his mince pie.

'What happened?' Tristan swept over to her.

Lola put down the plates and used the edge of her apron to dab at her eyes. 'I think I've just upset Alf,' she said, her lip trembling as she allowed Tristan to pull her into his arms.

'Ah, I see.' Tristan exhaled as he gently rubbed her back and made soothing sounds.

Lola melted against him. Burying her head in his shoulder, she inhaled the scent of him, his citrus shower gel, his washing detergent, and the feeling of coming home washed over her. Standing in the café with Tristan's arms around her felt like the safest place on earth.

'What if I have ruined everything?' she mumbled into his shoulder.

Tristan stroked her back. 'You've not ruined anything, Lola, it was probably just a bit of a shock, that's all. I still think you've done the right thing. Alf adores you. Give him a few days and he'll be back again with some quip about Cathy.'

Lola looked up at him even though she didn't share his positivity. 'I hope you're right, he's been like a grandfather to me. I hardly remember my own, they both died when I was small. I hope no one else finds out I upset him, they'll definitely run me out of town with pitchforks if they do.'

Tristan gave her a squeeze. 'I won't let that happen. You're far too precious.'

Lola managed a smile but as their eyes met all responses fizzled into nothing. She wondered how right Alf had been because as Tristan gazed down at her there was an undeniable bond between them, like they were two halves of a whole that had found each other. Time slowed down and waited like a paused breath. Lola didn't know who moved first but as her hand came up to Tristan's face, he lowered his lips towards hers. Her eyes closed as she leaned into the moment.

Chapter Twenty-Eight

Lola was glad of a busy day as it gave her something to think about other than upsetting Alf. Freya had covered the morning to mid-afternoon rush before bounding off to Bayview where she claimed she had a special project waiting. The over-the-top wink left Lola in no doubt that it was something to do with her forthcoming birthday celebrations and for once, she was glad of one less thing to plan.

Clinging to Tristan's reassurance that Alf would be OK, Lola's heart sank the following morning when Alf didn't show up at breakfast. Tristan gave her hand a squeeze but when the third morning rolled round without any sign of Alf, Lola asked Tristan what she should do.

'I think you need to leave him be, let him come round himself. I'll check on him on my way back,' he said, kissing her forehead before he left.

At the end of another busy day, Lola wiped down the café and made a list of what to bake in the morning, then bundled herself up and headed home, determined to lose herself in her knitting. Once home she turned on the fairy lights, followed by the radio, where gentle carols played. Lola prepared herself for a night in finishing Scruff's jumper. She was just settling into her stiches when a knock came at the door. Three purposeful raps that didn't sound familiar. Putting the jumper away, Lola made her way to the front door and unlocked it. Alf stood there, bundled up against the cold, an anxious look on his face as if he wasn't sure he should be there.

'Alf? Are you OK?' Lola almost sagged against the door frame in surprise. 'Where's Scruff?'

'At home, snug in front of the fire. Are you going to let me in, it's perishing out here?'

'Of course.' Lola stepped back to let him in and watched as he took in the interior of the house.

'I like what you've done,' he said, 'you've made it very homely. These places were very basic back in the day, loads of us crammed in, not much privacy.'

'Go through to the living room. Would you like a drink or anything?'

Alf shook his head as he settled himself into the chair. 'No, I don't need anything. I can't be too long, you know, what with Scruff being home alone. He might get ideas.'

Lola laughed despite herself. This definitely seemed like an improvement from the other morning. She settled back on the sofa and waited for Alf to begin.

'The thing is, Lola, I've been sitting at home these past couple of days thinking about what you asked me. Yes, the past is an upsetting place to visit and mostly it should be left well alone. But I'm almost ninety and I don't know how much longer I have left and I've lived a lot longer than my brother Charlie did, God rest his soul. Your questions got me thinking that maybe it's not right to keep his story locked up in the past, that maybe you do have a right to know what happened, especially as it involves your grandmother.'

Lola swallowed and nodded encouragingly, sensing she shouldn't say anything lest she put Alf off his stride.

'It was after the war, I see now that I was really only a boy, but I felt grown up. It was summer, these three young ladies turned up to stay in the village for their holidays. They seemed so glamorous and sophisticated, and I think all the village boys were half in love with them, much to the disgust of the village girls.' Alf chuckled. 'Charlie was older than me and I worshipped him. He was everything a boy could want in a brother. Kind, caring, had all the time in the world for me. Here, I've found a picture.' Alf held it out to Lola who reached across and took it.

Staring back at her was a black and white studio portrait of a handsome young man. Lola could see why her grandmother would have fallen for him. His face had natural charm, a strong jaw and despite the mono-chrome photo, she could tell his hair was thick and fair, his eyes light as the Cornish sea.

'He was quite the handsome devil, wasn't he?' Alf said as he took the photo back. 'All the girls were in love with him. But it was Ruby who stole his heart. It's a long time ago now, Lola, but I remember her being a lot of fun, very vibrant, very much like you in a way. I hate to admit it, but I was jealous, not only of Charlie getting the girl, but of Ruby taking him away from me. I was only a lad, remember, and Charlie was my role model. I thought it was just a passing fad but after Ruby left, Charlie told me he was planning on saving as much money as he could so that they could set up home somewhere.'

'I'm not proud of how I reacted, Lola, I'm really not, but I was devastated. How dare this woman turn up and turn Charlie's head, convince him that there's more to life than Cornwall? Although I was all sullen, Charlie made sure he taught me all he knew in his last months so that when he left, he could pass the business over to me.' Alf grew silent as he reflected. 'I got the business but not under any happy circumstances. You were at the memorial and you've read the letters so you know about the shipwreck.'

Lola nodded.

'There's only the memorial, they never recovered the bodies. Do you know what that's like?' He paused. 'My poor mother never recovered. Charlie was the apple of her eye. Especially as we'd only lost my dad two years before. My sister couldn't face staying here so she moved and we lost contact. Charlie dying meant any plans I may have had were put on the back-burner as I had to step up and run the business and help support the family. Oh, Lola, you know I've had a long, happy life here, but I never got the chance to discover if there was anything else out there for me because Charlie put paid to that with his dreams of a life with Ruby. He would never have gone out that night if it hadn't been for the fact he was desperate to scrape together the last bit of money he needed to leave and one of the other lads had mentioned he'd heard a huge shoal was coming in.' Alf shook his head sadly. 'Charlie was a bit of a daredevil, you know, I think it's what the girls liked. Anyway, they never came back. My mother cursed Ruby's name because she'd managed to take her favourite son away and ruin the family.'

'Oh Alf!' Lola gasped. 'I had no idea. Ruby never said anything other than alluding to the fact she had a wonderful summer by the sea, and then always looked a bit sad about it afterwards. I had no idea she left all this destruction in her wake.'

'She did write back, you know, after I told her about Charlie being lost at sea, despite me telling her not to. She asked to visit, to come to the funeral, but my mother didn't want her here, so she never came. Such a waste.' Alf shook his head. 'I do sometimes wonder what things would've been like had Charlie lived, but we'll never know. Tell me, did Ruby have a good life?'

'She had a wonderful life, she married my grandfather the following year, they had children, went on holidays and she taught me all I know about baking and reading palms,' Lola said, acutely aware of the sadness attached to a life that went on, the full life Ruby lived whilst Charlie remained a memory to all those who loved him. 'I'm so sorry about Charlie, he sounds like a good man, he must've been if my grandmother was willing to make a life with him. I have her diary – she really enjoyed her time here, I can tell that, and I think her feelings were true. I'm sorry if my curiosity brought you any pain, it wasn't intentional.'

'I know it wasn't, love, it has been good to reminisce. That was a glorious summer, it truly was, post war, everyone full of the joys of life. It's small consolation but I know Charlie died happy. He carried her photo with him everywhere, you know.'

Tears pricked Lola's eyes. 'Don't get me started, that's the most adorable thing I've ever heard.'

Alf rolled his eyes and then reached into his shirt pocket, pulling out a pile of faded pink envelopes. 'I want you to have these. I think you know who they're from. The whole village did with that colour paper!'

The letters still smelled faintly of the perfume Ruby had sprayed on them and it struck Lola that she was holding a piece of her grandmother's life that no one had ever known about. Pastel pink evidence of Ruby as a lovesick girl writing to her charming fisherman boy-friend. A young woman worlds away from the grand-mother she'd known. The writing on the envelopes was small, looped and girlish as Ruby had etched her dreams onto paper and sent them off into the world.

'I think you were always meant to come here, Lola, serendipity or fate or whatever you want to call it, but it seems you were meant to come full circle.' Alf pulled himself up. 'I'm going to leave them with you to read at your leisure. I have never read them so I don't know what they say, but there is one thing I need to say to you. I saw Ruby and Charlie lit from the inside with love, with promise, that's why she came here. But why are you here? Truly here? If you believe in all this mystic stuff, all this fate, destiny and tarot cards, then why are you here, and I don't think it's just to keep me in tea and scones in my old age, is it?' Alf said with a wink and when Lola went to get up, he stayed her with a hand on her shoulder. 'I'll let myself out. I'm here if you want to talk about anything. In another life things would have been different, I might have been your uncle, fancy that!'

Lola squeezed his hand back. 'I rather think of you like a surrogate grandfather,' she admitted in a choked voice. 'Thank you for looking after me so well, Alf.'

'Think nothing of it, I'm just hoping you'll make me an extra-special cake for my birthday next spring. Three tiers, I think. Ninety, you know, got to celebrate with a bang. Now you just sit and read those letters and remember, if there's one thing people seem to find in Polcarrow it's love.'

'But—'

'Don't fight it, Lola, and don't keep Tristan waiting. Or any of us for that matter. I'll see you in the morning.'

Lola listened as Alf let himself out, his words of advice and his tale of Ruby and Charlie settling around her. She reached for her phone. There was only one person she wanted to share this with, but as her finger hovered over his number, Lola decided not to make to call. She needed to read these letters alone. She picked up the top letter and pulled out the sheets, flowery with declarations of love and brimming with youthful hope. One by one she read them, immersed herself in her grandmother's love story, searching the words for guidance on her own.

Chapter Twenty-Nine

Ruby's gushing letters filled Lola's heart with so much joy, followed by a sweeping sadness to know that her love hadn't had the chance to bloom. Once she'd read the final one, Lola put it back into its envelope and thought about Tristan, wondering what it would feel like if he was to suddenly vanish just as they were having their first taste of happiness. Chills ran down her spine. Lola wasted no time in texting him, inviting him round, so she could share with him the next, unexpected part of Ruby and Charlie's romance. Not to mention reassure him that everything with Alf was fine.

'He kept dropping hints about us,' Lola said as she watched Tristan make up a couple of ham and cheese omelettes in her kitchen a short while later. 'It's like he knows!'

'Of course he knows,' Tristan said, 'Alf knows everything. Let's just tell him in the morning.'

Lola sipped her wine and nodded her agreement. There didn't seem much point in keeping everything under wraps and they weren't being particularly good at taking things slowly.

Alf arrived at the café early the following morning, Scruff in tow, Tristan bringing up the rear. He'd left Lola's late the previous night, after an extended goodbye kiss at the door. Tristan beamed at Lola as he held the door open for Alf, who went in, sat straight down and told Scruff, 'Now, give me a bit of peace so I can finish this crossword. Maybe I'll slip you a crust of toast.' The promise of toast made Scruff sit down more obediently than any of them had ever seen before.

'Morning, bit brisk out there, but despite whatever they're saying on the television, I can't see a storm brewing. I can usually feel them in my bones. This grey cloud is just going to blow around for a bit, dampening everyone's spirits,' Alf said, glancing between Lola and Tristan, his brow furrowing. 'Now, why are you all jittery this morning, Tristan?'

Lola placed a tray full of tea and toast on the table and smiled as Alf did his usual shake of the head at Tristan's Earl Grey. A wonderful warm feeling of having found her home washed over her. After all her years of travelling around the country, of taking herself off to far-flung destinations for brief exotic flings, there was nothing on earth that compared to sitting around the breakfast table in her own café with two men who'd come to mean the world to her.

Alf cut off his crust and slipped it under the table to Scruff. When he looked back up surprise, joy flashed across his face to see Lola and Tristan sitting side by side, hands clasped. 'Oh my, you two finally seen sense then? I knew you would.'

Laughing, Lola snuck a glance at Tristan only to find him gazing back at her adoringly. He gave her a quick kiss before turning back to Alf.

'Yes, we've finally come to our senses,' Tristan told him, 'and it might be brand new but I don't think I've ever been happier.'

'We just didn't want to ruin the friendship,' Lola explained.

Alf wiped a tear from his eye. 'Well look at that, you two making an old man cry. I couldn't be happier, two of my favourite people finally together is certainly the best Christmas present I could ask for. And friendship is the best basis for a relationship, at least you know you already like each other.'

'We'd like to keep it to ourselves for a bit,' Lola said, 'you know, to enjoy it without anyone else having their two pence worth.'

'Of course, but I'm pretty sure most people's tuppence worth would buy you a whole load of blessings.' Alf sipped his tea and fixed Lola with a look. 'Now you've come to your senses about each other, any chance you could help him come to his senses about what a proper cup of tea should be like?'

Lola and Tristan laughed. 'I would, but I think he's perfect just as he is, Earl Grey and all.'

Chapter Thirty

It was a week before Christmas and all over Polcarrow residents were frantically trying to pull together their festive plans. Parents were whizzing their kids from school party to school performance and trying not to panic when their children updated their Christmas lists last minute. Steve was experimenting with making his strongest mulled wine ever and was threatening to bring it along to the solstice ritual in the hope it would inspire some naked dancing. The mums who met regularly at the café had started asking for extra shots in their gingerbread lattes and people were enquiring about adding a dozen mince pies to their Christmas cake order.

Lola was starting to wonder where she'd find the time to fit everything in. At least she'd managed to finish Alf and Scruff's matching Christmas jumpers. She couldn't wait to see their faces when they opened them, or how long Scruff would manage to keep his clean. The biggest task on her list was finishing off the Christmas cakes and she was keeping her fingers crossed that winging the solstice festival would work. There was something different about a last-minute panic at Christmas time, everyone was united in it but also experiencing it in their own ways. Lola adored the way Tristan presided over all the panic with a calm air of religious reassurance. His bit was relatively easy, although she knew he was secretly struggling with his Christmas Day sermon, but nobody else needed to know that.

Lola had quickly backtracked into the kitchen when she'd discovered Freya and Tristan, heads together over the countertop, frantically whispering at each other. She knew she shouldn't have, but Lola couldn't resist standing behind the kitchen door, listening in to their plans for her birthday. Freya was in charge of balloons, banners and music and since Freya had discovered that Tristan had already successfully dipped his toe into baking, he had rather reluctantly been assigned birthday cake duties. The thought of her friends putting in the effort to plan a party for her touched Lola's heart. She'd thought she'd found a community amongst all the people she'd travelled with, but they were nothing compared to what she'd found in Polcarrow. Sometimes being in the village felt like living in a huge hug.

Freya's parents were all set for their visit, having booked the rooms above the pub, which meant Angelo was nervously trying to get Bayview House as presentable as possible. Having been up for a nose around, Lola and Tristan had kept to themselves the fact that Angelo would need a Christmas miracle of his own to make the house look like a cosy home and not a work in progress.

Lola eventually got round to sending out information about her solstice ritual and had asked everyone to bring along something to throw on the bonfire in the hope that they would have a big supply of wood. She wanted the bonfire to be spectacular, something for the village to gather around for quiet reflection before the shiny wrapped, beribboned festivities exploded over people's lives. A moment of stillness for everyone to breathe, to just be.

Lola's relationship with Alf had grown stronger. Far from dragging up Ruby and Charlie's ill-fated romance dooming their friendship, it had cemented it. Two people they had loved had once loved one another enough to dream of a life together. The ice had broken on Alf's refusal to discuss the past and he was suddenly regaling them over breakfast with tales from his youth, complete with the occasional sea shanty that Scruff tried to join in with. Villagers who had popped in for a take-away coffee or to collect a cake lingered to listen and some wove their tales in. Alf's and Polcarrow's fishing history was no longer just a ghost on the dawn tide.

Contentment settled over Lola. Every morning as she walked along the harbour to her café, she had an abundance of things to be thankful for. She ticked them off as she watched the light tentatively creeping along the horizon. Thankful for the friendships she had found, the fact that she was bringing joy to so many people with her Christmas cakes, that she was still friends with Alf, but above all, she was grateful for the love she had found. A love that was still very much wrapped in tissue paper and kept in a box, waiting to be opened. The word love seemed grand and big, terrifying but right. Lola kept hold of it knowing the four letters would change everything.

To distract herself, Lola busied herself with the café and ordering the ingredients for Christmas dinner, wondering if she should make a cheesecake rather than just the Christmas pudding. She picked up pencils and paper for the solstice ritual and scouted the beach for the best place to hold it. Excitement fizzed through her every time she thought about sharing the more spiritual side of her life with Polcarrow. All these activities were made even better by the fact Tristan accompanied her on them or lent a listening ear as she was thrashing out ideas, pointing out that maybe a mince pie cheesecake might be taking the festive theme a bit too far before kissing away any further discussion of the notion.

It seemed like nothing could disturb her bliss. It was late afternoon, the sun going down over the bay, leaving a trail of pink floating across the sea like rose petals. Having sent Freya home, Lola relaxed into the end-of-the-day ritual, wrapping the cakes, wiping down the coffee machine, the carols on the radio were playing low and soothing. Tristan was coming to meet her with a vague plan of trying another pub he'd read about, that he assured her had a sticky toffee pudding on the menu. They'd hatched a plan to travel around Cornwall rating them.

Lola was just thinking about closing early when the door opened and a young woman with impossibly golden blonde hair, wrapped in faux fur trimmed winter wear stepped into the café. She looked like something out of a magazine. Lola didn't think she'd ever be able to keep that much cream wool clean.

'Sorry, I know it's late, but I've come a long way, you're not closing are you?' the woman apologised.

Unable to turn away a lonesome traveller, Lola flashed her a broad smile. 'Of course not, take a seat. What can I get you?'

The woman peered into the counter, her eyes wide with indecision as she took in the selection. 'There's so much to choose from! Oh! Rocky road, I can never resist that. And a hot chocolate, please.'

'Sure, take a seat,' Lola said once the payment was through.

Lola got the order together as the woman made a beeline for the window seat with the sea view.

'It's beautiful here.' She sighed at the sunset. 'Thank you.' Her eyes brightened as Lola set the treats down. 'I have such a sweet tooth,' she confessed before looking at Lola sheepishly. 'Um, I saw in the window that you do tarot cards, how does that work? Can I have a reading?' She put her phone down and smiled nervously. 'I'm here to meet someone who was once very special to me. Oh, not here at the café, I'm just trying to calm my nerves before seeing him. I'm hoping things can go back to how they were.'

'How lovely, I'm sure it'll all be fine.' Picking up the woman's nerves and suddenly curious herself as to why she was so anxious, Lola replied, 'I'll just get my cards.'

When Lola emerged from the kitchen the hot chocolate topped with whipped cream and marshmallow snowmen was on the receiving end of a photoshoot and Lola hoped she'd be tagged in the social media photos.

'Your café is so adorable,' the woman gushed, 'I love all this vintage cuteness. It's so kitsch.' She snapped a selfie before putting her phone down with a giggle.

'Here's the cards.' Lola placed the box on the table, her own stomach suddenly lurching with a warning. She pushed it away and told the woman how much the reading would cost.

'That's fine. What do I do?'

Lola handed her the cards. 'Shuffle them well. As you do, think of what questions you want answered. When you feel happy with what you've asked, make three piles.' Lola sat down on the chair opposite her, watching as she squeezed her eyes shut and directed all her energy into silently asking the cards her questions.

The woman shuffled for a long time before opening her eyes and with a quick glance at Lola, created three piles on the table between them.

'Which one do you feel most called to?'

She took a sip of her hot chocolate and studied the piles before tapping the middle one.

Lola took the other piles and placed them back in the box. For some reason the cards felt cumbersome in her hands, as if they didn't want to reveal their secrets. Lola began to lay out the cards. 'Yes, I can see you've travelled a long way. You're at a crossroads in your life and have a big decision to make in regard to where you are going to live. You feel torn but are keen for something new. You've seen how moving away has had a positive effect on others in your circle and you're keen to try it.'

'Will it work?' she gasped.

Lola laid down the next card. 'It will if you move for the right reasons,' she said vaguely, turning over the next card but getting no clearer answer. 'Your destiny is in your hands.'

'And what about my special person?' The woman raised her eyebrows and leaned in. 'Are we getting together?'

Lola dealt two more cards, a furrow across her brow. 'You will reconnect with a past love, but the choice will be his. He's expecting you but is unsure of a future between you. You will need to work to win him back.'

Her face fell. 'But it's not hopeless, is it?'

Lola fixed her with a look and laid down the next card, which gave nothing away. Instead Lola bluffed, 'Nothing is ever hopeless.'

The young woman clapped her hands together. 'That's marvellous! He was so lovely and I loved him so much, but when he moved away our relationship ended and I was heartbroken. I tried to forget him . . . but you know how it is, you never forget true love.'

Lola gave her a tight smile before standing up. 'I'll leave you to it. I hope you find what you're looking for.' There was something tickling away at the hairs on the back of her neck, like a warning sign to get away from this young woman.

'Thank you.' The woman's smile stretched across her face like a cat who had been promised it would get the cream.

They both went back to their business of eating cake and tidying up. Something in Lola's stomach churned, causing her to have to catch her breath. She snuck a glance at the customer. She had a slight accent, she couldn't be . . . could she? No. It was a very long way to come just on the off chance. Just as Lola had reassured herself, the door opened and Tristan came in, wrapped in his black coat, a bunch of winter flowers in his hands.

No sooner had he walked through the door than the woman bounced off her chair and launched herself at him. 'Tristan! Surprise!'

Lola watched as a mixture of shock and horror washed over Tristan's face before a familiar recognition settled there. He had no choice but to hug the woman back.

'Anna? What are you doing here?' he asked, his voice shaking, trying to hide his bemusement as he let her go.

Anna. Lola's stomach plummeted. Anna was his ex-girlfriend. Frozen to the spot, Lola was unable to do anything other than watch their reunion unfold in all his horrifying awkwardness.

'I've come to surprise you.' She beamed. 'I've been thinking about how things were and since we've been back in touch I thought I'd come and see you. You said I was welcome any time! I've missed you.' She touched his arm, smiling up at him adoringly.

Back in touch? Welcome any time? Lola threw a glance at Tristan, which he caught but ignored.

'But why have you come all the way to Cornwall?' he asked, bemused.

'My sister's moved here. She's teaching in a school in Penzance and I've come for the Christmas holidays. I've been thinking about what you did, about moving somewhere quieter and my sister has encouraged me. Apparently, there's a vacancy at her school. I could be here by Easter.' She rubbed his arm territorially.

Tristan threw a look at Lola. 'Anna, I still don't understand.'

Anna laughed as if it was obvious. 'If I move to Cornwall, Tristan, we can try again. We can get back together. I've missed you so much,' she said again, clinging onto him like a limpet, burying her face in his chest, oblivious to the fact he wasn't hugging her back.

The colour drained out of Tristan's face. Lola's heart began to race. Surely, he wouldn't be tempted to go back, would he? Tristan threw Lola an apologetic glance.

'Erm, Anna, I think we'd better talk about this in private,' he said, still clutching the flowers as if he didn't quite know what to do with them anymore.

Anna spotted them and made a grab for them. 'It's like you knew I was coming!' She pulled them from his hands and buried her face in the blooms, inhaling their scent, 'And roses, my favourite!' She threw her arms back around Tristan, before thrusting the flowers back at him so she could grab her coat and bag.

Tristan and Lola stared at her, speechless. Oblivious to anything other than her own agenda Anna started to chatter to Tristan as she pushed him towards the door. As he was being herded away, Lola caught his confused, apologetic face and wondered briefly why he hadn't just told Anna the truth there and then. The thought that he might have missed Anna, that he might welcome her moving to Cornwall crumpled Lola's heart.

Chapter Thirty-One

'Lola I can explain everything,' Tristan implored the second Lola opened her door later that evening.

'Really?" Arms folded, she took him in, the harried desperation on his face. Her own heart was clenched like a fearful fist, tight and constricted. The panic that everything with Tristan had been too good to be true had palpitated through her since she'd locked up and café and come home, checking her phone every minute, waiting for something, anything, she didn't know what. Now he was here, desperation etched across his features. Lola resisted the temptation to slam the door in his face. Reasoned with herself that she needed to hear him out.

'Can I at least come in? Please?'

Lola inhaled, exhaled, pretended to think about it, before opening the door wider. 'Come on, no point broadcasting it to the whole of Polcarrow,' she said coldly.

She led the way into the living room, Tristan unwinding his scarf as he followed. Dropping into her favourite armchair, Lola curled her legs up under her. She studied Tristan as he perched on the sofa, his eyes skittering over all the trinkets and Christmas decorations that adorned her home, as if hoping to find support in them. Lola said nothing, just watched him flounder before he eventually managed to try and explain.

'That was Anna,' he began. 'Yes, ex-girlfriend Anna. The one I told you about on the beach.'

'The one you weren't quite ready to make a commitment to,' Lola recalled.

'Erm, yes, as you can see, she's a bit full on,' he said with a nervous laugh. 'Sort of bulldozes her way through life. I don't think she ever takes no for an answer.' He paused. 'I'm not making this better am I?'

Lola shook her head as he collapsed back against the cushions. 'Was she right? You got back in touch with her?' She tried to keep her voice calm, measured.

'No!' Tristan protested. 'She contacted me. And I was just being friendly. We had a shared past and in a way it was nice to hear how everyone was doing, old friends, her family . . .' His eyes widened as he realised he must've given her some false hope. 'I think she might have gotten the wrong end of the stick.'

'She seems pretty adamant that you and her are getting back together.' Somehow Lola kept her voice measured. There was no need to tell him about the cards. They hadn't exactly said they'd rekindle their relationship, Lola desperately reminded herself, but they had stated Anna should make a go of it.

Tristan's face was aghast. 'What? Never. Although she might take a bit of convincing.'

'Where is she now?' Lola prayed he wasn't going to say at the vicarage.

'She's just gone back to her sister's. She tried to stay.' He fell back against the cushions, exhausted.

'Will she be back?'

Tristan let out an exasperated exhale. 'Who knows? I hope not.'

'Did you give her any reason to believe she'd be welcomed back?'

Tristan hesitated.

'Did you?' Lola's voice was like ice.

'Erm, the thing with Anna is,' he floundered, 'that she doesn't take no for an answer. If she's got her mind made up about something then it's hard to dissuade her. It's one of the reasons I moved so far away, so she'd get the hint.'

'Get the hint?' Lola almost exploded. 'She was your girlfriend, you told me she wanted to settle down with you! It's more than her just getting the hint, it's about you manning up and being brutally honest with her.'

'I don't want to hurt her feelings, Lola, she doesn't take bad news well.'

'Her feelings? What about my feelings, Tristan?' Lola flung at him. 'We had plans this evening. What about them? You dropped me for her! You gave her my flowers!' Lola fought back the tears. After Jared she'd vowed never to let a man see her cry.

'Oh Lola, I know, I'm sorry, we could still . . .' He checked his watch. It was gone nine. 'I'm sorry, I tried to get her to go, but she wanted to talk about old times and . . . time just . . . It's hard, very hard, to get her to listen.'

'What are you going to do? Just marry her now because she doesn't like bad news?' Lola scoffed.

Tristan opened his mouth and closed it, as if that hadn't dawned on him.

'Well, would you?'

'No, of course not,' he rushed to reassure her, 'of course I wouldn't. But it's going to take a bit of effort to extract her again.'

Standing up, Lola shook her head. 'It shouldn't take any effort. I thought what we had was something special, that you'd moved on, but what I'm seeing, what you're saying is that keeping Anna happy is more important than keeping me happy, more important than us, more important than even yourself.'

'Lola, no, that's really not it.'

'Tell me, is she never going to set foot in Polcarrow again? Honest, Tristan. Did you tell her never to come back? That you're with someone else now?'

Tristan shook his head slowly as he followed her out into the hallway.

'I see.' Lola opened the front door and folded her arms. 'I think you'd better leave and decide who you really want.'

Tristan tried to protest some more, but Lola steeled herself, unable to tell who she was most angry with. Tristan, Anna or herself for believing this time everything would be different.

Chapter Thirty-Two

December twenty-first, the day of the solstice, dawned clear and bright, as if the world was presenting Lola with a clean slate. She stood on the still dark seafront, bundled up under her scarf, and inhaled, then exhaled, pulling the soft magic of the morning into her body, allowing it to spread through her on what she always felt was one of the most sacred days. The winter solstice, the shortest day, the time when the veil between worlds was at its thinnest. The day after which the light would slowly return as the world rolled towards another spring.

Lola briefly wondered what spring would bring. Everything this year had been brand new, her life totally reborn in Polcarrow. She'd spent the spring decorating her café and setting up the boundaries of her new life. Lola cast her mind back to those first few mornings, the sun warm with promise as it streamed through the café windows, Alf shuffling along to see how she was doing and checking up how long it'd be until he could sit with a cup of tea and watch the world go by. Then there was Tristan, doing his local vicar duty, popping in to say hello as she painted her new chairs. There was no denying now that something had been starting to brew between them even then. Lola had convinced herself that she looked forward to him popping in because he was easy company, now she knew it was something more. Tristan had always made her feel safe, equal, all the things she had struggled to find in her life. For the first time she felt someone had her back.

Or at least she had until Anna had made her appearance. That had only been two nights ago and Lola was rather frustrated by Tristan's Mr Nice Guy approach to putting Anna off. Why on earth Tristan couldn't just tell her he had a new girlfriend, Lola didn't know. Unless, of course, they'd got their wires crossed somewhere. Lola swallowed down the fear that they'd never had the exclusivity chat. Could Tristan be seeing how things might pan out with Anna? Was Anna going to slowly wear him down until he had no choice but to get back together with her? Her little red Fiat had been pulled up along the seafront both days and Lola had had to bite her lip and smile through the pain as Anna came into the café for more extra-sugary treats.

'I'm trying, Lola,' Tristan said as he paid for his breakfast that morning, reaching out to take her hands in his. Lola pulled hers back. Shock flashed across his face.

'She's just not listening. She never listened in fact. I now think I got swept up in her enthusiasm and it was easier just to go with it. Oh gosh, does that make me sound bad? It does, doesn't it? She means well . . .'

'Stop apologising for her,' Lola hissed, biting her tongue so as not to snap at him to just tell Anna where to go. Tristan's sweet side had always been a balm after the scoundrels she'd previously dated but now she was finding it slightly irritating.

Tristan took a deep breath and warned Lola, 'Anna wants to come to the solstice ritual, but she said she is bringing her sister. I tried to put her off, but it was like trying to stop a steamroller.'

Lola glared at him. 'I need to do your toast.' Reaching for the kitchen door, she glanced back. There was a look of confusion on his face, like he knew something was off-kilter but not how to put it right. Lola prayed Anna wouldn't manage to steamroll her way back into Tristan's heart.

After all the indecision about making a move on Tristan, about not wanting to ruin their friendship, the appearance of Anna made Lola regret not moving sooner. Exhaling away the fear that Tristan might choose Anna, Lola put her palms together in semblance of prayer and asked for the ritual to be a success.

'You ready for later?' Alf asked as he stirred his tea when Lola brought toast out to him and Tristan.

Lola let out a harried puff of air. 'No. Well, yes, but no, ugh, there's been so much to do.'

'Is there anything we can help with?' Tristan asked.

Lola was about to say everything was fine, that she had it all under control, but instead she dropped onto the vacant chair between them. She desperately needed a hand. 'Actually, could you pick up some logs for the fire. I decided I can't just hope people will bring along enough bits to burn. I've got the logs on order and I was hoping to nip out, but . . .'

'I'll do it.' Tristan reached to put a hand over hers, but pulled back. Lola's own hand suddenly yearned for his touch before remembering she was the one who'd drawn the barriers up between them.

'Thank you, I'll text you the details of where to collect them.' Lola stood up, her eyes darting all over Tristan looking for a sign, silently asking for everything to be OK between them. Seeing her own pain echoed in his eyes, she opened her mouth to speak but the arrival of Sue and her brood, who were now on school holidays, put paid to that.

'Morning! Bread's gone stale so I thought it was a perfect opportunity to grab breakfast here before we go last-minute shopping,' she said as she directed her kids to a table. 'All set for later?'

'Yes,' Lola said as she passed them menus, 'I think I am now.' She might have imagined it, but on the horizon there was a flash of light, as if someone up in the heavens was giving their blessing.

Chapter Thirty-Three

The arrival of the school holidays helped boost business. Their little corner of Cornwall had been blessed with bright winter sun and people were keen to make the most of the fine weather. Children ran around on the beach whilst parents perched on the harbour wall with takeaway coffee and cake. As distant family members began to arrive in the village, a proper holiday feeling descended and Lola briefly wondered if her plan to close between Christmas and New Year was a wise one. But she reasoned she deserved the rest, plus, she was looking forward to seeing the back of all the mince pies and getting her New Year baking plans ready.

As the last customers left, Lola locked the door and leaned back against it, her eyes trailing over the state they had left her café in. Chairs askew, a smear of cake on the wall from an excited small child, teacups that needed tidying away. However, it was a sight that made her happy, the mess an indicator of her success. Freya had headed back to Bayview to fetch Angelo so Lola turned the radio up and bopped around to the Christmas tunes as she embarked on her end-of-the-day cleaning routine – filling up the dishwasher, mopping the floor and wiping down the tables.

Once everything was straightened out, Lola pulled off her apron and nipped into the toilet to change out of her holly-print dress and into something much warmer, much more suited to spending a winter evening on a beach. She'd updated her social media earlier advising everyone to wrap up and bring blankets so they could make the most of the event. As she retouched her makeup, she couldn't deny that she was both excited and terrified. It had been a very long time since she'd run any spiritual practices other than palm and card reading. Smoothing down her jumper she tried to soothe the butterflies in her stomach as well, unsure as to whether they were dancing due to nerves or excitement. After a few calming breaths Lola decided it was a bit of both and surrendered the success of the evening to the universe. Whatever would be, would be.

She'd just finished her preening when a loud knock at the door came. Hurrying to open it, she found Freya, Angelo and Tristan standing there. Tristan had two bags of logs at his feet and in Angelo's arms was a very large round bowl.

'What's that?' Lola asked as she stepped aside to let them in, enjoying the thrill of Tristan's eyes catching her own.

Angelo placed the drum in the middle of the floor. 'I found this out the back of Bayview and I wondered if you could use it to light your bonfire later? I removed the legs and have turned it into some sort of fire bowl. Keep the fire contained inside. I think it'll be much better than laying it on the beach and far easier to tidy up. Maybe you can use it again next year?'

Moved by his thoughtfulness, Lola gave him a quick hug. 'Oh, Angelo, it's perfect. I think you might've saved the day, I've been so distracted by all the Christmas cakes and stuff that I'm not as organised as I'd like to have been, which does not sit well with me at all. After all, as you all know, I'm usually a planner. Thanks for getting the logs, Tristan, I'm sure with that many we'll have quite the fire going,' she added, unwilling to catch his searching eyes.

'I'm sure it will all turn out wonderfully,' Tristan said, in his usual reassuring way. 'I think people are just expecting a bit of a bonfire, a bit of mulled wine and some nice words.'

Her heart thawing at his kindness, Lola turned to him, her grateful smile tight. 'Maybe I can just claim I'm doing the ritual organically, you know, feeling the vibe and going with the flow.'

'That would work!' Tristan laughed. 'I have to confess sometimes that's what I do. If it wasn't for Cathy watching me with her hawk eyes I sometimes think I could slip in something about pink elephants dancing on the church roof and no one would bat an eyelid.'

'I'm sure they're all listening intently,' Lola reassured him, her resolve to stay angry at him fizzling.

Freya coughed to remind them they weren't the only two in the café. 'I think we should start setting up, don't you? I mean it's gone five and everyone is coming for six so we need to get the fire going. Chop-chop!' She stood back and opened the door indicating for everyone to move. Tristan and Angelo picked up their cargo and went ahead.

Lola pulled her coat, gloves and scarf on and hauled her bag onto her shoulder. 'When did you become the bossy one?' she asked Freya on her way out.

'When I was craving s'mores more than I wanted to listen to you and Tristan coo over each other. Although I don't see much cooing going on. Is everything all right?'

Lola shook her head as she locked the door then dropped her voice. 'His ex-girlfriend has tracked him down wanting to get back together and I don't know, he just doesn't seem very good at telling her firmly that it's a no. Apparently she's coming tonight.'

Freya's jaw dropped open. 'Why didn't you say?'

'I was trying to be the bigger person and not let it get to me. I don't think anything will come of it, but, what if he does get back together with her?'

Freya pulled a disapproving face, 'I wouldn't worry about that. He clearly adores you. Anyway, you know what they say, an ex is an ex for a reason. Unless, of course, you've dumped him?'

Lola was silent.

'You haven't, have you?'

'Not quite. I told him to get rid of her, but he doesn't seem to have managed that. It's really shaken me. What if he does choose her?'

'Uh-uh, not happening, no way.' Freya shook her head. 'I've not met her, but he is besotted with you. It's obvious.'

Lola smiled her gratitude at Freya but decided not to explain that Anna was determined to get her little claws back into her man at any cost. 'Let's just concentrate on getting this bonfire built and the ritual going well.'

Freya clapped her gloved hands together. 'Woohoo! That's more like it! The sooner Steve arrives with the mulled wine, the better.'

'Oi, you're meant to be warmed up with the fire and the setting of good intentions, not by half a barrel of rum and some dodgy Shiraz.' Lola linked her arm through her friends. 'We all need clear minds to focus on what we wish to manifest.'

They followed Angelo and Tristan onto the beach and once they'd found the perfect position for the fire bowl, started to fill it up with logs before Tristan, Freya and Angelo rushed back to behind the café where the excess wood they'd collected was waiting to be burned. Lola burrowed into her coat and wished she'd squeezed on an extra layer. The air was biting and the fire not yet large enough to take off the chill. She was transfixed as the orange flames licked at the wood and the fire began to tentatively take hold until it was glowing like a beacon to show everyone the way.

When the others returned, they started to feed in the extra wood and for a few moments simply stood watching the bonfire, collectively admiring their work. There was something calming about the crackle of flames against the splash of the waves. Primal, ancient. Lola imagined their ancestors gathered in similar fashion and the thought gave her comfort. She didn't mind if no one else turned up, if the ritual had poor attendance, standing in front of her solstice fire with three of the people who'd come to mean everything to her over the recent months set peace in her heart. Taking some deep calming breaths, Lola dragged the winter coldness into her body, allowing it to centre her.

'I hope you've all wrapped up warm,' she said to break the silence.

Tristan waved his thick gloved hands in Lola's direction as if seeking approval for his attire. 'If anything I'm starting to feel a bit too warm.'

Angelo patted his coat. 'Three layers. Freya is the one who's living dangerously with less. I keep telling her it's not London out here.'

Freya stuck her tongue out at him. 'I'll just have to snuggle up to you if I get too cold, won't I?'

'Just save the canoodling until later, please,' Lola advised them.

Sue was the first attendee to arrive. Wrapped in a furry hat, two hand-knitted scarves and leather gloves, she brimmed with excitement. 'I've never done anything like this before, it makes a change from all the other Christmas stuff.' She plonked down a picnic bag. 'I didn't want to be presumptuous, but I brought some flasks of non-alcoholic mulled punch. We all experienced Steve's mulled wine back at the carol concert and the rumours he was going to make it stronger had me worried.'

'It's all tittle-tattle,' an old voice dismissed.

Lola turned to see Alf ambling across the sand all bundled up.

'Alf! You should've said you were coming, I'd have got a chair for you.'

'Pft, I'm almost ninety, not an invalid, you don't think I can't stand round a bonfire for half an hour or so?' He shook his head and Lola knew he was determined to prove to everyone that age was just a number. Still, Tristan took a blanket over to him and a bit of fussing took place until Alf allowed the vicar to wrap it around his shoulders to keep him extra snug.

More people began to gather, some boldly crossing the sand, others approaching more nervously, as if they weren't too sure what to expect. Lola greeted them all, welcomed them, and pulled the few who had come from outside the village into the local embrace. She noticed Anna, in full fake fur regalia, tiptoeing across the sand, clutching onto her sister's arm. Tristan was too busy talking to Alf to notice.

Anna came straight over to Lola. 'Isn't this romantic,' she sighed as her eyes began to dart around, looking for Tristan.

Lola fought the urge to tell her to back off.

'I guess, but it's not meant to be romantic,' Lola pointed out. 'This is a way for us all to feel calmer, more in touch with our inner selves,' she said, but Anna was only half listening as she scanned the crowd. 'I'll be starting soon but there's a couple of people who I know said they were coming but are yet to arrive. Go and circulate.'

Anna didn't need to be told twice, she grabbed her sister's arm and marched her over to Tristan, immediately engaging him in conversation. Hmm . . . Lola's brow furrowed and her hackles rose as she noticed Anna briefly touch his arm as she laughed extra loudly at something he said. Tristan had the good grace to take a step back. As she watched Anna step closer to Tristan, Lola wondered why on earth she hadn't just told Anna to get lost.

'Where do you want this?' Steve caught her attention by dumping something at her feet. He'd invested in an insulated urn to keep the mulled wine warm for the occasion. 'It's super strength to get the naked dancing going. I reckon if that fire gets any bigger we'll all be stripping off.'

Lola rolled her eyes. 'How many times do I have to tell you there's no naked dancing, it's a solstice ritual not a nudist one. But you know, if that's how you wish to express your gratitude for the year, then by all means go ahead.'

Steve laughed. 'Let's see how the evening pans out. Shall I just leave this here or do you want me to start serving?'

'Leave it there. It's important to approach the ritual with a clear mind, it's all about grounding yourself, reaching deep inside and getting in touch with nature.'

Steve looked at her as if she was crazy, which made Lola chuckle. With an affectionate pat on his arm she sent him off in the direction of Alf and then took her place at the fire. Lola scanned the crowd and counted roughly twenty people, which was more than she had expected. She allowed everyone a few moments to greet each other and settle down. When she was sure no one else was coming, she clapped her hands together to get their attention. 'Welcome everyone. Come on, let's all sit down, huddle up, it's going to be cold.'

As people settled onto the blankets they'd brought, the chattering dropped to anticipated whispers until the loudest sounds were the whoosh of the waves and the crackling of the fire. Lola knelt in front of it and fed some more wood to the flames, transfixed by the way they leapt hungrily, taking her time to give gratitude that so many people were supporting her event. Lola paused, glanced around at the gathering and smiled warmly at everyone.

'Welcome and thank you for coming tonight, this is my first winter solstice ritual but I hope it won't be my last,' Lola began as she found her voice. A few people gave a little round of applause. 'Thank you. I believe it's important at the closing of the year to give thanks for what has come to pass and also to set intentions for what we want from the coming year. Today is the short-est day, our darkest hours, a time to reflect but also a time of hope. Going forward the days will grow lighter as we head towards spring's rebirth.' Lola passed a box to Freya. 'Please take a pen and two slips of paper, but keep them safe. I'll explain what they are for.'

The box was passed around and everyone dutifully took their supplies. Once the box came back to Lola she continued. 'What I'd like you all to do is to take a few minutes to think of something you are most grateful for from this year. Then I want you to write it down. Once you've done that I invite you to screw the paper up and put it in the fire, to release that gratitude.'

Lola stared at her slip as everyone around her slowly began to write. Love was the first thing that sprang to mind. The love she'd received from Polcarrow, the love she'd helped Freya and Angelo find, and another kind of love, one she hadn't expected to find herself. Seeing that everyone else had finished, she leaned forward and tossed her piece of paper into the flames. Everyone followed suit.

'Now we're going to do a short meditation. Please don't feel any pressure to travel anywhere through this. All I really want you to find is a moment of peace and stillness, a moment where there are no other demands on your life. A moment to reconnect with nature, with the ancient spirits. If you want to focus on something maybe focus on what you would like to bring into your life next year. Meditate on it, imagine what that thing would feel like, that you are worthy of receiving it. Close your eyes, I will bang this drum three times to begin the meditation and then three times to end it.'

Lola watched as everyone settled in. She wondered how many people were here because they believed in the practice, how many were simply curious or wanted to try something new. She noticed Freya and Angelo had linked their hands together and the sight touched Lola. Confident that everyone's eyes were closed, she beat the little drum three times and then closed her own eyes.

Almost instantly she settled into the moment, her tired brain giving up to the peace of meditation. Her eyes closed off to visual stimulants her soul began to respond to the natural ones it sensed. The crack and warmth of the flames, ancient and dependable. The notion that for thousands of years people had gathered around fires for companionship and togetherness swelled in her heart as Lola reconnected with the simplicity of human nature. In the background the waves continued their eternal ebb and flow, providing the rhythm of life since the world began. Lola retreated into a calm, centred place. A place that was comfort and love, where the embers of hope still burned. She fed them with her secret desires for the year ahead, mentally nurturing the life she wanted to live. Emotion swelled in her chest and the overwhelming sensation to cry, to release, ran through her as her soul travelled somewhere deep but safe. Strength flowed back through her fingers, the warmth emanating into her body and a wave of positivity washed over her for the future. It was as if her grandmother was there, speaking directly to her, tucking a stray hair behind her ear and telling her she'd made all the right choices. A blessing from the heavens.

A crackle of flames brought Lola swimming back up to the present. Surfacing, she picked up her drum and beat it three times. 'Come back to the light, to the darkness slowly. Take your time.' She watched as her gathering rubbed their eyes, yawned, stretched and came back to the present. Lola smiled to herself, pleased at how peaceful they all looked. Briefly her eyes met with Tristan's, snagging on a moment of truth that was larger than them both.

'Now, I hope whatever journey you have been on that you travelled somewhere nice. Somewhere safe. I invite you to write one wish, or something you wish to manifest onto your second piece of paper. We will then offer it to the fire and pray that our wishes come true.' Lola scribbled without daring to look or confront what she was writing, then balled it up tightly, less her secret desire snuck out.

'I'll go first.' She knelt forward. 'I give thanks and gratitude for everything that has been given to us this year. Community, friendship and love, these things all enrich our lives. I am blessed by everything you have bestowed on us. I thank you for watching over us this past year and offer up a prayer for love and protection for the year to come. Hear our desires for the year ahead, please guide us to help make these wishes come true. Namaste.' Lola bowed her head in silent contemplation for a few moments before throwing her paper in the flames, watching as the fire devoured her wish, turning it to ashes.

Sitting back, she wiped away the tears that were leaking from her eyes. She hadn't expected to have her emotions stirred so much. She was stronger, empowered, the universe had her back and the coming year loomed less ominously.

'And now,' she announced once everyone had thrown their papers into the fire, 'it's time to properly celebrate.' The cheer that went up was like an embrace, a confirmation of her place in Polcarrow.

Chapter Thirty-Four

People emerged from the ceremony yawning and stretching, their eyes readjusting to their surroundings. Lola watched as they smiled at neighbours, heard their nervous laughs and felt the deep contentment that had fallen over the gathering. She sensed in her soul that the event had been transformative, that the group had enjoyed it.

Sue made her way over and yawned. 'That was so relaxing, do you think you could do more of this?'

Lola hadn't thought about it previously but instantly brightened at the idea of a new business venture. 'I don't see why not. Maybe not on this scale with the huge bonfire, but I don't see why we shouldn't form a little circle here in Polcarrow. Leave it with me, Sue, something else to tuck up my sleeve for the New Year,' she said. 'You'll definitely sleep well tonight.'

'You have no idea how thankful I'll be for that, I've been lying in bed writing mental lists of all the things I need to do for Christmas and wondering if my mother-in-law will like the lilac jumper I've bought her, or worrying about the turkey being dry—'

'Stop right there, it will all be fine. Who doesn't love a lilac jumper and turkey is always a bit dry, so no point worrying about it. It's supposed to be the season of love and joy so it always amazes me how so many people tie themselves up in knots over it.'

Sue nodded. 'Very true. Right, well, if your meditation wasn't enough to knock me out, I better go and sample some of Steve's mulled wine. Do you want one?'

Lola shook her head and didn't have the heart to tell Sue that post spiritual practice it was usually best not to reach for the alcohol. However, the mulled wine had gained almost legendary status ever since Steve had announced he was making it, so she didn't think anyone would heed her advice. Lola was relaxed and floating on air enough without it. Popping all her materials back in her tote bag, she scanned the crowd, watching as Freya cracked open the biscuits and marshmallows and started to dish out s'mores to anyone who wanted one.

'Well, that was quite something,' Alf said as he sidled up to her. 'I never thought I'd get involved with any of this sort of hippy stuff and certainly not at my age, but, well, that was very peaceful. I've not felt as calm as that in years but maybe that's because I've left Scruff at home. Speaking of which, I think I better go back to him, let you young'uns have your fun. Watch out, that young woman seems to have her claws into poor Tristan.'

Lola's eyes followed to where Alf indicated and she swallowed back a lump in her throat as she saw Anna laughing as she got melted marshmallow in her long wavy hair. Lola's stomach churned as she witnessed Anna's over-the-top flirty behaviour. Peering through the darkness she was only somewhat reassured to see Tristan wasn't reacting. Alf gave her a quick pat on the arm before making his way back towards the road, using a torch he'd pulled out of his pocket to light the way. Tristan caught her eye, turned to Anna, said something and made his way over to her. Anna's eyes narrowed at Lola.

'I've tried many different things in my life, observed many different ways of worshipping, but tonight has been something very special. I can't quite explain it, but I feel it in here.' He put his hand on his heart. 'It feels like I've returned to an ancient time, to whatever predated all the things I do. It's been . . . beautiful,' he said sincerely.

Lola stepped towards him, as if pulled by an invisible thread. 'I'm glad you enjoyed it. Sue's asked me to do more.'

'That's certainly an idea I can get behind,' he said without removing his eyes from hers. 'I think we could all do with getting back in touch with our roots more often.'

Lola fought the urge to lean into him. She could feel the warmth of his body and, completely ignoring the fact that she'd spent the past couple of days shutting him out, willed him to step closer. No one reached her quite like Tristan did. He gave her hand the briefest of squeezes, longing shining in his eyes. She swallowed back the temptation to ask about Anna.

'Are you sure I can't convince you to come to the pub?' he asked.

As tempting an offer as he made it, Lola shook her head, overcome with a sudden fatigue. She didn't much feel like partying. Deep meditations always left her wiped out and in need of sleep. 'No, I have some cakes I need to finish off and I would never normally drink after such a deep practice,' she told him.

Tristan looked aghast and frowned at his cup of mulled wine. 'Should I not be having this?'

'It's fine, honestly, it is. I'm pleased with how many people have turned out, how much of a party this looks like it'll become. I feel such a deep sense of peace, of belonging that I want a chance to reflect on it.' She reached out and put a hand on Tristan's arm. 'Thank you for everything. For guiding me with the whole Alf, Charlie and Ruby triangle. It won't bring either of them back but it's brought Alf and me closer and I can't complain about that.'

'I think your grandmother would be proud of what you've done, Lola.'

'I think so too.' She hesitated before adding, 'I felt her here tonight, like she'd come to give me her blessing, I don't know if that sounds daft. I often feel her with me but tonight even more so. I think she would've loved this. She would've approved of me getting you along, luring you over to the dark side.'

Tristan laughed. 'It's not the dark side, Lola, if anything your side is very bright and beautiful. Soft and gentle. It's made me think we've all lost our way a bit. I could learn a lot from you about how to be a better man, a better vicar, too.'

Lola batted the notion away. 'You don't need to be a better man or vicar. In fact, I think you're perfect, just as you are.'

Tristan was about to say something but before he could get the words out Anna bounded over to them.

'There you are!' she exclaimed in an over-friendly way before turning to Lola. 'I really enjoyed that. I'm not very good at relaxing, too much going on in my brain.'

Lola smiled at her, determined not to let a hint of irritation show. 'Thank you. I think everyone enjoyed it.'

'It's not my normal cup of tea, but I think it's important I experience all sorts of things before moving down here,' Anna gushed, glancing adoringly up at Tristan before looking hopefully at Lola.

'And this was definitely a wonderful one,' Tristan interjected. 'But it's not all bonfires on the beach,' he said, trying to put her off. 'There's a lot of sideways rain and it can take a while to be accepted.'

After their closeness moments earlier, Lola's heart sank as she watched Tristan stumble around the issue of Anna moving. Lola shot him a venomous glance before taking a step back.

Anna remained oblivious to the tension. Instead, she glanced from Tristan to Lola as if seeking reassurance. 'Erm, yes, totally. I get that. I wouldn't just swoop in.'

Lola glared at Anna and Tristan looked at her in disbelief.

'You mentioned the pub, didn't you? I definitely need a wine or two!' Anna laughed. 'I'll go and find my sister and we'll come along.'

'Why didn't you tell her?' Lola said through gritted teeth as Anna bounded across the sand.

Tristan's laugher faded. 'I don't think she means any harm and I don't really think she'll move here. She's always jumping from one idea to another without settling.'

Lola turned to him in disbelief. 'Tristan, can you not see it? She's already told you she hopes you'll get back together. It's obvious. In fact, I reckon she thinks you already are back together.' She didn't like the way jealousy coloured her voice but she had reached the end of her tether with Tristan not sorting the situation out, for leaving her floundering whilst he pandered to Anna.

Shock washed over Tristan's face. 'I thought I made it clear to her.'

'I think you need to make it clearer, for her sake at least.' Lola's voice softened as the fight went out of her. 'I get the impression that unless you make it very clear she'll be moving here in January and that would be awkward for everyone. If you don't sort it out tonight, Tristan, then there's no future for us. I can't be with someone who can be so easily swayed by another woman. Or who'd put her needs above mine.'

The request hit Tristan square in the chest. Lola saw him blanch as the strike landed, saw the threat of losing her completely flash across his face. He reached for her, but Lola pulled back.

'Sure you don't want to come to the pub as backup?' He laughed nervously.

Lola shook her head. 'No. You need to do this alone. You need to choose.'

Tristan gave a tight nod. There was a pause as they gazed at each other and it was as if the rest of the beach had ceased to exist. The look was raw with longing as they drank each other in, the risk Anna posed to both their futures hanging between them. Lola resisted the urge to throw her arms around him, to pull his lips towards hers, to bury herself in the safety of him. To remind him of what they'd shared. She couldn't give herself any more to him until she knew she was his choice. Couldn't risk falling deeper for him if he wouldn't, couldn't be brave enough to choose her.

'I'll sort it.' His voice was soft, his face solemn.

Lola watched him walk away before gathering her stuff together. Once everything was packed up she searched out Freya, finding her handing out melted marshmallows to whoever would have one. Lola took one. 'Having fun?'

'Yes, I had to demote Angelo as he was burning all the marshmallows. I'm guessing you weren't expecting us to use your big spiritual cleansing fire to make s'mores.'

Lola shrugged. 'It would be a shame to waste such a fantastic bonfire.' She studied the flames that were starting to burn themselves out and popped the perfectly melted marshmallow in her mouth.

'It would. Tonight has been lovely, Lola, I've really enjoyed it. You should do more of this. Everyone has been saying the same. How about a big one for the summer?'

'Oooh, I'm sure I could rustle something up for that,' she said, 'it'll be much warmer then.'

'Better for the naked dancing!'

'Not you too!' Lola laughed. 'What is it with everyone and naked dancing around the bonfire?'

'I guess it feels a bit woo-woo,' Freya giggled, 'though it's far too cold. Are you coming to the pub?'

'No, I feel like I need some space to absorb tonight, it's been a lot deeper than I expected. I also think it's far too late to say to everyone that meditation and excess alcohol probably aren't the best mix, but you know, I'm not one to be a killjoy.' Lola studied the crowds who were still huddling around the fire, chatting, laughing, sipping their super-strength mulled wine. 'It's amazing to have created all this for everyone. It warms my heart.'

'But I still can't tempt you to the pub?'

'No, my lovely, not tonight, I'm saving myself for my birthday.'

Chapter Thirty-Five

It took Lola another forty minutes to leave the beach due to everyone stopping her to comment on how relaxed they felt following the meditation and dropping hints that they'd like to repeat it sometime. Pleased she had another string to her bow, Lola didn't mind leaving the party early. By the time she got back to her café the bonfire was just embers and being presided over by Angelo and Freya. As she unlocked the kitchen door, Lola smiled as she heard the singing that accompanied the revellers back to the pub. After flicking on the lights, Lola removed her coat, washed her hands and pulled on her apron. She had two cakes left to finish, the most important ones that she had saved until last. Alf's and Tristan's.

Humming along to the radio Lola set about covering the cakes in marzipan but not before she'd added an extra tot of brandy to Alf's. The combined aromas of almonds and brandy warmed Lola's heart, conjuring up happy memories of being with her grandmother. Ruby's presence still lingered like woodsmoke and it had contributed to Lola eschewing the invitation to the pub; she hadn't wanted the feeling of being close to her grand-mother again to be wiped away by a gin and tonic or two, even though she knew Ruby would've approved of a double-strength one after a chill winter night on the beach. Lola suspected Ruby would have taken one sip of Steve's lethal mulled wine and dished out advice as to how he could improve on it.

The thought of how well her grandmother would have settled into modern Polcarrow was stirring. Lola sensed her watching over her shoulder as she smoothed the icing onto the two cakes, making the top of Alf's tex-tured like choppy little waves. She'd found a plastic boat online and it was the perfect fit for the design she had in mind. Singing along to the radio, she crafted two figures from sugar paste; an old man dressed like Santa and a dog. She'd sit them in the boat and have little gift-shaped boxes strewn across the sea. It was a pleasure to make and Lola couldn't wait to see Alf's face when she lifted the lid on Christmas Eve. He'd specifically requested a Christmas Eve collection so he wouldn't be tempted to eat the cake before the big day, although Lola had told him cake was for eating and not keeping.

Pleased with the result, Lola made herself a cup of tea and warmed a portion of the spiced butternut squash soup that had been going down a treat in the café that week. As she ate it, wiping out the bowl with thick gra-nary bread, she stared at Tristan's undecorated cake, sitting like a blank canvas on the kitchen island. It was important that she got this one right, that she somehow found a way of showing what he meant to her through sugar paste. No pressure, she reminded herself as she set about getting the cake ready.

Not wanting any distractions, Lola switched the radio off and allowed silence to settle over the kitchen. The icing on the top of the cake was almost set but Lola managed to swirl a path from the bottom left corner towards the top right. Reaching for her tools, she set about creating a tiny, delicate sugar paste replica of the church, complete with shimmering shells pressed into the mortar around the door, on which she placed a tiny red and green wreath. There was something therapeutic about decorating Tristan's cake, about smoothing over the edges and making it beautiful, as if she was somehow paving the way for their future.

Carefully, Lola eased the church onto the cake, before adding a couple of plastic, snow-topped Christmas trees along the path. After dusting it with a little shimmer of silver, she stepped back and studied it. It was one of the most beautiful things she'd ever made. She hoped Tristan would like it. Tristan, who was currently sitting in the pub with his ex-girlfriend who was enthusiastically trying to get back together with him, when she should be the one sitting next to him, telling him she loved him.

Loved him? The thought stopped her dead as she carried the implements she'd used over to the dishwasher. No . . . she didn't . . . did she? The L word had been bouncing around in the back of her mind for a while.

Lola tried to wipe the thought away but it was written across her soul in permanent marker.

'I love him.' She tried the words out loud, giggling as she crammed them back in with her hands. 'Oh gosh, I'm in love with Tristan!' She whooped with joy as a smile broke across her face and she did a little shimmy. 'I love him and I've left him to Anna,' she gasped, panic rising in her throat as she stopped mid happy dance. Lola glanced around the kitchen, at all the decorating debris strewn across the counters. Why on earth hadn't she just gone along for that gin and tonic and enjoyed Tristan's company? She could almost hear Nannie Ruby tutting her disapproval.

Lola dumped the dishes haphazardly in the sink. Getting to the pub became the most urgent thing in the world. She'd physically haul Anna off him if need be. The washing-up could wait. Lola pulled her scarf and coat on over her sugar-dusted apron, pausing just long enough to reapply her signature red lipstick in the desperate hope that it was about to be passionately kissed off.

Chapter Thirty-Six

Lola darted out of the kitchen and hurried along to the seafront. She'd go to the pub, she'd haul Tristan outside and tell him how she felt. Hell, she'd even pull the plug on the pub jukebox and spill it all with everyone listening. Now the truth had bubbled up there was no squashing it back down. She wanted to shout it to the world. Pulling her coat tighter around her, Lola ran along the harbour wall, only briefly cursing the fact she'd not stopped to pull her gloves on, when she ran smack bang into something tall and solid.

'Woah! Slow down!'

Large hands closed around her arms, holding her firmly in place. Looking up, Lola's eyes met with Tristan's, as they both paused, the anticipation ignited like fireworks in her belly. Straightening up, he stepped back and let her go. Untethered, Lola tucked a stray lock of hair behind her ear and pressed her lips together. She took in everything about Tristan, the way the night stars twinkled in his eyes, the bit of hair that flopped over his forehead that she always itched to push back. The smile that was tugging at his lips. The way he looked at her as if she was the most precious, most beautiful thing on earth. It stilled her, centred her. The moment was so perfect Lola wanted to freeze it, encase in a snow globe so she could always tip it up and let the magic rain down upon the memory. As they studied each other, time slowed right down, like the world was waiting with bated breath to see what they did next.

'What's got you running along the seafront at this time of night?' Tristan asked, amused, as if he already knew and was testing her. 'I thought you'd be all tucked up at home.'

'You,' she said before she could change her mind. 'You've got me running along the seafront at this time of night.'

'Me?' He feigned puzzlement as a smile spread across his face. As he stepped closer, he cupped Lola's face in his hand. 'Why me?'

Lola leaned into his touch, absorbed the comfort of it as the words fizzed like sherbet on her tongue. 'Because . . .' She paused and even though she was almost on tiptoes with anticipation she couldn't resist asking, 'Why are *you* running along the seafront at this time of night?'

Tristan laughed then grew serious. 'Because of you.'

Lola stepped forward, sliding her hand up his arm until it came to rest on his shoulder. Anchoring herself to him, she slipped it around his neck, pulling him in close, stroking the short strands of hair at the nape of his neck. 'Me? Why me?' Lola echoed, bracing herself, all her nerves tingling as she waited to hear what she hoped to.

Tristan took her other hand, linked his fingers through hers. 'Because, Lola, I'm in love with you, I've been in love with you from the moment I first saw you. That's why. I couldn't sit there with Anna any longer. I told her straight. I love you, Lola.'

Lola swallowed back the words. Time stopped. Tristan loved her. Hearing it was better than she'd expected. They were more than just the cherry on the top of the cake, they were a whole box of sprinkles and a dusting of glitter. She squeezed his hand back whilst planning on never, ever letting go. 'Well, that's quite handy,' she began, 'because the thing is, Tristan, I've realised I'm in love with you, too.'

A grin broke across his face and he let out a whoop of joy, before pulling her to him. 'Does this mean we don't have to take it slowly, or keep it from everyone anymore, because frankly, I've been struggling so much.'

'No, I don't think we should keep it to ourselves any longer,' she said, 'after all, romance is the extra sparkle on the Christmas cake.'

A smile broke out across his face before he closed the gap between them and kissed her, his lips lingering on hers like an invitation until she kissed him back. It was brandy and tinsel, fireworks and stardust all rolled into one. For Lola, it was absolutely perfect.

Chapter Thirty-Seven

The day following the solstice ritual dawned crisp and bright, reminding the residents of Polcarrow that from now on the days would slowly grow longer, lighter. Lola's alarm sounded through the still dark of the morning, rousing her and Tristan from a few snatched hours' slumber. He groaned in complaint and Lola silenced him with kisses before getting up, jumping in the shower and getting ready for the day ahead. Even if she wasn't quite ready to forget the blissful night they'd shared, her mind was already mentally compiling a to-do list.

'I have a new-found respect for you getting up each day at this time.' Tristan yawned as Lola locked up the cottage door.

She slipped her arm through his. 'I've always been an early-riser, sunrise is one of the best parts of the day. It's where the magic really happens,' she said as they made their way over to the harbour wall, where a flicker of golden light was breaking through on the horizon, stretching like a blessing over the calm waves. Lola had the notion that everyone was exactly where they were meant to be. She snuggled into Tristan and gave silent thanks to Ruby for leading her to Polcarrow and into the arms of someone who truly loved and cared for her.

'I love winter days like this,' Tristan said, 'where it's cold and clear and if you get the sunlight at the right angle, you can sometimes believe it's summer.'

Lola shivered. 'Might be a bit nippy for that but I did see the forecast is for blue skies, which I think is much better than a white Christmas. Imagine how all that snow would ruin people's travel plans?'

Tristan laughed. 'That's a very practical thought.'

'Hmm. Well, I am looking forward to hosting Christmas and after all the work Freya and Angelo have put into Bayview it would be nice for her parents to actually get here. Anyway, has Freya said how my birthday plans are going?' She raised her eyebrows at him and fixed him with a look she hoped would melt him into revealing what was going on.

'They're . . .' Tristan stopped. 'No, I'm sworn to secrecy.' He kissed her as a distraction. 'I'm not telling you anything other than you have nothing to worry about. Nothing,' he reiterated as Lola's face wavered.

Lola's instinct was to press him – not being in control was strange for her – but as she watched him wrestle with keeping the plans under wraps, she knew she could trust him and Freya. 'Come on, I better get baking. It's school holidays, it's sunny, I want to do all the fun things. Reindeer and snowman cupcakes, gingerbread fishermen. Do you think I could get away with culling the mince pies this early? Surely everyone has had their fill?'

Tristan winced. 'Oh, I don't know about that. There's still three days of annual mince pie scoffing left for this year, some people might be trying to squeeze in as many as they can still. Like Alf.'

Lola laughed and pulled away from him to make her way to the café to unlock. 'I guess you're right. I wouldn't want his, or Scruff's, complaints. But I can't wait to make all sorts of new things in the New Year. Proper comfort food bakes, none of this post-Christmas dieting. I even found a recipe for a sticky toffee cake . . .'

'Well, if you need a taster, you only have to say,' Tristan offered.

Lola kissed him. 'I hope you're not only after me for first dibs on my baking.'

'Well, there have to be some advantages to dating the local café owner,' he said, pulling her to him.

'In that case, I better get on with some of that baking then,' she said, giving him one last kiss. As they crossed the road towards the café they spotted someone attaching a 'To Let' sign above the door of the shop next door. 'What's happening?' Lola asked the man.

He shrugged. 'Owners have decided to rent it out. Obviously think it's worth it now.' He didn't elaborate but went back to his work.

Lola tugged Tristan's arm and they headed back towards the café. 'I hope it's not going to be a rival.'

'No one would dare,' Tristan reminded her as she unlocked the door. 'Alf would chase them out of town for one.'

Lola laughed. 'True. Come and keep me company, I promise not to sing along to the radio. Alf won't be here for a while.'

Tristan made them both a cup of tea and some toast whilst Lola got stuck into that day's baking. Lola adored the way he patiently sat on the kitchen stool watching what she was doing with awe. He asked questions as she went along about where she got her ideas from, about baking with Ruby, if there was anything he could do to help with Christmas dinner. The companionship between them was something Lola had never experienced before and she found she liked it a lot more than the hot and cold passion she'd experienced with Jared. Talking about their days, exchanging views on the solstice festival, taking in a little bit of calm before the Christmas rush, was exactly what Lola had been looking for without realising it. Freya had been right, friendship really was the best basis for a relationship.

Chapter Thirty-Eight

It was the twenty-third of December and Polcarrow was divided into two camps: those panicking that they still had last-minute Christmas bits and bobs to buy and those who had already cracked open the mulled wine having accepted that they had done everything they could. The whole of the village was in a flurry – wrapping last-minute gifts, catching up with friends over gingerbread lattes and snowman cupcakes, preparing for the crib service at the church or getting ready for relatives to descend. The morning had been bright which meant the café had been busy with people buying hot chocolates and pastries to consume on the beach while the kids ran off some of their pent-up holiday energy. Now with soft grey clouds rolling in over the bay, people had headed for home to get on with various Christmas chores.

'Freya, stop it, you're making me nervous!' Lola exclaimed as she brought out a fresh batch of mince pies and some brownies. 'Calm down, it's only your parents.' As the day had worn on, Freya had grown twitchier and twitchier about her family's arrival. They were now due any moment.

Freya reached for one of the brownies before pulling her hand back. 'Exactly! And they're meeting Angelo for the first time.'

'From what I've observed, Angelo is perfectly capable of being charming, I'm sure they'll love him.'

'But the bike and the tattoos—'

'He sold the bike, remember, to help fund Bayview. As for the tattoos, well, unless you're planning on whipping his jumper off, they don't need to see them, do they?' Lola pointed out. 'Stop flapping, it will all be fine. They'll see how much he looks after you and that will win them over. What time are they arriving?'

Freya glanced at the clock. It was five past three. She sucked in a breath. 'If traffic is good then they should be arriving any time now.'

'Right, I'll leave you to it, I've got a few things to finish.' Lola gave her a smile and a shoulder squeeze. 'It will all be fine, trust me, I'm the local oracle,' she said with a wink.

'Angelo's making dinner for us all later, he's doing some lasagnes, you and Tristan are more than welcome to join us, unless, of course, you have other plans?' Freya said with a wiggle of her eyebrows.

'If you're making those sort of insinuations about me and the local vicar, young lady, then I think it's only right that we join you and prove that we're perfectly capable of keeping our hands off each other for an evening. What time?'

'Seven.'

'Great, looking forward to it. I'll text Tristan, pull him away from the Christmas Day sermon he's been agonising over for the last couple of days,' Lola said.

'I'm not sure you should be leading him that astray,' Freya warned.

'Me, lead him astray? Never!' Lola quipped as she popped her phone back in her pocket.

Chapter Thirty-Nine

Although most of the residents of Polcarrow had gone for a nose around Bayview House when it went on the market, Lola had only stepped foot inside once, just after Angelo had bought it. The house had been dusty and in need of a lot of love and care. Having listened to Freya outline the trials and tribulations of turning an ageing fixer-upper into a forever home, Lola was impressed with the amount of work they had managed to achieve in just six weeks. The house had been stripped back and painted white, a blank canvas ready to be explored. Tinsel with fake holly leaves had been wound around the curving banisters and in the corner sat a small Christmas tree twinkling with fairy lights

Lola gazed around in awe to think this was where her grandmother had stayed that summer. Any ghosts of that holiday had been swept away with the cobwebs. It must have seemed like a palace to Ruby, who grew up in a slightly damp two-up two-down in north London. On the way to Bayview House Lola had decided that if the right moment arose, she would tell everyone the remarkable story about Ruby and how they both came to be in Polcarrow. Alf had given her his blessing to share the story whenever it felt right to.

Angelo took them all on a tour of the ground floor, explaining what they hoped to do with each room before leading them into a large, old-fashioned, but cosy kitchen. Rather than turn on the glaring overhead lights, Freya had dotted candles everywhere, creating a warm glow. The atmosphere was so festive, so romantic that no one minded that they were sitting around a rickety plastic table on mismatched chairs. There was red wine, Christmas crackers and a tiramisu to top it all off. Everything about it was divine. Lola gave Freya a thumbs up. It seemed that her family approved of Angelo.

Nobody minded that there weren't enough wine glasses, or the plates didn't match, or the table was a bit wonky because what really mattered were the people gathered around it, sharing food and stories, all of them looking forward to the next few days. Lola watched as Freya relaxed. It was exactly as she'd predicted, Freya's family warmed to Angelo and they had all been left speechless when Freya bounded outside to show them the shed he'd turned into an art studio for her. Lola had given her friend a squeeze and tried not to get too sentimental about how far they'd all travelled in their lives that year. The studio was gorgeous, created with love, and Lola would only ever admit to herself that she'd miss having her friend painting in the room up above the café. This was the next step in Freya's exciting career. The flat would be put up for rent, someone else would move in and hopefully Polcarrow would work its magic on them.

After dinner they sat around the table, squeezing in brandy chocolates and sharing stories of Christmases past. Olivia, Freya's older sister, seemed keen to regale Angelo with tales of Freya's youth, which she bore with an affectionate grimace. As the conversation lulled, Lola exchanged a glance with Alf and used his nod of encouragement to slowly unwind her own tumultuous family links to Polcarrow, telling everyone about Ruby, her romance with Charlie and how it had allowed her to grow closer to Alf. By the time she had finished there was not a single dry eye around the table, everyone's emotions stirred by the story of heartbreak and hope shared at such a special time of year.

It was almost eleven o'clock when Lola caught Tristan yawning and found her own mouth being tugged in tiredness. 'I think it's time we head off,' she announced, 'I'm sure tomorrow will be a busy day.'

They were seen off with kisses, hugs and good cheer. Lola slipped her arm through Tristan's as they ambled down the hill towards the seafront. Polcarrow was quiet, all hunkered down, waiting for Christmas Eve to arrive and all the magic and anticipation of opening the final door on the advent calendar brought.

'They've done a good job at Bayview,' Tristan said. 'It's not a project I'd have liked to have taken on.'

'Nor me,' Lola admitted, 'and I'm not sure how much Freya enjoyed taking it on either, but it does look smashing all stripped back. There is a tiny, tiny part of me that would like to get my hands on it, but I think my vision would be very different from Angelo's.'

'Yes, I can't see him going for floral curtains personally.'

They wandered in companionable silence for a while, the distant whooshing of the waves a gentle, soothing backdrop after the noise of the dinner party.

'Would any of us have imagined this a year ago?' Lola mused. 'There's four of us who've all found a home here, a life, and love. It's like Polcarrow really is magic.'

'Well, I'm going to let you into a little secret, I think you are the magic, Lola. I think you turned up and dusted this whole village with it. No, don't be modest, you know your café has given the village a new hub and I'm sure everyone will turn out to celebrate at the pub tomorrow.'

'Come on, give me one little hint, please.'

'No! You're not wheedling it out of me now, just one more sleep.' He kissed her.

'I'm sure it will be perfect.' Lola looped her arms around him and pulled back to look him in the eyes. 'Even if it's just some bubbly, a few sausage rolls and no Christmas tunes, it will be absolutely wonderful. I'll probably fall asleep at the bar I'm so tired, but I honestly cannot wait.'

Tristan dipped his head and kissed her, pulling her in close. 'How does it feel to have less than an hour of your thirties left?'

Lola sucked in a breath. 'I thought I'd be terrified, but you know, the last few weeks have shown me that life truly doesn't end as soon as the clock strikes midnight on your thirty-nineth year, if anything it's shown me that life still has lots of wonderful surprises up its sleeve. One of which is standing here right now.' Her voice grew serious. 'You know, Tristan, I never expected this. Not just you or us but romance again. I was so relieved to be done with Jared, so pleased to have put myself first, to get an opportunity to create a life I love that I thought there was nothing else left. But you, you are the cherry on my cake.'

Tristan gave her a squeeze. 'I could say the same, but I think it'd be a bit sickly if I used the cherry analogy. I've never quite recovered from scoffing half the tub I used to make that upside down cake.' Lola laughed as he pulled a face. 'How about I love you instead?'

'That works. But promise me something – that it will always be like this. That you won't try to change me or take away my freedom. I have no intention of ever leaving here, I've put my bags down and unpacked for one final time. I love my café, I love the people, I've had so many requests for more meditation sessions, I know our beliefs don't always align but . . .' She trailed off.

'It doesn't matter. We both believe in caring for our community, in providing support either with pastries or prayer, we'll figure life out together, Lola, because there's no one I'd rather do this with, than you. We're a team, we've always been a team even when we didn't realise it.'

Stretching onto tiptoes Lola pulled him closer and kissed him. As Tristan kissed her back, she had the sensation that this was how she was meant to be kissed, with care and true intent. Above them the sound of the church bells chiming half past eleven sounded, shattering the peace of their moment.

'Only half an hour to go,' Lola whispered.

'Do you want to wait and celebrate right on the stroke of midnight?'

Lola shook her head. 'No, I want to go to bed like I used to and wake up to it being my birthday and Christmas Eve with all the promise the day holds waiting for me to unwrap.'

'Well, as you only have half an hour, I better get you home, like a Cornish Cinderella.'

'Cinderella?' she quipped as Tristan grabbed her hand and started to run along the seafront. 'I thought I was the fairy godmother.'

'I think it's high time that you get to be a princess.' Then catching the look she cast him, he quickly corrected, 'Queen, I mean, queen.'

Lola smiled with satisfaction and allowed him to pull her along. A year ago she would never have believed it if someone had said she'd be running head first into her fortieth year, pulled along by the sheer force of someone who loved her. But life, as she'd come to realise, was full of surprises.

Chapter Forty

Lola woke on Christmas Eve full of an excitement she hadn't felt since childhood. After pushing back the duvet and opening the curtains, she peered out to sea, where the dawn was just starting to show promise on the horizon. Christmas Eve always felt far more special in her opinion than Christmas Day. It was in the magic Father Christmas spread across the skies from his sleigh, the unusual-shaped objects still shrouded in bright paper under the tree and the anticipation of gathering with loved ones where arguments over how to cook the sprouts hadn't yet happened. Plus, today was her birthday.

Glancing in the mirror, Lola gave her face a satisfied pat, pleased with the way life had treated her. Forty had come round far more quickly than she would've liked, however she wouldn't swap the knowledge and life experience she'd gained to be twenty again for anything in the world. Staring at her reflection, Lola reflected on the path that had led her here: the parties, the quick fiery relationships, the friends she'd loved and lost along the way. All the accumulated memories, shifting in her mind like a kaleidoscope, refracting brightly like a montage of her life. She smiled to herself. It hadn't all been bad, in fact, it had been very good for the most part. Now, thinking of Tristan, she knew the best bits were still to come.

Makeup applied, hair rolled back and adorned with fake holly and ivy, Lola slipped into the dress she'd bought specially for the day. Deep green and figure hugging it was sprigged with dark red poinsettias. She adored it. Bundling herself up against the winter morning, she stepped out of her cottage and breathed in the damp, cold air, the scent of the sea undisturbed by any other aromas.

As she made her way along the early-morning sea-front, she knew this next chapter was going to be the best one, cosy and comforting, as close to a happy-ever-after as she could wish. Stopping to admire the view, and being secretly thankful that now the solstice had passed the days would be slowly getting longer, Lola set about her morning ritual of gratitude. Making her way onto the soft sand, she walked right up to the edges of the waves and was momentarily tempted to go for a paddle until she remembered she had on the special dress she'd bought for her birthday and a pair of tights. Hardly dipping a toe attire. There'd be plenty of time later for a paddle in the sea. She'd heard several people discussing a Boxing Day swim over their lattes the previous week. Lola shuddered at the thought. Instead, she took some deep inhales and exhales, pulling in the briny cold air and hugging her own life to her. She was blessed, pure and simple, in every area of her life.

'Thank you, Ruby, for leading me here. I know it was complete madness to up sticks and come to a tiny Cornish village, but you knew it'd bring me happiness. And it has. I'm so thankful that Angelo and Freya have been able to make a home here. That Alf has become like a surrogate grandfather. He says he's sorry, Ruby, and I believe him. All water under the bridge now. Thank you for bringing me Tristan, he is rather lovely and he makes me so happy.' Lola blew three kisses and imagined them being carried over the waves before turning her back on the rising sun and getting herself ready for what she suspected would be a very busy day of running a seaside café.

Unlocking the café door, Lola paused to take stock, and if truth be told, give herself a little pat on the back. It was the complete dream. It was something no one could take away from her. She wondered briefly what Jared would make of her achieving her 'beside the sea café' dream before realising that his opinion no longer mattered. The scent of coffee lingered in the air, warm and comforting, greeting her with the same rich embrace it had done for the past nine months. Below the glass domes sat little piles of brownies and a couple of left-over mince pies. Making a fresh batch would be the first order of the day, Lola thought, as she made her way into the kitchen, musing that she'd be glad not to see another mince pie for a whole year.

Turning the Christmas music up loud, she set about her baking, rocking along to the tunes as she rolled out pastry, filled the pies, made a batch of scones and finished it all off with a gooey chocolate fudge cake. It seemed right to start her birthday with cake for breakfast, there was no way she was going to wait until the evening for some, even if Tristan was making it.

Once the cake was baking in the oven, Lola made herself a cup of tea and a slice of toast and perching on a stool, pulled a stack of coloured envelopes out of her handbag. She'd received a few cards from family and old friends and set about opening them, reading their sentiments as the smell of baking curled its way around her. Breakfast finished, Lola checked the clock and realised it was time to open the café. As she unlocked the door she was surprised to find Freya standing there, a balloon and a bunch of flowers in her hands.

'What are you doing here?' Lola asked. 'I've given you today off because of your family.'

Freya passed her the flowers. 'Happy birthday. Anyway, that's nonsense, you know you'll be busy. They're all still asleep anyway. I told them to text me when they're up and about.' Freya pulled out her phone and waved it in Lola's direction. 'See, nothing.'

Unable to admit how pleased she was to see her friend, Lola took the flowers. 'They are gorgeous, thank you.' She pulled Freya in for a hug. 'I'll find a vase to put them in and put them out on the counter for everyone to admire.'

Freya sniffed the air. 'Is that a cake baking I can smell?'

'Yes, a chocolate cake. I'm hoping it'll be ready for second breakfast,' she said as she swept into the kitchen.

Rummaging around in the cupboard under the sink, she turned out a large glass vase, filled it with water and tried to arrange the flowers as artfully as she could manage, which wasn't very artfully at all. Still, they were so beautiful that it didn't matter. When Lola placed them on the counter they added a cheerful pop of colour. She headed back into the kitchen and after checking that the cake was cooked, she removed it from the oven and set it down to cool, pushing the window open slightly to hasten it.

The bell dinged and she heard Alf wishing Freya a good morning. Lola waited a bit until he was seated, listening as he gave Freya his order, requesting two mince pies, fresh ones, if they had any. Lola slipped a couple onto a plate – they were still a bit warm – and balanced the plate on top of the box containing his Christmas cake.

'Morning, Alf!' she called as she exited the kitchen and almost ground to a halt as she saw Tristan sitting next to him, the biggest bunch of red roses Lola had ever seen in a florist's box on the table beside him.

Spying the pies, Alf chuckled. 'They're right about you being psychic!'

Lola laughed as she placed the plate on the table. 'That or the doors are thin.' She winked then placed the box down on the table as well.

'Is that my cake?' Alf's face shone with anticipation.

Lola nodded. 'Yes, I decorated it especially for you, but don't open it yet, let me just grab something.' Lola rushed back to the kitchen and returned balancing two squidgy-looking presents on top of another cake box.

'Tristan, you might as well have your cake too,' Lola said as she set the box down on the table.

'It's your birthday, aren't we the ones supposed to be giving you gifts?' he asked, indicating the roses.

'Go on,' Alf urged, 'these will keep.'

Tristan passed Lola the gorgeous deep ruby red roses. She inhaled their scent before leaning over to give him a kiss, which earned a round of applause from Freya and Alf. 'Thank you, they're the most beautiful. I better find somewhere safe to keep these,' she said, glancing around the café. 'I don't want them to get ruined and there's no space on the counter for another bunch.' She gave them another sniff as she hugged them to her.

Freya took them from her. 'Shall I pop them back in the cottage?'

'Thanks, lovely,' Lola said, 'that would be wonderful, don't want them wilting in the heat of the kitchen.'

Freya pulled her coat on and took the roses from Lola before hurrying back to cottage.

'Can I open it now?' Alf asked as he started to fiddle with the box.

Lola nodded and watched as he carefully lifted the lid and set it aside. Scruff sat up on his back legs as if trying to get a look. Lola gave him a scratch behind the ears. A smile, bright as a summer's dawn, spread across Alf's face as he took in the decoration on top of the cake.

'Lola.' He shook his head, almost speechless. 'Well I never. Is that . . .'

'Yes, it's you and Scruff.' Tears sprang into Lola's eyes as she took in Alf's amazed reaction to the little figures she'd crafted in sugar paste. An old man dressed like Santa and a dog in matching red jumpers sat in a boat, little icing presents strewn all around them. Tristan gave Lola a round of applause at her skills, before pulling her in to perch on his knee. Lola curled herself around him and watched Alf's reaction.

'Well, that is just grand!' Alf announced. 'I will not be eating that.' He reached out and squeezed Lola's hand and she passed him the present. 'What's this?'

'Open it.'

Alf carefully undid the present, mumbling something about taking care to savour the moment. Lola watched as Alf pulled out the Christmas jumper.

'A Christmas jumper! Did you make this?' Amazement shone on Alf's face.

Lola nodded and wiped a tear away. 'There's one for Scruff too, so you can match.'

Alf whooped with laughter. 'Lola, this is wonderful, probably one of my best Christmases. You see, no matter how old you are, there's always something left to surprise you.' He pulled the jumper on. 'How does it look?'

'Smashing.' Lola stood up and turning to Tristan declared, 'Your turn now.'

Tristan reached for the present, then the box. 'Which one should I do first?'

295

'Like Alf, the cake, then the present,' Lola suggested as Freya opened the door and began to unwind her scarf.

Tristan glanced at Lola as if seeking reassurance before gently lifting the lid of the box. He froze midway as he saw what Lola had created, looking from the cake to Lola and back again. 'Lola, you made this?' He put the lid down. 'It's exquisite.'

His reaction brought happy tears to her eyes, so Lola could only nod as Alf stood up to peer into the box, their expressions equally as impressed.

'Will it come off? I really don't want to eat it. Or break it,' Tristan said. 'You've even got the tiny shells around the door. How on earth did you do that?'

Lola couldn't resist. 'Magic,' she quipped, making them all laugh. 'Now, enough of the cake, on to the present.'

Tristan made a big show of squeezing the package, pretending to give it a shake even though he knew it wouldn't give its secrets away like that. He tried, but failed, to unpick the generous amount of tape Lola had secured the gift with, and in the end he had to accept defeat and rip through the paper. Out spilled a blue and white jumper with a snowflake motif on the front. He held it up.

'I'm sorry it's not hand knitted, I ran out of time, but I know how much you like a Christmas jumper and I couldn't resist this one.'

'That's marvellous, Lola, thank you. I don't have one as tasteful as this.' Standing up, he pulled it on before modelling it to his audience.

Tristan pulled her in for a kiss. 'Happy birthday, my love. And Happy Christmas.'

'Happy birthday, Lola,' Alf said as he gave his tea a satisfied slurp. 'If you could have any wish you wanted, it being Christmas and your birthday, what would you have?'

Lola glanced at all her friends and snuggled into Tristan. 'For everything to always be like this. Happy and easy. Now, it might still be a bit warm to stick together but I'm going to rebel and do it anyway, so who's for chocolate cake second breakfast? I think with it being Christmas and a birthday all rules are officially out the window for the next forty-eight hours. Don't you agree?'

Scruff was the first to bark his agreement.

Chapter Forty-One

Lola hadn't planned to stay open until four but a flurry of customers and the general uplifting cheer of Christmas had kept the café busy well into the afternoon. For the final hour and a half Lola had been serving by herself, insisting Freya enjoy some time with her family before the party kicked off. Lola was getting more and more excited. It had been a long time since anyone had organised anything specifically for her birthday. There was usually just a balloon or an extra cake amongst all the Christmas Eve bits and bobs.

When closing time rolled round the gingerbread syrup was all used up and Lola didn't want to see another mince pie until the following year. Flicking the door sign to 'Closed', Lola turned the latch and dimmed the lights. Leaning back against the door, she took in the café, the chairs all a bit out of place, a few cups still left on table-tops, the Christmas tree twinkling cosily in the corner, 'Mary's Boy Child' coming out of the CD player adding to the festive feel. Joy rushed through her as she took it all in, her café, her achievement. Her first year had been more of a success than she could have dreamed of. Yes, there was still a lot to learn, but she was very pleased with how it had turned out and liked knowing she still had space to grow.

A quick sweep of the floor, followed by sticking the dirty crockery in the dishwasher and Lola was ready to leave. After Christmas she planned to give the café a deep clean and refresh. She checked everything in the kitchen had been turned off and made her way through the café, unplugging the Christmas tree and straightening the chairs before letting herself out. The darkness draped like luxurious velvet across the bay. Lola breathed in the fresh sea air and checked her watch. She had half an hour to freshen up before the party started. That was the trouble with a Christmas birthday, trying to squeeze everything in. Still, after the previous lonesome year, she couldn't find it in her to complain. Maybe from now on she'd have a second birthday in the summer. Double the celebrations sounded like double the fun.

Letting herself into the cottage, Lola picked the post up off the mat. A couple of cards and a charity circular. She carried them through into the living room. Flopping onto the sofa, she kicked off her shoes and sank back amongst the cushions. With a yawn she closed her eyes, figuring taking a few minutes out of the hectic schedule wouldn't do any harm.

The sound of knocking at the door roused her. Who on earth was calling at this time of night? Lola struggled up and glanced at the clock on the mantelpiece. Sugar! It

JENNIFER BIBBY

was gone half past six, she was meant to be at the pub half an hour ago. The knock came again, more insistent this time. It clearly wasn't Freya, as she had a key.

'All right, all right, I'm coming,' she called as she hurried down the hallway, pulling open the door to find Tristan standing there looking relieved that she'd answered.

'We were getting worried you'd forgotten,' he said.

Lola rolled her eyes. 'As if I'd forget the first proper birthday party I've had in years! I just put my feet up for a bit and the next thing you know I'd drifted off. I need to freshen up. Come in, I can't have you catching your death out there while I fix my makeup.' She tugged him by the scarf, reeling him in for a kiss. Tristan kissed her back and for a few moments Lola wondered if they should just skip the party and stay in together. Then his phone started to ring. Lola stepped back with a sigh.

'It's Freya wondering where the guest of honour is.'

'Tell her she's too busy canoodling with the local vicar. Right, I'll be five minutes.' Lola smacked one last kiss on Tristan's lips before rushing upstairs. In the bathroom she teased her victory rolls back into place, tidied up the smudged mascara and reapplied her red lipstick. Deciding that she loved her poinsettia print dress too much to swap it, she slipped into some heels and doused herself in perfume, before slinking back down the stairs, enjoying the way Tristan's eyes widened at the sight of her.

'Lola, you are stunning.'

Lola preened a bit before reminding him, 'I've only added some heels to the dress I've had on all day but thank you.'

'Well, then, I was remiss not to tell you earlier how stunning you looked. I was distracted by your amazing cake icing abilities.' He pulled her in and gave her a quick kiss. 'Come on, if we don't get a move on Freya will be on our case.'

Pulling her coat and scarf back on, Lola followed Tristan outside, locked up and slipping her arm through his, they slowly wandered along the seafront towards the pub, slowing to a halt in front of the twinkling lobster pot Christmas tree. Around them the village glowed with the season.

'Before I came here I never even knew places like this existed,' Lola said. 'Communities that actually care for each other. People like Alf. I never thought I'd find my forever home, somewhere to settle. I feel so lucky, I can't imagine ever leaving here.'

Tristan squeezed her hand. 'Me neither. I always worried I'd find Polcarrow too small or quiet after the city, but actually it's been nice to slow down a bit.' He smiled down at her. 'And it's brought us together. I don't know how much I considered God having a grand plan for me, but it seems someone wanted us both to be here at the same time.'

'Serendipity,' Lola whispered and when his brow furrowed she added, 'a happy accident. That, or Ruby's

301

work. Come on, we better get going or whatever happens next will not be all that happy.' She leaned in to him. 'I have to confess, I'm very curious to see what Freya has done. Also, about the cake.' She raised her eyebrows.

Tristan pulled an anxious face. 'I don't want to get your hopes up too much but I was pretty pleased with how it turned out even if your chocolate cake this morning did make my confidence waver.'

'Oooh! In that case, why are we lingering out here when there is cake to be had, come on.' She tugged him towards the pub.

Lola pushed open the pub door and stepped inside to cheers, whoops of joy and a round of applause followed by a rendition of 'Happy Birthday'. It was absolutely fabulous and she clapped her hands together in delight as she took it all in. The pub was decorated with blue balloons and 'Happy Birthday' banners hung from the old beams. A buffet was set out on a table in the corner and it looked as if the whole village had turned up – even Scruff was getting in on the action, barking along to the singing.

Lola wiped away some tears and bundled Freya into a hug. 'This is fantastic, thank you so much.'

'And not a Christmas tune in, erm, hearing. Happy birthday, Lola.' Freya squeezed her back. 'I really hope you enjoy tonight.'

'I'm sure I will, it looks fabulous, you've done a great job. I'm dying to try Tristan's cake.'

'You are going to have to do some circulating first, the grand cake reveal is scheduled for a bit later. That man would literally do anything for you and he's also managed to impress Mum and I with it.' Freya nodded in his direction.

Lola followed her gaze to where Tristan was showing off his Christmas jumper to Sue and Jan. His eyes caught with Lola's and he beamed back at her, which made her insides roll over with happiness. If the village hadn't cottoned on to their romance before now then by the end of the night it surely would no longer be a secret.

'He's more than I ever expected to find, he's absolutely wonderful.' Lola gave her friend a squeeze and turned to place her order with Steve. 'A glass of Prosecco please. Freya, what are you having?'

'The same.'

Steve gave Lola a once-over. 'What's your secret, you don't look a day over thirty.'

Shimmering with happiness at his compliment, Lola leaned over the bar and whispered, 'I couldn't possibly tell you that, but let's just say a little sprinkling of magic always helps.'

Laughing, Steve plonked a bottle of Prosecco on the bar. 'On the house, my lovely. We don't get to celebrate many big birthdays around here. Although apparently Alf turns ninety next year.'

'He may have mentioned it.' Lola winked. 'I don't think we can let him get away without a fuss, can we?'

303

'I don't think you'll have a hard time convincing him to have a party,' Steve pointed out as he passed her two glasses. 'Look at him.'

Alf was sitting by the fire, Scruff at his feet. Someone was playing a fiddle and he was singing along, entertaining his small audience with the sea shanties he grew up with. If anyone deserved a fuss then it was Alf. Lola turned back to the bar and poured Prosecco into the two flutes and passed one to Freya.

'Here's a toast to an unbelievable year.'

Freya chinked her glass against Lola's and took a sip. 'Hopefully with a few more unbelievable things left to happen.' She nodded over Lola's shoulder to where Tristan was hovering. 'I'll leave you to it.' She departed with a squeeze of Lola's hand.

'Showing off your new jumper? I hope you're not pretending I managed to knit it,' she asked as she sipped her drink.

'Sue was very impressed. I did have her fooled for a moment.'

Lola reached out and stroked his arm. 'You'll get me banned from the Women's Institute if you carry on like that. Isn't there something in the Bible about not lying?' she teased.

'Hmm, maybe, but it was just too tempting. Do you have a Christmas jumper?'

Lola shook her head. 'Very remiss of me, isn't it.'

'I'm sure it's forgivable. I have something for you, I meant to give it to you when I came to collect you, but

I got distracted.' Putting his glass down, he reached into his pocket and pulled out a small green box.

Lola's eyes widened as she took in the shape and size. Surely not . . . ? She didn't know if it was panic or excitement that flashed through her, but she managed to quell them both.

'Sorry I didn't get time to wrap it, but, here, Happy birthday, Lola.' With a quick kiss on the cheek he passed her the box.

She glanced up at him as she made a show of slowly opening the lid only to gasp in delight at the box's contents. Lola gasped, her eyes flickering from the contents to him and back again. Nestled on the black velvet was a pair of sparkling star-shaped earrings. 'Oh Tristan, they are beautiful.'

'I have to confess they're not real diamonds, but they are vintage.'

'It doesn't matter, they are perfect. Here.' She pressed the box into his hand. 'Let me put them on.' Lola quickly fastened them before turning her head left to right. 'What do you think?'

'Absolutely beautiful,' Tristan said, his voice full of wonder, 'the earrings and you.'

Lola stepped towards him. 'What have I done to deserve someone as adorable as you?' Suddenly it didn't matter that they were in a pub full of people on Christmas Eve, that everyone was jostling to get to the bar, or singing along with the eighties pop classics Steve was playing, all that mattered was that they were here together. Lola glanced down at her hands held in Tristan's and knew she never wanted to let him go. Who cared if the whole village knew?

As they stepped towards each other, the bar bell began to ring. Lola threw Steve a questioning look.

'Don't worry, it's not last orders, Freya's just got something up her sleeve.'

'Ooh!' Lola wiggled free of Tristan. Taking his hand, she pulled him forward through the crowded pub.

A cheer went up as Freya exited the kitchen, balancing a cake ablaze with candles in her hands, and the singing started up again. It was the most raucous rendition of 'Happy Birthday' Lola had ever heard.

'Is that your handiwork? Three tiers? I am impressed. It looks fabulous!' She squeezed Tristan to her.

'Yes, but I left the decorating to Freya.' The cake was adorned with pink roses and a golden 'Happy Birthday' topper which sparkled in the candlelight.

'Don't be so modest, it looks amazing, I cannot wait for a slice,' Lola said as she stepped in the direction of the cake. 'Freya! Are you trying to burn the place down?' Lola laughed as she blew on a stubborn candle. A round of applause went up and Lola glanced around, revelling in the moment. She began to slice the cake and realised she was ridiculously happy and surrounded by more love than she ever believed she'd find. Someone called out for a speech.

'All right, all right.' Lola licked buttercream off her finger from where it had oozed onto her hand when she'd started to cut the cake. Someone turned the juke-box down. 'Thank you, everyone, for coming tonight. It's not every day a girl turns forty and you've made it all feel so fabulous.' Lola glanced around the pub at everyone looking back at her fondly. 'You've made me feel so welcome here, it's been more than I expected and I have a whole host of treats up my sleeve for the new year. Thank you, Freya, for organising me such a lovely party.' She paused so Freya could receive a round of applause. 'And thank you, Tristan, for, well, just being your wonderful self and for being brave enough to bake me this cake.' Another round of applause, which was accompanied by some whisperings. 'Now, I think I've said enough, who wants some cake?'

The question was met by an enthusiastic cheer.

Chapter Forty-Two

It was no hardship for Lola to get up early on Christmas morning to do the Christmas dinner prep as she'd been awake half the night reliving the party and fizzing with excitement for Christmas Day. Tristan had ducked out of the party early to head for the more solemn calling of Midnight Mass. It had still been taking place, the church windows glowing with gentle candlelight, as Lola had strolled home, happily full of prosecco and cake. She'd loitered, wondering if she could slip in at the back, pay witness to the service he confessed he'd always loved. In the end, tiredness had swept over her, and the chill winter air had sent her scurrying for the cosiness of her duvet. She was tired, her emotions all over the place and she was fuzzy around the edges from all the glasses of Prosecco she'd been passed. She'd wait until morning. They would have plenty of time together after Christmas. Plus her feet had been freezing lingering in the chill December air.

Dressed in her festive poinsettia dress again, the star-shaped earrings twinkling in her ears, Lola busied herself in the café kitchen peeling potatoes, carrots, parsnips and getting the sprouts ready. The turkey had been delivered the previous morning and she had whipped up the stuffing the previous afternoon in-between customers. Happiness buzzed through her; this is what she loved, cooking for people, feeding families and creating special moments. After covering the massive turkey in foil, she placed it in the oven, knowing it would take several hours to roast.

As she retrieved the Christmas pudding from the top shelf, memories of the day they'd all come together to stir in their wishes flooded through her. It was more than just a pudding, she thought, as she placed it in the steamer, it was symbolic of the little family she had gathered together in Cornwall and she couldn't wait to share the day with them. Having made herself a cup of tea and a slice of toast, Lola opened the kitchen door and stepped into the courtyard. The sky was a pale, soft grey after days of winter sunshine. Leaning back, she listened to the gulls calling to each other and thought about Polcarrow waking up for Christmas, the children eating chocolate for breakfast whilst opening their presents, the glasses of Buck's Fizz sipped by harried parents as they tried to smooth over the days frantic preparation.

Her mind wandered to Tristan getting ready for one of the biggest days in the church's calendar. He was the biggest gift of her year. It wasn't just the breathless kisses or the physical attraction, but the companionship and friendship. Thinking about Tristan warmed her up from the inside. He made her feel she could take on anything, that she no longer had to weather life alone. Lola knew it was exactly the sort of love her grandmother had wanted her to find – safe and secure, not wild and untamed. Lola crossed her fingers and hoped it'd last forever. That they'd grow old together, shuffling along the seafront. Having Tristan by her side made the future feel slightly less daunting.

The service was due to start at half past ten. Lola had arranged to meet Freya, Angelo and Freya's family at quarter past. Lola finished her breakfast and checked herself in the mirror, applied a bit of concealer under her eyes and touched up her lipstick. Coat on, scarf wrapped warm around her neck, Lola left the café and made her way to the lobster pot Christmas Tree, where they'd all agreed to meet. Her stomach churned with nerves; a proper church service was a totally different commitment from singing along to Christmas carols.

Surprised to see them already waiting for her, Lola kissed Freya and Angelo in turn. 'Merry Christmas, my lovelies.'

They returned the greeting and Freya raised her eyebrows at Lola. 'So? How are you this morning?'

'Absolutely fine, despite all the Prosecco. I should turn forty more often.'

'I'm not sure I want to add party planning to my CV just yet though,' Freya said.

'Oh, but you did a splendid job.'

Freya's family arrived and more festive exchanges took place, kisses, wishes and checks about how everyone felt after what had turned into a brilliant party. They made their way up to the church, Lola sandwiched in between Angelo and Freya's family. Her stomach flipped as they made their way up the path. Tristan was standing at the doorway, all decked out in his religious finery, ready to greet them all. Lola was pretty sure she wasn't meant to find religious robes sexy but her knees went a little wobbly.

'Merry Christmas,' he bestowed along with smiles and handshakes. Lola waited as he passed from Freya to Angelo and then it was her turn.

'Merry Christmas.' Lola beamed at him, her smile spreading from ear to ear.

'Merry Christmas, you look gorgeous.' Tristan dropped his voice and held her hand for a moment longer than necessary. 'Go in, I think Alf's saved you a seat.'

One final squeeze of each other's hands, and they parted. Lola made her way inside. Alf was sitting in the front pew, with Scruff at his feet chewing a stuffed shark, trying to get the squeaker out. They looked adorable in their hand-knitted Christmas jumpers. Lola hurried to join him, giving him a kiss and a hug and exchanging season's greetings.

'Don't you both look handsome,' she said, signalling to their jumpers.

'I was a bit worried he'd look better than me, but I think I've just pipped him to the post,' Alf preened.

'You certainly have,' Lola said as she settled in beside him.

'How are you this morning after your party? Smashing it was, haven't had a night like it for ages. You'll have to organise my ninetieth in the spring.'

'It was, wasn't it? We have Freya to thank for that. We'll do an even better party for you, Alf.' Lola gave him a quick kiss on the cheek before fiddling with her order of service, folding it up like a fan.

Alf placed a hand on hers. 'Stop worrying, it'll all be fine, you'll see.'

'I've never been to church on Christmas Day before,' she told him. 'I'm not sure what to expect.'

'Well, I've been every year so I'll look after you.' Alf's smile was warm and kind.

Lola watched as the church filled up, the whole community of Polcarrow gathering in their festive finest. Alf continued to hold her hand all through the carols and the prayers, anchoring her, as if he knew she might take flight. The spirit of community, of togetherness touched Lola and she was surprised to find herself wiping away stray tears. Even Scruff behaved himself for once, lying over her and Alf's feet to keep them extra warm.

Tristan made his way to the lectern and Lola watched as he surveyed the gathered villagers, noted the relief in his eyes for a good turnout.

'Merry Christmas to you all,' he began, to which everyone shouted 'Merry Christmas' back. Smiling, Tristan took a moment to compose himself. Lola couldn't take her eyes off him as he looked at his notes, then back over the congregation, taking in everyone until his eyes

CHRISTMAS AT THE LITTLE CORNISH BAKERY

found hers. Her heart skipped several beats and the only thing that reminded her that she was still in the church in Polcarrow was Alf squeezing her hand, anchoring her to the spot.

Without breaking her gaze, Tristan lifted his sheet of paper, stared at it for a few long seconds before putting it back down again. 'I spent the past few days agonising over what to write, what to tell you, what to wish you. But all the words that came seemed trite.' He turned to address the congregation. 'But there is one thing that is never trite and that is community, harmony and love. Three things we have in abundance in Polcarrow. I thank you all for welcoming me as your vicar this past year, and I thank you all for weathering the changes other newcomers have brought to the village. This is an exciting time to be in Polcarrow and I hope moving forward we can embrace the changes we are blessed with and find a way to live in harmony.

'Harmony is important, it's the gentle flow of the waves against the shore, the keeping rhythm of the day. The sea reminds us of this daily and I am thankful to be so humbled by its ongoing presence.' Tristan paused. 'But what I want to speak to you about today is even more important, even more precious. Something that makes us richer than we can ever imagine. That thing is love.'

Lola swallowed as his eyes rejoined hers, softened with emotion. Almost as if she knew what was coming her hand went to her mouth, tears in her eyes.

'One thing I didn't expect to find here was love. But love was waiting for me in the most spectacular, unexpected way. We all read about or watch films about love that comes in and sweeps us off our feet, a love that will never allow us to be the same. I was content with the gentle love I had for God and for my parishioners to carry me through my days. In fact, I counted myself lucky to be blessed with this peaceful love. I never believed the other more romantic love was there for me until I arrived in Polcarrow and was dazzled by a woman with a vision, one she wasn't going to let anyone deter her from. A vision that included the most marvellous scones most of us have ever eaten and a passion for the village she had found herself in. This enthusiasm was infectious, it rallied against all the odds and quite frankly, Lola, when I saw you, it was love at first sight.'

Lola gasped with shock at the public declaration, which made Alf chuckle and pull her in for a hug.

'I know some people may not have matched us together but you do not get to choose who you love, if anything, love chooses you and I wouldn't want to change anything about who it chose for me. Lola, I realise in you it isn't just love I've found, but a confidante, a friend, in fact, the best of friends. Without you, I am only half a being. Everything in life is much more fun knowing you are by my side. This might seem unconventional, but I believe that when you meet the one, you know, and I think we both know, Lola, that we're meant for each other.'

Lola watched, wide eyed as Tristan made his way down from the lectern and, kneeling in front of her, took her hand from Alf.

'Lola, will you marry me?'

Somewhere behind them Freya let out a whoop of delight as Lola totally and utterly dissolved. 'I don't know why I'm crying, sobbing and laughing at the same time.' Lola attempted to wipe the tears away. She took a few deep, composing breaths as she looked at Tristan, the love she had never expected to find. Reaching out, she pushed his hair off his face and with a slightly wicked smile, accepted with a wink, 'Thanks for asking, you know, I do rather fancy being a vicar's wife.'

To a round of applause, Tristan swept Lola off the pew and into his arms. She knew once and for all that this was exactly where she was meant to be, her own happy-ever-after just as she was meant to find it.

Epilogue

Lola paused in the kitchen doorway, and smiled at the scene before her. Her dream for the café had always been for it to be more than just a place for people to grab a cup of tea, but a place for people to gather. Somewhere lost souls would feel safe, where people could sit and make new friends, exchange stories and impart wisdom. She observed Angelo bravely being interrogated by Freya's sister, Tristan talking animatedly to Freya's parents and Alf, head of the table, regaling Freya with stories. These people, her friends, her chosen family, were the heart any successful business needed. Watching them chatter as they passed the starters around, Lola was thrilled to think of what the next year would hold. A big birthday for Alf, the final work on Bayview and, of course, a wedding to plan. She caught Tristan's eye. First thing to do after Christmas was shop for a ring, Tristan had promised her a proper diamond, even if Lola was rather taken with the glorious piece of costume jewellery he'd presented her with to seal their engagement.

She waved away any offers to help and went back to finishing off the cooking, pleased with how everything had turned out, enjoying a moment of peace in her kitchen. She'd made a copy of the photo of Ruby with Alf and Charlie and tacked it onto the noticeboard where she kept the weeks' planned bakes. Lola touched the photo, her talisman, and thought it appropriate that her ring should have a ruby in it. After all, without her grandmother's legacy she would not be here. She would not have met Tristan.

Once everything was ready, Lola transferred the food onto serving plates and carried them through into the café where gentle Christmas music played in the background.

'Dinner's ready!' she called, as she placed the large plate of turkey on the table, which instantly caught Scruff's attention.

The tables in the seating area had been pushed together in a long line by Angelo and Freya's dad that morning. The crockery was a bit mismatched but Alf was lording it up at the head of the table, Scruff by his side waiting for a stray pig in blanket. Freya was curled around Angelo, who was the only one not wearing a paper cracker crown, despite Freya's mum trying to convince him to put one on. Olivia was rearranging the table settings, stuffing the empty cracker tubes into a bin liner her dad was holding out. Freya got up and helped Lola carry the rest of the dishes out before slipping back beside Angelo. Lola smiled at Tristan as she placed the roast potatoes on the table.

'Do you have enough wine? Cranberry sauce? There's more gravy,' Lola called out as everyone began to help themselves.

Tristan tugged at her hand, instructing her to sit down. Once she was seated and helping herself to roast potatoes, Tristan tapped the side of his wine glass. 'I propose a toast, to Lola—' he beamed at her as everyone raised their glasses '—my future wife, whose magic has made today that little bit extra special.'

Blinking back a fresh set of happy tears, Lola kissed him, which was greeted by a round of applause and some whoops of joy. Snuggling up to him, she gazed around the table, at her adoptive family, her chosen home and the people who helped bring her sparkle to life.

Acknowledgements

Hello and thank you for choosing to visit Polcarrow at Christmas time. Firstly, I'd like to thank you, the reader, for choosing this book. If you've returned after reading *The Cornish Hideaway*, welcome back! If this is your first trip to Polcarrow, I hope it also won't be your last. The enthusiasm of romance readers is marvellous and keeps me going. Authors wouldn't be anything without you.

If my gratitude was a (mince) pie then the largest slice would be going to my agent, Saskia Leach. It is purely down to her belief in this book and her championing it when I had long lost hope, that you are reading Lola and Tristan's story. Saskia has been absolutely wonderful support on this stage of my writing journey and I couldn't be happier with everything she has done. Thank you.

Second serving goes to my wonderful editor Claire Johnson-Creek at Zaffre for falling in love with Lola, Tristan and Polcarrow and deciding to take a chance on this book. Lola and Tristan have found their perfect home. It's been such a pleasure to work with you on this book and I'm looking forward to the next one. Thanks also to everyone else at Bonnier Books UK, I'm very happy to be one of your authors.

Special mention to Joanna Kerr for producing such a gorgeous cover. I am obsessed with it! It's beautiful. Especially the enormous mince pies!

I'd also like to share out the thank you pie amongst my writing friends, particularly the Surrey buddies who've been there with a consoling ear or a congratulatory cheer. Writing books can feel very lonesome so I am grateful for all the support I've received from my fellow romance authors, especially from Alison Sherlock, Julie Haworth, Leonie Mack and Susie Hull.

Of course there is still enough pie to share out between all my friends, both in real life and online, who've supported me through a couple of tough years, not just in the writing of this book, but in some tricky real-life stuff that transpired. Lashings of brandy sauce for Carla, Essi, Helen, Laura and Liz. Thank you to Desiree, Lucy and Margaret for all the bookish support. Special mention to all my University of Bedfordshire colleagues who've enthusiastically supported my non-admin side hussle. I think we can all agree this is more exciting to read than exam board minutes.

Last but not least, and there is definitely enough pie left so don't fret, thank you to my parents, John and Diana for all your love and support and to Chris, Kristina, Amelia and Henry for bringing some extra sprinklings of joy. Thank you also to my wider family for your encouragement and enthusiasm all along the way.

Return to Polcarrow in . . .

HOT CROSS BUNS AT THE LITTLE CORNISH BOOKSHOP

Effie has always loved her quiet life in Cornwall – sea swims, beach walks, reading and knitting. After university in London, she returned home, craving the calm of the coast. But while her friends move forward, Effie feels stuck. So when she's offered the chance to open a bookshop in the seaside village of Polcarrow – with a flat above the shop – Effie leaps at the opportunity. A bookshop by the sea? It's the dream.

Adjusting to life on her own is tough at first, but she soon finds friendship in Lola, the local café owner, and her warm circle of friends. Then there's Jake – a globe-trotting photographer – who stirs something in Effie that she didn't expect. As Easter approaches and the shop's grand opening nears, Effie's new life begins to bloom. But a difficult local author and a misunderstanding with Jake threaten to upend everything. Can Effie find the courage to fight for the life – and love – she's always wanted?

Coming March 2026. Pre-order now.

A Recipe for Lola's Famous Mince Pies

Why not join Lola this festive season and make your own mince pies? Pop on some Christmas tunes, put on your best Christmas jumper and get baking!

For this recipe you'll need:

- 300g of plain flour and some extra for dusting
- A pinch of salt
- 150g of butter, cold from the fridge and cut into cubes
- 3 tbsp of icing sugar
- 1 large egg, beaten with 1 tbsp of cold water
- 300g of mincemeat

And for the top of the pies:

- 1 medium egg, beaten
- 1 tbsp caster sugar

Method:

1. Preheat the oven to 190C/170C Fan/Gas 5.
2. To make the pastry, place the flour and salt in a food processor and add the butter. Mix it up until it resembles breadcrumbs. Add the icing sugar and mix again. Add the beaten egg mixture and mix briefly to a rough dough.

3. Tip the pastry out onto the work surface bring the dough together into a ball with your hands and wrap in cling to chill for about 20–30 minutes.

4. Brush a 12-hole muffin tin with melted butter and set aside in the fridge.

5. After chilling, turn the dough out onto a lightly floured work surface. Roll out into a circle of around 4mm thick. Use a round cutter to cut out 12 discs of pastry that are about 6mm bigger than the size of the holes in your tin.

6. Press a round of pastry into the bottom of each hole. Fill each pastry case with a level tablespoon of mincemeat.

7. Cut out 12 lids with a smaller pastry cutter, re-rolling the pastry as needed. Brush a little beaten egg around the base of the lid and stick it down onto the pie edge, pressing gently to seal.

8. Brush the tops of the mince pies with egg wash and sprinkle lightly with caster sugar.

9. Use the scraps of pastry to decorate the tops of your pies with stars and holly leaves.

10. Return the pies to the fridge for half an hour or so.

11. Bake the mince pies for 20–25 minutes, or until golden-brown and crisp. Set the tray on a wire rack to cool for 5 minutes, and then turn out the mince pies.

12. Enjoy!

Introducing the place for
story lovers – somewhere to share
memories, photographs, recipes and
reminiscences, and discover the very
best of saga writing from authors you
know and love, and new ones we
simply can't wait for you to meet.

·MEMORY LANE·

The address for story lovers
www.MemoryLane.club